"What's the matter, Brix? I thought you liked bold and brazen women."

"And it's not as if I'm about to start seducing every man in sight." She lowered her voice so that only he could hear. "Just you."

His green eyes seemed to reach right into her heart and make its rhythm erratic. "If you're going to try to seduce me, Fanny, you've got a lot to learn."

She struggled to remain cool and calm. "Do I? Will you teach me?"

"If you'd like."

She could easily believe this was the way he sounded when he was in bed with a woman. After they'd made love.

Her throat constricted. Breathing wasn't easy. Yet she mustn't give him the satisfaction of thinking he could affect her in any way. "Perhaps not."

He gazed down at her with a look that was even more potent than his voice. "Why don't you ask the man who taught you how to kiss for lessons in seduction?"

She instinctively moved back against the counter table, seeking out its solid support. "I can't."

His lips curved in a victorious smile. "Why not?"

"Because that would be you."

Other **AVON ROMANCES**

Coming Soon

And Don't Miss These
ROMANTIC TREASURES
from Avon Books

MARGARET MOORE

Kiss Me Again

AVON BOOKS

An Imprint of HarperCollins*Publishers*

This is a work of fiction. Names, characters, places, and incidents are products of the author's imagination or are used fictitiously and are not to be construed as real. Any resemblance to actual events, locales, organizations, or persons, living or dead, is entirely coincidental.

AVON BOOKS
An Imprint of HarperCollins*Publishers*
10 East 53rd Street
New York, New York 10022-5299

Copyright © 2004 by Margaret Wilkins
ISBN: 0-06-052621-1
www.avonromance.com

First Avon Books paperback printing: February 2004

Avon Trademark Reg. U.S. Pat. Off. and in Other Countries, Marca Registrada, Hecho en U.S.A.
HarperCollins® is a registered trademark of HarperCollins Publishers Inc.

Printed in the U.S.A.

10 9 8 7 6 5 4 3 2 1

Always, Bill

Chapter 1

London, the third of May, 1819

Dear Aunt Euphenia,

I'm so sorry you weren't well enough to attend the baptism yesterday, and I hope you're feeling better today. My sweet boy acquitted himself in a manner I don't expect will surprise you, given that I'm his mother. He cried loudly throughout. I shall give you a detailed description later in my letter, because first I must tell you that however distressing D'Arcy's crying was at the time, it was nothing compared to what happened afterward. . . .

Lady Diana Westover Terrington

His green eyes twinkling, the Honorable Brixton Smythe-Medway spread his arms across the back of a cabriole sofa in the library of Viscount Adderley's town house. A merry smile on his pleasant face, he surveyed the decidedly masculine room furnished with the aforementioned sofa and comfortable oval-backed chairs, shelves of leather-bound volumes and walls pan-

1

eled in age-darkened oak. He felt at peace with the whole world and the equal of anybody, including the other gentlemen who were there with him, for he had the special privilege of being the godfather of the son and heir of his best friend, Edmond Terrington, Viscount Adderley.

At the moment, Edmond was upstairs with his wife Diana and, judging from the wails wafting from above, he wasn't having much luck helping her and the nursemaid getting little D'Arcy Douglas to nap.

Brix glanced at Lord Justinian Bromwell, Buggy to his friends, who was deaf to the baby's crying and the conversation in general as he studied the various books on the shelves near the door as if looking for the secret of El Dorado—or perhaps an interesting spider, as arachnids were his specialty.

Lieutenant Charles Grendon of His Majesty's Royal Navy stood properly at ease in front of one of the tall, narrow windows. He had the air and attitude of a commander and, Brix reflected, the uniforms of naval officers couldn't have been better designed to highlight Charlie's impressive physique.

While Charlie didn't lack for female admirers, it was no secret among the group of former schoolmates that Sir Douglas Drury, baronet and barrister, could claim to have conquered more hearts than any of them.

Brix watched the most famous attorney in London as he poured the brandies, finding himself once again slightly perplexed as to Drury's attraction. His sardonic friend wasn't particularly good-looking, and he never dressed with any regard for fashion, preferring plain black wool and white linen. On the other hand, Brix could see that Drury's dark hair and angular features, his propensity to brood since he'd returned from being interred in a French prison during the war, and the fact that Drury had never lost a case might render him an object of some fascination to the fairer sex.

Not that he was jealous. Far from it. He had had a few conquests of his own, despite his mop of unruly straw-colored hair that was his valet's bane, his average features and lean build. Indeed, he had some cause to wish he was even less attractive, at least in one case.

But this was not the day to have unpleasant thoughts about anybody.

Drury handed round the brandies, and once all the men had their drinks, Brix held up his glass. "To the Honorable D'Arcy Douglas Brixton Bromwell Grendon Terrington!"

The toast drunk, Brix set down his brandy on the pedestal side table near him. He'd had a fair bit of wine at the breakfast and didn't want to be foxed.

"That name has quite a ring to it, doesn't it?" he mused aloud as he made himself comfortable. "I did feel for the poor vicar, though, having to remember it all. I'd have had to write the names on my cuff."

The other men exchanged rueful smiles, except for Drury, who rarely smiled at anything.

"Edmond looked proud enough to burst the buttons on his vest, didn't he?" Charlie said after finishing his drink. He set the glass on the console table beside him and returned to his habitual attitude, hands clasped behind his back. "Even when little D'Arcy was screaming fit to wake the dead."

"That merely proves the infant has strong, healthy lungs," Buggy noted as he wandered closer, past the large globe.

Brix laughed. "Try telling that to the vicar, Buggy. I thought he was going to drop the little fellow in the font."

"I appreciate being second on the list of names," Drury remarked in the deep voice that many of his legal enemies claimed was the sole secret of his success. He settled in the chair nearest the marble hearth. "But how the devil did Edmond and Diana come up with that spelling of D'Arcy? I don't recall any family names of D'Arcy, and as far as I know, neither one of them has a drop of French blood in their veins."

There was a moment of awkward silence before Brix stepped jovially into the breach. Although he appreciated that Drury had suffered at French hands, this was no time for grim denunciations. "I daresay it was Diana's idea. Sounds like the sort of name a romantic woman would pick, and she does write those novels, you know."

Drury's broad shoulders relaxed. "I suppose the boy should be grateful she didn't name him after that villain in her book. What was he called?"

"Korlovsky," Buggy supplied.

"Egad, yes!" Brix seconded. "Wouldn't that have raised a few eyebrows among the *ton*? As it was, I tried to warn Edmond that the boys at Harrow would probably tease the lad no end. I can hear them now—Arssy D'Arcy." He sighed melodramatically. "Alas, he refused to heed my sage advice, so the boy's stuck with it, I'm afraid."

"Perhaps the boys in his class at Harrow won't think of that," Buggy suggested.

Brix snorted. "If they have an ounce of brains between them, they will. Still, perhaps D'Arcy will be the stronger for it, eh? Or maybe he just won't care. It never bothered me when anybody called me Middling Medway, but then, they were right," he finished with a broad grin. "Middling I was, and middling I continue."

"I did inquire about the name," Buggy gravely remarked. "Edmond says they simply liked it. He assured me they chose the order of subsequent names not with any sort of ranking in mind. It was all about the rhythm."

"I'm flattered any way you look at it," Charlie said, rocking back and forth on his heels. "To think a viscount's son shares any part of his name with me! My family still can't quite believe it, and neither can I."

"Diana looked lovely, didn't she?" Brix said, deciding to move away from the topic of names altogether, for in truth and despite the explanation, he'd been a little hurt that his name had come after Drury's. "A wife who adores you, a fine healthy son . . . it's nearly enough to make a man contemplate marriage himself."

Charlie stopped rocking. "Don't tell me you are?"

"Not at all," Brix assured him. "Edmond got lucky when he found Diana—or she found him. Not many people are so fortunate. For most of us, marriage will be no more than a duty or a financial arrangement." He shivered with mock horror at the very notion. "I have no desire to tie myself to a woman under such conditions until I'm too old to care about, well . . ." He gave them a knowing wink. "Much of anything. Then I'll find myself a placid little wife to provide me with an heir."

"We've heard this all before," Drury reminded him. "You bet us you won't marry until you're fifty, remember?"

"I most certainly do," Brix replied, straightening. "I'm glad to hear *you* do."

"A bet of fifteen hundred pounds does rather stay in one's mind," Buggy observed.

"Especially since I have every intention of winning it," Brix replied. "I have absolutely no desire and no need to tie myself legally to a woman until I have to. I'm going to remain free, and carefree, until I'm at *least* fifty."

"What about the other part of the bet?" Charlie asked, walking away from the window toward the fireplace, where Edmond kept a box of cheroots on the mantel. "You're still adamant you'll never marry Fanny Epping?"

"I can assure you, gentlemen," Brix replied with complete conviction, "that no force on earth will ever compel me to marry my annoying little shadow, despite the oft-stated wishes of my family."

"Come, Brix, tell us how you *really* feel," Drury said with a hint of a smirk as he reached for the brandy at his elbow.

"I don't understand your abhorrence of her," Buggy said, regarding Brix as studiously as if he were planning to write a treatise on men opposed to marriage with Fanny Epping. "She may not be a beauty, but she's quiet and sweet and—"

"Too quiet, and too sweet," Brix declared, smacking his hands on his knees as he hoisted himself to his feet and headed toward the brandy decanter on the mahogany side table to refill his glass. "Too bland, too boring."

"Unlike those actresses you're always consorting with?" Drury asked, one dark brow slightly raised.

"Exactly!" Brix cried. He went to pour more brandy into his glass, then realized he'd never finished the first. Regardless, he topped it up, then turned toward them, grinning and not the least bit embarrassed. After all, Drury was hardly chaste. Rumor had him in a different woman's bed every week.

"Doesn't it at least flatter you that she's infatuated with you?" Buggy asked. "She *is* the daughter of a duke."

"Perhaps I might not mind her hounding me if she were a beauty," Brix allowed. "But she's not. You don't know what it's like to have a woman like that following you about, making a nuisance of herself."

"You're right, I don't know," Buggy gravely agreed. "I've never been so lucky."

"Lucky?" Brix scoffed. "Ask Edmond how it feels—he'll tell you, and he only had to deal with Diana for a few weeks. It's been damned annoying being shadowed by a mousy little creature without an ounce of vitality for the past fourteen years."

"Then perhaps you shouldn't have kissed her," Charlie suggested.

"It was only once, and I was just trying to cheer her up because our brothers had been teasing her again, yet she seems to think one kiss means I belong to her for the rest of our lives," Brix explained, regretting that he'd ever told his friends about that day in his mother's rose garden when he and Fanny were twelve years old.

At least he'd refrained from revealing anything more, such as how he'd felt when Fanny had looked up at him adoringly, her big blue eyes still moist with tears, her lips parted, a little breathless. How he'd immediately acted on the sudden, overwhelming impulse to press his lips to hers.

He pushed that memory away.

"Even though I try to ignore her, she still trails after me at parties and balls and receptions," he went on. "Gad, I can't even avoid her at Medway

Manor. Mother invites her every year, so I'm forced to stay in town or go to Bath or Brighton."

"You hate visiting your family in the country anyway," Charlie said, sitting on the wide windowsill. "You wouldn't go whether Fanny was there or not."

Brix laughed. "Oh, all right. I don't get along with my family, so I probably wouldn't." He gave them a magnanimous smile. "If you all feel so bad about the wager, I'm willing to end it—provided you concede defeat and give me my winnings."

"You don't need the money, do you?" Charlie asked warily.

"Not a bit," Brix breezily replied. "I've got a fine income from my investments, and you all know I never gamble more than I can afford to lose. But a win's a win, gentlemen, and I do have my pride."

"I'm not willing to concede defeat," Drury said, twisting his brandy glass in long, somewhat gnarled fingers that had been broken more than once. "I'm sure you'll succumb to a woman's charms in the next twenty-two years, and attractive or not, I have every hope that Lady Francesca Cecilia Epping will be the one to reel you in. If she does, I'll consider you fortunate. She's a sensible young woman who'll do you a lot of good."

"Oh, yes, that's what we all want in a wife, isn't it—somebody to do us some good," Brix replied, his tone grave, but with a roguish sparkle in his eyes. "Especially you, Drury. You'd love some chaste, dutiful nunlike woman to constantly point out the error of your ways, I'm sure."

Brix's grin widened when Drury didn't answer. "There's nothing in our wager about a vow of chastity," he said, "so I may very well succumb to a woman's charms, as long as marriage isn't part of the bargain. As for Fanny, here's hoping she'll soon realize how ridiculous she looks and how hopeless her feelings, and leave me alone."

"*You could have told me.*"

Definitely exhibiting signs of vitality, Lady Francesca Cecilia Epping stormed toward Brix across the crimson-and-blue Aubusson carpet. Her face was flushed, her plain, Nile green silk gown swished about her ankles and the simple crucifix on a thin gold chain around her neck bounced with each furious step.

Brix wanted to both disappear and stare with fascinated horror at the enraged young woman striding toward him, her blue eyes fairly dancing with rage as she came to a halt in front of him, their noses nearly touching.

"You think I'm *annoying*?" she demanded, her usually soft and dulcet voice stern and low-pitched, as if she were fighting not to shout. "You want me to leave you alone? Why didn't you have the decency to tell me? In private?"

Being caught in a tornado might be as disconcerting as being upbraided by Fanny. But surely a harmless agreement between friends didn't warrant this extreme reaction. "Fanny, you don't under—"

She cut him off. "Instead of doing the honorable thing, the *kind* thing, the *Honorable* Brixton

Smythe-Medway decides to make a wager, to both enrich and amuse himself at my expense, as if my feelings are nothing but a joke!"

Well aware that his friends were looking on and dismayed by this unexpected turn of events, Brix decided they didn't need an audience. He put his hand on her elbow to steer her out of the room. "We can discuss this—"

She wrenched herself free of his grasp. "You saw fit to make fun of me and my feelings in front of your friends, so we'll discuss this here and now."

Still hoping to placate her, he gave her his very best smile and spread his hands. "It's just a bit of sport among the four of us, Fanny. I never meant to hurt you."

Her expression grew even more murderous. "And that makes it all right? Four men I considered my friends know that the thought of marrying me is absolutely abhorrent to you, and I'm not supposed to be hurt and humiliated? I'm supposed to be *amused*?"

Brix didn't appreciate being chastised, by anybody. And it wasn't as if she were completely innocent of wrongdoing. "You wouldn't have had your feelings hurt if you hadn't been eavesdropping. You know what they say about people who do that. They rarely hear anything good."

"So now it's *my* fault?" Fanny cried, her hands balling into fists.

For an instant, Brix thought she might actually hit him, and he took a step back. "Fanny, you're getting all worked up over nothing," he said, still struggling to maintain some semblance of calm. "It was just a friendly little wager between Buggy, Charlie, Drury and me. Nobody else knows, so there's no need for these theatrics."

"Actually, it isn't just between the four of us anymore," Drury noted, standing by the Doric-inspired chimney piece. "Somebody wrote the wagers in the betting book at White's yesterday."

Brix stared at the lawyer with shocked dismay. A lighthearted bet between friends was one thing; a wager that all the *ton* would hear about was quite another.

Even worse, one of these men, friends he thought he could trust, was responsible for this terrible turn of events. "Which one of you wrote our wagers up in White's?"

Buggy immediately shook his head. "Not I."

"Nor I," Charlie added, obviously taken aback by both what had happened, and the accusation.

"Any number of people could have done it," Drury said with a shrug. "You talked about the wagers that night in our club after Edmond's son was born."

As dismayed as Brix was to hear that his loose tongue was responsible, he was relieved to think that none of his friends had made those wagers public knowledge.

"What does it matter who actually wrote it there, or when people first heard of it?" Fanny demanded. "What's important is that this *disgusting* wager is now known among the *ton*."

"Well, it's not as if you've been accused of treason, Fanny," Brix replied, using the same tone as when she'd been upset in the past and come to him for comfort. "If we just keep quiet about it, I'm sure it will all blow over in a few days and be forgotten."

For once, his comforting tone had no effect. "Perhaps there'll be no serious repercussions for *you*," she charged. "But *I'm* the unattractive, annoying Fanny Epping who the amusing Smythe-Medway has vowed to never, ever marry. While this may be nothing more to you than a light-hearted anecdote to tell at dinner parties, I've been made to look a complete fool."

She straightened her shoulders and her eyes burned with indignant resolution. "Care to make another wager, Mr. Smythe-Medway? I'm willing to bet that I, ridiculous, annoying Fanny Epping, can break your heart in a year. No, six months." She thrust out her chin. "No, six *weeks!*"

Brix managed to answer with a calm composure distinctly at odds with his inner state. "Really, Fanny, you astound me. I would think you'd had enough of wagers."

She sniffed derisively as she crossed her arms. "I don't call *that* a very sporting remark."

"Fanny, don't be silly."

"What's the matter, Mr. Smythe-Medway? Afraid you'll lose?"

"Fanny, Brix, I think you ought to reconsider—" Buggy began, but she interrupted him.

"I don't. Well, Mr. Smythe-Medway, do you agree to accept my wager?"

Brix felt his friends' eyes upon him, especially Drury's. He couldn't back down now without it looking as if he'd been intimidated by a slightly hysterical young woman, even if she sounded quite determined. Besides, the idea that he could lose such a wager was laughable, so he decided to play along. "Far be it from me to refuse a lady. I accept your wager."

He stuck out his hand, then raised a brow when she stared at it as if it were a poisonous snake. "We ought to shake hands on it."

Fanny's gaze darted to his face. Her lips turned up into a smile, and she got what Brix would have described as a devilish gleam in her eye if it'd been anybody but Fanny.

She grabbed his hand with a remarkably firm grip and tugged him forward. Pulled off-balance, he half stumbled, half fell. She put her arms about him to steady him, or so he thought, until her mouth captured his as if she needed his lips to live. That was shocking enough—but then she thrust her tongue into his mouth.

Excited and overwhelmed in spite of himself, his embrace tightened around her, and he returned her kiss with equal fervor. Holding her lithe, trim body against him, he inhaled the sweet scent of her skin—roses. She smelled of roses, and she kissed like . . . the most intoxicatingly passionate woman in England. His blood throbbed with heated urgency, and he hardened, his whole body anxious for closer, more intimate contact.

The memory of that first kiss arose, unbidden.

The first time he'd ever kissed a girl. The first time he'd ever felt desire, although he hadn't realized what it was.

The first—and only time—he'd been embarrassed by his body's response. Because it was Fanny, his innocent little acolyte.

This passionate woman wasn't his juvenile admirer, the girl with the perpetually worried expression who'd come to him in tears so many times.

Nor was she the gawky adolescent, all eyes and legs and skinny arms, who'd trailed after him at parties like a wraith.

This was a Fanny who stirred his desire as no woman ever had in his life. He'd made love with experienced courtesans who didn't make him weak at the knees, yet he was certainly weak at the knees now.

Fanny finally broke the kiss. Panting, she stared at him, her lips slightly swollen, her eyes glowing. He'd never have guessed in a hundred years that Fanny could look like this.

Or kiss like that.

"So we have a bet, then, Mr. Smythe-Medway?" she demanded.

Although he was—for once—speechless, he managed to recover enough to nod his agreement.

"Good!" She headed for the door, then hesitated on the threshold and looked back over her slender shoulder. "And good day to you, gentlemen."

She went out, slamming the door so hard, the windows rattled.

The sound was like a thunderclap, releasing the men from their stunned, motionless state.

"My God, Brix, what the devil have you done?" Buggy whispered.

Words still failed Brix as he tried to regain his internal equilibrium. He'd seen Fanny upset, distressed, sad, but never enraged. He wouldn't have believed it was even possible for her to get so angry, let alone so fiercely angry she would raise her voice.

As for that kiss . . .

He'd never experienced anything like the passionate sensations she aroused, or the overwhelming urge to pick her up in his arms and carry her to the nearest sofa. To caress and touch her and make love.

Thank God they hadn't been alone, or he wasn't sure what he might have done.

And for *Fanny* to make him feel that way . . . It had to be the unexpectedness of it, the surprise when he felt her tongue in his mouth, the sheer shock of being kissed in that bold, wanton way by a fiercely angry Fanny. To think that she could kiss like that . . .

Good God, wherever had she learned to kiss like that?

"There for a moment, I thought our little Fanny was going to murder you," Drury observed, cutting into Brix's ruminations. "Or sue you for slander."

Brix would rather spend a year in the country than admit he could be flustered by a woman, so he managed to put a genial smile on his face. "Oh, it's not as bad as all that. Not that I blame her for being upset. I wouldn't be delighted if somebody bet that I *couldn't* marry until I was fifty. But there was no need for such hysterics."

He sat back down on the chintz sofa and resumed his usual casual posture. "I'm sure she'll realize that and be absolutely mortified when she calms down and realizes what she's done. She'll probably be desperate to call off that wager and forget it ever happened."

"I wouldn't be so sure of that, if I were you," Drury said, strolling over for another brandy. "She looked fairly determined to me, and I understand a woman scorned is a terrible enemy."

Trust Drury to make everything sound like a matter of life and death.

Brix inclined his head. "In general, I bow to your superior knowledge of the fairer sex, but I don't think general rules apply to Fanny, and I ought to know. I've been acquainted with her since we were both babes in our mother's arms."

"So you weren't at all surprised by that kiss?" Drury asked, as if daring Brix to deny it.

Brix blushed and wished he wasn't. After all, it wasn't as if he hadn't been passionately kissed before, and by women more seductive than Fanny could ever be. "Well, naturally I was surprised. I mean, to think little Fanny would ever do anything so bold as to kiss a man in front of other people . . . it's like discovering England's not really an island."

He grinned, to show he was more amused than anything else by her uncharacteristic action. "I must say, if I'd been aware she could kiss like that, I might have let her catch me alone now and again."

"I don't think this is a joking matter, not anymore," Buggy said as he wandered over to the window overlooking the square. He kept his back to them as he spoke. "In fact, I wish we'd never made that wager at all. It was cruel."

Brix refused to feel guilty for a harmless bit of fun. "That's a bit harsh, don't you think? As I said, I didn't do it to hurt her."

Buggy turned around and regarded them all with a woeful expression. "No, none of us did. That's the worst thing of all. We weren't thinking of her as a person, with feelings to be hurt."

Charlie stared at the buckles on his shoes, and Drury silently drank his brandy.

"Oh, there's no need for these long faces, gentlemen!" Brix cried, sitting up straight. "It's just a tempest in a teapot. She'll get over it. Really. I'll have a word with her in the next few days. Smooth things over, as it were."

"You sound sure she'll forgive you," Drury said as he returned to his chair by the hearth.

"I've jollied her out of her little sorrows plenty of times before."

Drury didn't seem impressed. "Don't you think this is a bit different?"

In a way, Brix supposed it was. This time, he was the one who'd upset her. But he still refused to believe this was a serious problem. "Granted, it may not be so simple as a few little compliments and jokes, but I'm sure she'll come round."

"Well, whatever happens," Drury dryly observed, "you've accomplished one thing. I don't think Fanny will be following you around anymore."

Brix smiled as if he'd just been given his heart's desire. "And that's the way I want it."

"What the devil's going on in here?" a voice demanded from the door.

Damn, Brix thought as he jumped to his feet, knocking over his brandy. Fanny must have said something to their host, the father of D'Arcy Douglas Brixton Bromwell Grendon Terrington, who was now standing on the threshold.

Brix pulled out his handkerchief and started to mop up the spilled drink.

"Fanny just ran past me on the stairs," Edmond said as he entered the room, his handsome face sternly concerned. "She's very upset."

She obviously hadn't spoken to Edmond. That was a relief, even if Charlie and Buggy were exchanging guilty looks. Drury didn't look guilty; he looked mildly interested, which for him was the same as another man's avidly curious stare.

Ignoring them, Brix tossed his damp handkerchief on the side table, then strolled toward the brandy decanter to pour Edmond and himself a drink.

"It's like this, Edmond," he began, speaking as if telling his friend a funny story he'd heard at Almack's or White's. "Last year on your wedding day, we four got to talking about marriage, and somebody questioned my resolution not to wed until I'm fifty. Well, of course I couldn't let that pass, so one thing led to another, and I made a wager that I wouldn't."

"I see," Edmond said, slowly crossing his arms over his broad chest, his expression betraying his certainty that this was *not* going to be an amusing anecdote. "Go on."

"Well," Brix continued, trying to steady his slightly trembling hands as he poured, "somebody said Fanny would get me sooner or later. You know how I feel about Fanny, so of course I denied that possibility. One more thing led to another, and there was an addition to the wager, that I wouldn't marry Fanny. We were joking about it here, and Fanny—who must have been listening at the door—heard us."

Drinks in hand, he started toward Edmond, noting that Drury had returned to his chair, and Buggy and Charlie had taken seats on the sofa. "She was a little upset—"

"A little?" Edmond interjected. He hadn't moved at all, but still stood like some sort of irate king. "She was a damned sight more than a *little* upset. I had to look twice to make sure the young woman dashing up the stairs even *was* Fanny."

"All right," Brix conceded as he held out Edmond's brandy. "She was very upset, because it also seems that somebody has written the bet in the book at White's."

Edmond's eyes widened. "Gad." He took the drink and downed it in a gulp, then sat in an upholstered oval-backed chair close to the sofa table. "No wonder she was so distraught."

"It's hardly the end of the world, as I tried to explain to her, although I'll admit our little joke has gotten a bit out of hand," Brix said as he sat in the nearest chair, which was beside the table inlaid with a checkerboard pattern holding Edmond's chess set.

"There's more," Drury remarked, his expression as enigmatic as usual. "She made a counter wager. She's bet Brix she can break his heart in six weeks."

Edmond stared as if he couldn't believe it, which wasn't so surprising, Brix thought. He could hardly believe it himself, and he'd been here.

"And then she sealed the bet with the most astonishing kiss, Edmond," Charlie said.

"She kissed you?" Edmond asked Brix incredulously, as if it was a shocking thing that any woman should want to kiss him.

To be sure, Brix wasn't known for his sexual conquests, but he was hardly repellent to the female sex.

Nevertheless, he'd caused enough dissension that day, so he subdued any annoyance, and replied with his usual jaunty good humor. "Right on the lips, my friend. I confess you could have knocked me over with a feather."

"It didn't look that way to me," Drury said, regarding Brix with his intense, dark-eyed stare. "You seemed quite involved in the proceeding."

"What would you have had me do? Shove her off?" he protested. "That wouldn't have been very gentlemanly. I was only trying to be polite."

"I don't think etiquette was uppermost in your mind."

"You've become an expert on reading minds now, have you?" Brix answered, struggling not to get angry.

"Whatever you were thinking at the time, this is a bad business, Brix," Edmond declared, steepling his fingers and laying them against his chin. "To make Fanny the brunt of one of your jokes—"

"While your treatment of Diana prior to your engagement was exemplary?" Brix demanded as he shot to his feet. "It's not as if you're a saint, you know. If I recall correctly, you weren't exactly a model of chivalry when you first started pursuing your wife."

His friend colored, as well he should. "You're absolutely right. So I'm very aware of the serious, unforeseen consequences of something that seems no more than a harmless bit of fun."

Brix's gaze swept over his friends, who suddenly seemed like a jury there to condemn him. "You all seem determined to put the blame solely on me, but *I* wasn't the one who wrote it in the book. *I* wasn't the one who made the counter wager. All I did was make a joking wager with my friends. It wasn't intended to publicly humiliate Fanny, and it wouldn't have, if it had remained between us."

Edmond rose. "Nevertheless, don't you think you ought to reconsider? Remove the bet from the book at White's and ask Fanny to nullify your wager."

"I'm not a child, Edmond, and I resent being scolded like one," he retorted. "If you all want to concede a loss—and Fanny, too—then I'll gladly call an end to these bets. Otherwise, I won't withdraw my wagers. I do have my pride, the same as any of you, even if I don't flaunt it most of the time. So I'll stand by my bets, come what may. I will *not* marry until I'm fifty, I will *never* marry Fanny Epping and she will *not* break my heart in six weeks."

He bowed stiffly to his host. "I'm sorry if I've cast a pall over the celebration of your son's baptism, Viscount Adderley, and to ensure I don't cast more, I'll give you good day!"

With that, he walked out of the viscount's library, slamming the door behind him.

Chapter 2

*I was simply astonished. I had no idea quiet, de-
mure Fanny possessed such a temper. I daresay
neither did Brix, or the others. Unfortunately,
that was not the end of it.*

     Lady Diana Westover Terrington

Fanny stood silently on the threshold of the
 gaily painted nursery. Despite her distress,
she hesitated to disturb the peace of this comfortable chamber that seemed the embodiment of Diana's determination to be a good, and present,
mother, not a distant maternal figure with little in-
volvement in the life of her own children.

The nursery was near the master bedroom, instead of on another floor entirely. Painted a lovely,
light peacock blue, pictures of storybook characters hung on the walls. The furniture was light
wood, or painted white, and the carpet was thick
and as green as grass.

Diana had also decided to nurse her child, unlike most mothers of the *ton*, and she was doing so

now, sitting in a low white rocking chair. Illuminated by a beam of afternoon sunlight that poured in through the muslin-curtained windows, her dark hair loose about her shoulders and cradling her dark-haired son, they looked like a Renaissance portrait of a Madonna and child.

Fanny had often pictured herself in just such a pose, except that the baby in her arms would not have black hair like little D'Arcy, but blond locks that wouldn't fall flat, just like his father's.

What a little fool she'd been. How simpleminded. How blind. To care so much for a man only to discover he thought her nothing but a nuisance, a silly chit . . .

She quietly turned to go. She would go home, back to her brother's house, and wait for the storm that was likely already brewing.

Diana looked up and saw her. "Oh, hello, Fanny."

Fanny couldn't ignore her, so she turned back into the room. "I didn't mean to disturb you," she said softly, still on the threshold.

She couldn't bring herself to ruin this quiet time for mother and son. "I just wanted to say thank you again for asking me to be D'Arcy's godmother, before I went home."

Diana regarded Fanny in a way that made her want to squirm. Diana's intense gaze was nearly as disconcerting as Sir Douglas Drury's stare.

"Something's wrong," Diana declared quietly, but firmly. She gently laid her sleeping son in the cradle beside the rocking chair, then folded her hands in her lap and regarded Fanny expectantly. "You're upset. What's happened?"

As much as Fanny wanted to tell Diana about the wagers, she still hesitated. What good would it do to burden Diana with her troubles on this festive day?

Yet Diana was going to hear about it anyway. She'd been obviously upset when she'd run past Diana's husband on the stairs. The men in the library might be telling Edmond their version of what had happened even now.

If *she* told Diana what had happened, she could try to explain the feelings that had made her behave as she had. Surely Diana, being a woman and her friend, would be sympathetic.

In spite of her belief that Diana would be on her side, Fanny nervously entwined her fingers. "I heard something very upsetting, and I did something rather outlandish as a result," she confessed.

Diana frowned with puzzlement. "*You* did something outlandish?"

Fanny's hands dropped to her sides as she started to pace. "Yes—but I was driven to it by Brixton Smythe-Medway."

"Oh, dear, you'd better tell me all about it," Diana said with a sigh, as if to say, "What's he done now?"

Considering this was Brix, who was notorious for his pranks at Harrow and in the years since, Fanny wasn't surprised by her friend's tone.

She also wondered if Diana had already heard about the initial wagers from her husband.

Turning on her heel, she started across the room again, staying on the carpet so her footfalls would be muffled and not wake up the baby. "Did you know Brix has bet his friends that he won't marry until he's fifty, and he won't ever marry me?"

Diana's expression revealed that this was news to her. Either Edmond wasn't involved in that odious business, or he hadn't told Diana. Given the close relationship between Diana and her husband, Fanny guessed it was the former.

"It's true, and that's not all," she continued, relieved to think her friend hadn't been keeping secrets from her. "The wagers have been written up in the betting book at White's."

"Are you sure?" Diana asked after a moment's shocked silence. "It's not that I doubt you, Fanny, but I've never heard a whisper of such a thing."

Fanny perched on the end of a chair across from the cradle. "Drury said they were written up in the book at White's yesterday. He wouldn't joke about something like that. Indeed, he never jokes about anything."

What optimism had been on Diana's face disappeared. "No, he doesn't." Her eyes filled with sympathy. "I don't really know what to say, Fanny. I'll talk to Edmond and see if he'd heard about this, although I think he would have told me if he had."

"I just learned of it today myself," Fanny said. "I'd left my shawl in the dining room and was going to get it when I passed by the study. Brix and the others were there, and I heard them talking. I stopped when I caught my name. I know it's wrong to listen at doors, but I couldn't help it."

As the feeling of shame and horror returned, she struggled to keep her voice low so that she wouldn't disturb D'Arcy. "Oh, Diana, I've never been so mortified in my life!"

"Brix can be rather heedless," Diana agreed, "but I never thought he could be so . . . so . . ." She spread her hands as she searched for the right word.

"Heartless?" Fanny supplied. "Callous? *Cruel?*"

Diana grimaced. "Thoughtless certainly comes to mind."

"It's not just the wagers, although that's terrible enough," Fanny said as she rose to pace once again. "Brix must hate me. He must have hated me for a long time."

"Oh, I'm sure he doesn't hate you," Diana protested.

"Why else would he make fun of me in such a way?" Fanny demanded, her voice rising as her anger and dismay grew. "Why else would he say I'm annoying and a mousy little creature without an ounce of vitality?"

Little D'Arcy gave a short cry.

"That doesn't mean he hates you," Diana said placatingly as she gently rocked the cradle with her foot.

In spite of Diana's attempts at comfort, Fanny heard doubt in her voice.

She regarded her friend steadily. "If he doesn't hate me," she said, keeping her voice low so she wouldn't wake D'Arcy again, "why did he make that hateful bet?"

"Perhaps he was embarrassed by something Drury or one of the others said," Diana proposed. "Maybe they teased him, or goaded him in some way. Maybe it started out as some jest or joke and went too far."

Fanny crossed the carpet toward her. "That doesn't excuse him. If he thought I was such a nuisance and my company such a bother, he should have told me to my face."

"I was simply trying to envision how this could have happened."

Little D'Arcy began to cry.

"I'm sorry I woke him," Fanny said, distressed by this, too.

"It's all right," Diana assured her as she bent down and picked him up. Putting him against her shoulder, she started to rock. "He'll settle down again in a moment.

"I'm so taken aback by this, Fanny," she continued softly. "I didn't think Brix had a malicious bone in his body."

"Until today, I didn't, either," Fanny replied as Diana began to sing softly to her infant son.

What else had she been wrong about when it came to Brixton Smythe-Medway?

Like Diana, she'd been convinced that Brix was the most genial of men. He was always pleasant and agreeable, an amusing companion and entertaining host. She'd rarely heard a cross word pass his lips, at least since he'd become an adult. He was well respected by his servants and the tenants of his family's estate, even though he was the younger son. Many times when she'd visited Medway Manor she'd come upon tenants telling him their concerns and worries, instead of his older brother, Humphrey, or his father.

It wasn't hard to guess why: Brix was known to be fair and to care about their welfare. His father only worried about his horses and hounds; his brother only wanted to make money and increase the size of the estate.

She would also have agreed with any woman who found Brix a very attractive man. To be sure, he didn't have the viscount's classical good looks, or Drury's air of mystery, or Charlie Grendon's commanding presence. She even supposed some women might prefer Buggy Bromwell's studious demeanor and lean, sharp features.

But Brix had something more, and rare among the men Fanny knew: when she was with him, he made her feel comfortable and completely at ease, as if her troubles would all disappear, and nothing bad could possibly happen.

Until today.

"Perhaps it's not as bad as you think," Diana offered. "Perhaps Drury was mistaken, or somebody only told him about the wagers being written up . . ."

Her words trailed off when she saw Fanny's expression.

"I wish I thought you could be right," Fanny said grimly, "but I don't. Sir Douglas Drury isn't known to make mistakes, so I think we have to assume the wagers are now common knowledge."

She decided to tell Diana everything. She couldn't keep the worst a secret anyway. "And there's more, I'm afraid."

Diana paused in the middle of laying D'Arcy back in his cradle. "More?" she mouthed.

Fanny nodded. She walked to the other side of the room, as far away from the cradle as she could get, then waited until Diana joined her. When she did, she spoke in a whisper, to be sure she wouldn't wake the baby.

"I didn't simply skulk away," she admitted. "I was so angry, I walked into the study and confronted Brix. And then I made a counter wager. I bet him I could break his heart in six weeks."

Diana looked utterly flabbergasted.

"I know. It's ridiculous," Fanny said, running her hand over her forehead. "Fanny Epping break any man's heart in six weeks? Impossible!" She regarded her friend woefully. "I'm going to be the laughingstock of the *ton*. I can see them now, laughing and tittering behind their fans."

"Gossip doesn't last forever," Diana said soothingly. "The scandal around Edmond and me has been forgotten."

"Because he married you after pursuing you. He wasn't going around telling people he wouldn't ever marry you. He wasn't making wagers about it."

Fanny looked down at her feet. "I didn't just make the wager." She raised her eyes to look at her friend, silently pleading for understanding. "Instead of shaking his hand to seal the wager, I kissed him. And it wasn't a little peck on the cheek."

She wasn't going to go into more detail, such as how she'd impulsively stuck out her tongue mid-kiss, as she used to do when she'd pretended to be annoyed with Brix when they were children.

She'd had no idea that doing so while kissing would feel so . . . would have such an effect . . . would make him hold her closer and move his mouth with such slow, intoxicating languor . . .

She covered her blushing face with her hands. "I don't know what I was thinking!"

Diana reached out and gently pried Fanny's hands away from her burning cheeks. "I can't say that I know what you were thinking, but I can guess what you were feeling. You were hurt and angry. Your pride was wounded, too. You reacted on those feelings, and in that, you're no different from most of us.

"I don't think this is the end of the world, Fanny, truly. I'll talk to Brix, or get Edmond to. I'm sure we can convince him to see your side of it, and he'll be glad to forget this wagering non-sense. All will be well. You'll see. Now let me call the nursery maid to watch D'Arcy. We'll go to my morning room and have a nice cup of tea."

"I'm not anxious to face Brix again today," Fanny confessed. "I should be on my way."

Diana put her arm around Fanny's shoulders. "As you wish. And you know if there's anything I can do for you, Fanny, about this or anything else, you have only to ask. I was very lonely when I came to London as Edmond's bride, and I haven't forgotten that you were the first to visit me and make me feel welcome."

Fanny was warmed by those words, and she tried to smile, but it wasn't easy.

Diana didn't have to face an older brother who had mentioned going to White's that very afternoon.

Fanny paused in the hallway of her brother's London abode and glanced at her reflection in the large and ornately framed pier glass. Being just over five feet tall, she had to look through the enormous bouquet of lilies set on the rosewood pier table below the mirror.

Upon returning from Diana's, she'd changed into one of her day dresses, a simple buttercup yellow muslin frock without any trim, something that didn't require any thought or concern. She had quite enough on her mind without worrying about wrinkles in her skirts, or catching a bit of trim on one of her sister-in-law's chairs. Elizabeth preferred her furniture with as much ornamental carving as possible, and pointy acanthus leaves were a particular favorite.

Fanny smoothed her slightly disheveled hair, patting down the few errant curls that had come loose. She didn't want any hint of a disheveled appearance, which might signal that she'd been upset or distraught. Questions were going to come, of that she was sure, but she didn't want to inspire any sooner than necessary.

Frowning, Fanny scrutinized the rest of her reflection. No mode of dressing her hair was ever going to change the fact that she wasn't pretty. Her nose was hardly classic, her eyes were too large, her lips too full. To be sure, she'd never been described as ugly, but she was certainly no beauty, either.

She lowered her gaze to her bodice and sighed. She had a noticeable lack there, too.

"Oh, Fanny, is that you?" Her sister-in-law's lazy drawl wafted toward her from inside the sitting room. "Come and tell me all about the christening."

After pulling a face at her reflection, Fanny put on a smile and entered the drawing room. As she'd expected, Elizabeth was reclining on the Grecian couch covered in expensive gold brocade. The damask upholstery on the couch matched the gold brocade swag draperies edged with long fringe and tied back with heavy tassels. They matched the gold velvet upholstery on the oval-backed and Bergere chairs. The various side tables were made of satinwood and harewood, some inlaid in intricate patterns. A Savonnerie carpet in crimson and gold covered much of the floor. There was a pianoforte in the far corner, and a gilded harp—which Elizabeth hadn't played since the day she wed—stood beside it. The walls of the large room were covered in very expensive wallpaper, also in varying shades of gold, and the white plaster chimneypiece was ornately decorated with festoons of leaves.

Whenever Fanny was annoyed with Elizabeth, which happened with some frequency, she tried to think of her sister-in-law as a bird in a gilded cage and feel some pity for her.

That rarely worked, because Elizabeth had eagerly thrown herself into her gilded chamber. The duke of Hetley had been considered quite a catch. Not only was he of high rank, Albert was not an ill-favored man, and he could be generous, as the decor of this room illustrated, for that had been all Elizabeth's doing.

Elizabeth had been considered quite a catch herself, a fact she never forgot, or let other people forget, especially Fanny.

As Fanny approached, Elizabeth raised herself slightly on her elbow. Bangle bracelets jingled with her languid movement. The amethyst broach she wore at the neck of her high-cut bodice caught the last rays of the sun, and more purple sparkled in her ears. Her gown, of mauve silk, was high-waisted and cut to emphasize her figure, which was well endowed.

Elizabeth's heavy dark hair was expertly dressed *à la grecque*, with braids and curls and ribbons, in a manner that had likely taken two hours or better at her dressing table, time Fanny preferred to spend reading, or sewing, playing with her nieces and nephews, or helping them with their studies.

Although Elizabeth clearly didn't approve of

Fanny's hair or dress, she no longer voiced her opinion of Fanny's taste, having tried for six years to get her to emulate herself, to no avail. Fanny had resisted every effort to wear garments abundantly trimmed in lace, tucks and embroidery. She was too petite; she'd look more like a doll or a child than a woman, and she'd very much wanted Brix to think of her as a woman.

In the days before she knew what he really thought of her.

"So, how was the baptism?" Elizabeth asked as Fanny sat beside the couch. "What was the child's gown like? And his mother's? Were all the viscount's friends there? Even Lord Bromwell? I hear he's mounting another expedition soon, to the Amazon or some other godforsaken place. Really, what he sees in spiders, I'll never understand, although that book of his did rather well, I understand. What was it called? *The Spider's Lair?* And Sir Douglas Drury? Was he there? What about that dashing naval officer? I hear he made a pretty penny in the war. I suppose they'll all be marrying now that the viscount has."

Elizabeth never raised her voice, and she didn't speak quickly; nevertheless, one had about as much chance of interrupting her as of interrupting a town crier in midbellow. Fanny had learned to wait for Elizabeth to draw breath before attempting to speak when sharing a conversation with her, which she finally did.

"The baby's gown was quite exquisite," Fanny dutifully reported. "Belgium lace, and white silk with blue satin trim. Lady Diana was also very prettily dressed. She doesn't worry about finery, as you know, but I doubt even you could find fault with her gown."

Elizabeth was not the most perceptive of women, so her expression didn't alter by so much as a raised eyebrow before Fanny continued. "It was a very lovely pale burgundy silk. Her bonnet was fairly plain, but it came from Paris, the ribbons were silk and perhaps, oh, two inches wide. Of course, the viscount looked handsome, and all his friends were there."

Elizabeth likewise failed to notice the change in Fanny's tone and the slight hardening of her expression.

"Lord Bromwell, whose book was *The Spider's Web*, made no mention of another expedition. I gather Lieutenant Grendon will soon be going back to sea, perhaps to the West Indies. Sir Douglas didn't say very much, but then, he never does."

Elizabeth smiled at the mention of the barrister. "No, he was always a quiet man. He spoke more with those marvelous eyes of his than with his marvelous voice."

Fanny didn't even attempt to reply to this, yet she had never for an instant believed Sir Douglas Drury had ever been seriously interested in the beautiful Elizabeth. Nor could she fathom what any woman saw in the barrister, although she heard all the rumors of his various romantic liaisons. Sir Douglas always made Fanny uncomfortable, as if he was about to ferret out her secrets.

That might explain his appeal to some women, but she much preferred to be comfortable, the way she always was with Brix. Or used to be.

"What about that other fellow—Smythe-Medway? The one you like so much, although I really don't see why. He's amusing enough, I suppose, and the younger son of an earl, but his hair! You'd think his man could cut it instead of letting it flop about like a bundle of wet straw! His nose is rather too large, although quite aristocratic, and his mouth—"

Fanny did not want to hear any comments about Brixton Smythe-Medway's mouth. "Yes, he was there."

Elizabeth looked startled, as indeed she was. "Are you quite well, my dear?"

"I'm a little tired. It's been a busy day."

"I do hope you haven't got a headache. Young Albert's been wanting you to explain geometry to him." Elizabeth sighed as if she carried the weight of the world. "I fear we were sadly mistaken hiring Mr. Heppleweight for his tutor. He can't seem to teach the boys anything. Albert doesn't understand the first thing about angels, or octapuses, or quadruplets after all this time, and Peter remains baffled by multiplication. *You* got him up to the five times table. And then Miss Mapples tried to tell me the girls were not applying themselves to their French. I said to her, 'My dear Miss Mapples, even Fanny could teach them some French before you arrived, so the fault cannot lie with *them*.' You should have seen her face."

When Elizabeth again paused for breath, Fanny took the opportunity to break in. "Perhaps if you made it clear to Clarissa and Geraldine that they must pay attention to their lessons and not tease each other so much, it would help."

"They are merely lively and spirited girls, Fanny," her sister-in-law replied, with an unspoken implication in her tone that Fanny would never understand lively and spirited girls, not being one herself.

And as if their mother wasn't the very opposite of lively or spirited.

"I think we might have to dispense with Miss Mapples entirely," Elizabeth continued. "You wouldn't mind taking over the girls' education, would you, Fanny? You've got nothing better to do. And perhaps we'll bid adieu to Mr. Heppleweight, too. He's certainly not earning his wages, and you're living here anyway."

Fanny stiffened. Ever since her parents had died and she'd come to live with her brother, she'd lived in dread of just such a fate.

Having foreseen this suggestion, however, Fanny was prepared. "Naturally I'm grateful for your hospitality, Elizabeth, and I'm pleased to think I've been of assistance to the children. Unfortunately, I'm not qualified to teach them what they ought to know if they're to succeed in society, especially the girls, or I wouldn't be living with you. I would have a husband and household and children of my own.

"As for the boys, I'm sure I'd never be able to manage them as they get older. As you're always noting, I'm too timid a creature. They would simply overrule me and learn nothing. No, Elizabeth, as loath as I am to admit it, I would be a very poor substitute for either Miss Mapples or Mr. Heppleweight."

Fanny put on a mournful face. "I regret that I'm such a burden. Perhaps it's about time I made my own establishment—

"*Fanny!*" Her brother's angry voice thundered through the house. "Where the devil is the chit?"

As Fanny cringed, Elizabeth sat bolt upright, and the drawing room door crashed open.

"Here you are!" Albert cried as he spotted Fanny.

She steeled herself for the battle to come. Obviously he'd heard about the wagers, for there could be nothing else that would explain the fury he was directing at her.

Still wearing his indigo great coat and tall hat, Albert strode into the room and came to a halt, glaring, his beefy hands on his broad hips.

"Why, whatever is wrong, Albert?" Elizabeth cried, wringing her hands. "You're scaring me!"

"I'll tell you what's wrong, my love," Albert declared as he began to wrestle off his coat. The butler, who'd been fidgeting anxiously behind him, hurried forward to help.

Laughlin only seemed to get in his employer's way, however, as Albert continued to speak and struggle with his garment. "My sister . . . the sister and daughter of a duke . . . Fanny . . . she's . . . you won't believe it . . . the shame . . . the degradation . . ."

Eventually Albert fought his way free of his coat. Laughlin took the offending garment and his master's hat and scurried away.

Straightening his disheveled cravat, Albert glared at Fanny as if she'd tried to assassinate him. "Fanny, you've disgraced us! And after all I've done for you!"

Fanny had long ago learned that the best way to end her brother's blustering tantrums was to remain calm and composed—and address her brother as if he were a very small, very sulky child. "I assume you've discovered that the Honorable Brixton Smythe-Medway has made a wager with his friends that he won't marry until he's fifty, and that he'll never marry *me*."

Elizabeth's mouth dropped open, while Albert muttered what sounded like a very earthy curse.

"I only found out about it this morning after the christening," Fanny continued.

Elizabeth made a noise like a distressed sheep.

Fanny decided it would be better to tell him everything before he heard it in a similar second-hand manner. "Naturally, I was as upset as you are. In fact, I was so angry and indignant over what he'd done, that I lost my temper and made a wager with Mr. Smythe-Medway myself."

Albert's face, already red, turned almost purple. "*Y-you*?" he bellowed like a wounded bull. "*You* made a wager?"

"Yes." She thought of the one reason Albert might comprehend to explain what she'd done. "I felt my pride was at stake, so I bet Mr. Smythe-Medway that I can break his heart in six weeks."

Staring at Fanny, her brother gasped for air like a landed fish and felt for the nearest chair, into which he collapsed. Elizabeth didn't speak or move or do anything, except breathe.

"Are you *mad*?" Albert finally gasped.

"I told you, I lost my temper. I admit I acted on impulse, but surely you wouldn't have wanted me to ignore—"

Suddenly invigorated, Albert shot to his large feet. "I would have wanted you to behave with dignity, as befits our family! Had you no thought of our honor, our standing in society?"

She should have known it was useless to expect Albert to share her feelings, or have any concern about how Brix's wager had upset her. "My pride was wounded, Albert. And many of the highest-born ladies of the *ton* gamble. I see little difference—"

"There's a world of difference!" he cried, flailing his arms. "They gamble at cards, or gaming tables. They don't bet men they'll break their hearts! They don't allow their names to be written in the book at White's."

Fanny rose and faced her brother squarely. "I didn't *allow* my name to be written at White's. I didn't make that wager, and I assure you, I would be delighted if it had never been made. But it was, and I responded in the only way—"

"You *responded* like a damned silly chit of a girl!" Albert roared. "You should have used your head!"

"And reacted calmly, as you are now?" Fanny countered.

She had the brief pleasure of seeing Albert's sails lose their wind—momentarily. In the next moment, he was back in full angry throttle. "You shouldn't have made that wager. It's degrading! Demeaning! Disgraceful! Disgusting!"

"Unlike the original one?" she charged. "Isn't that worthy of a few of your *de*-nunciations?"

"Of course I'm not pleased about it," Albert fumed, his fists clenching, "but I can't control that idiot Smythe-Medway."

"You don't con—"

"As your older brother, I *do* control you, Fanny," Albert interrupted, an arrogant gleam in his blue eyes that she knew all too well. "It's my duty, and one I didn't mind, until today."

Shaking his head, he walked to the doors leading to the garden. "I don't know what's come over you, Fanny, I really don't. You've always been a most amenable, amiable, sensible girl, except for your infatuation with Smythe-Medway, who's nothing but a useless, lazy dilettante."

"As if you're a model of useful activity," Fanny retorted. "All you do is discuss politics and politicians, or the latest political scandal. You constantly complain about the government, but you never do anything about it. And all your arguments only ever end in duels, not real change."

"What do you mean by defending that wastrel?"

Good God, what did she mean by it?

Having effectively silenced her, Albert clasped his hands behind his wide hips and assumed an even more pompous, patronizing air. "Fanny, it's clear to me that you've allowed your emotions to run away with you today. That would be bad enough, but you've also acted upon them in a way I simply cannot countenance, no matter how hysterical you become. Elizabeth and I have allowed you to live in our home, and we'll continue to do so, but only if you conduct yourself as befits the sister of a duke, no matter how distraught you may be."

Fanny glanced at her sister-in-law, to see her still staring at them slack-jawed with horrified disbelief. She looked back at Albert and envisioned a long, dull future under his broad thumb.

"And if I don't conduct myself as *you* see fit?" she asked, raising an inquisitive brow. "Will you toss me out into the streets?"

Albert scowled. "Don't talk nonsense, Fanny."

"Is it nonsense to want to be free to conduct myself as *I* see fit?"

Elizabeth made a disapproving noise, and that was the last straw for Fanny. Her temper, already more roused this day than it had been for years, burst forth again. "So it's live by your rules, and be happy with your bounty. Become nothing but an unpaid servant, and rejoice."

Albert gave her a warning look. "Fanny, calm yourself."

"I won't be calm!" Her whole body quaked with barely suppressed rage. "I've been calm for years, and what good has it done me? You've made me feel like a leech for living in your house. Your wife makes me feel like the ugliest woman in London. Your children make fun of me behind my back—but who's to blame for that except their father? You've been teasing and making fun of me all my life. Well, I won't stand it another moment!"

"Fanny, take care, or I'll wash my hands of you," her brother warned, wiping his hands together as if he was already doing so.

"Go ahead," Fanny declared as she marched toward the door. "Do whatever you like, because I won't be here to see it. I won't stay in this house as your lowly dependent, Albert."

"What are you doing?" he demanded, following her.

"I'm leaving this house. Now."

"Don't be ridiculous!" he cried, coming to an abrupt halt. "I'm not forcing you to leave. I'm not asking you to go. What on earth will people say?"

Her hand on the latch, Fanny turned back and glared at him. "That's really all you care about, isn't it, Albert? *Your* reputation. Well, I don't care what people say about me anymore. I've lived by society's rules, done everything my governess told me, and what good has it done me? I'm going to be gossiped about and laughed at anyway. But I won't stand idly by and do nothing except submit."

"Fanny, I *order* you to stay!"

"No."

Elizabeth suddenly hurled herself at her husband as if she feared Fanny was going to assault him. "Let her go, Albert! She's not in her right mind. What if she harms the children?"

That question was too ludicrous even for Albert. "Don't be a fool, Elizabeth. Fanny will listen to reason."

Fanny's eyes blazed. "If by that you mean I'll do as you say, I will not."

"You can't just walk out of this house!" Albert cried.

"No, I can't," Fanny snapped as she threw open the door. "First I have to pack a bag."

Quite oblivious to pedestrians, street sellers, horses, carriages and dogs, Fanny marched through Mayfair, her bag bumping against her leg. Resisting Albert's orders and pleas, ignoring Elizabeth's wailing and the servants' shocked stares, she'd packed a few of her things in an old traveling case, thrown on a short Spencer jacket, shoved a bonnet on her head and left her brother's house forever.

She felt like a servant finally free of a master's hated yoke. It was about time she'd told Albert what she really thought. It was past time she made her own way in the world and quit hoping Brixton Smythe-Medway would marry her and take her away from Albert's domineering patronage.

Her euphoria lasted until the perspiration began to trickle down her back, and her leg began to feel sore where the bag hit it. She came to a halt—and suddenly realized she had no idea where she was.

A quick survey of the area told her she was still in Mayfair, and she'd been walking generally north. Then she realized she wasn't very far from Diana and Edmond's.

Diana and Edmond would surely welcome her, and since they already knew about the wager, she wouldn't have to explain or answer questions about the cause of her quarrel with Albert.

She began walking toward their house on Curzon Street with renewed vigor. She wouldn't impose on them for long. As she'd been about to say to Elizabeth earlier, she was anxious to set up her own household. She'd saved most of her pin money for several years, and that would be enough to set up some sort of establishment for herself.

"Are you lost, my lovely?"

Ripped from her ruminations, Fanny raised her head and discovered two drunken, leering dandies standing in front of her, blocking her way. They were both wearing the most extreme form of popular male fashion. The tallest one, made taller by his beaver hat, sported a vest in a bilious shade of green and lazily twirled a silver-headed walking cane. His trousers and jacket were so tight, they looked about to tear asunder. His companion, shorter and rounder, grinned like a death's-head encased in the high points of his collar.

"Been dismissed from your place, have you?" the short one said, running an insolent gaze over her as she tried to remain calm. They were in a public street in a good part of town, after all. Surely that would offer her some protection.

Yet all she could think about was the tales her governess had told her illustrating how dangerous the world could be for a woman alone.

"I could use a new maid," the tall man said, smirking at his companion. "Especially one as pretty as this." He turned his leering, smarmy face toward Fanny. "What do you say, my dear? Fancy coming to my house?"

"I should think not," she said haughtily, taking defense in her breeding as her grip tightened on her bag. She straightened her shoulders. "Let me pass."

"Ooooh, my, isn't she the hoity-toity one?" the tall man cried. "Been listening to your mistress, eh? Picked up how to speak from her, did you?"

"Wonder if she picked up anything from the master," the short man speculated in a way that made Fanny's flesh crawl. "Maybe that's why she had to leave, eh? Bet you were more friendly with him."

She glanced around, seeking aid, but the street was deserted, and the curtains were already drawn in the nearest houses.

"Come on, my dear, come home with me. I'll give you a hot supper," the tall man murmured, forcing her back against the iron railing that separated the row of limestone-fronted town houses from the walk.

"I'll give you something else," the short one promised, licking his lips as he reached out to take hold of her arms.

Energy surged through Fanny and she swung her bag as hard as she could, sending the short man staggering. The other one grabbed her arm, but she kept swinging, catching him on the side of the head and knocking him sideways. He stumbled back, swearing.

Fanny didn't hesitate. Clutching her bag, she ran down the street as fast as her legs could take her. She kept running until she could hardly draw breath, then stopped and, panting heavily, looked around. There was no sign of the men, or anybody else giving chase.

She dropped her bag and held onto a railing for support as she tried to regain her breath and calm her shattered nerves.

A couple walked by on the other side of the road, glancing at her warily.

She must be a sight, and if she didn't find shelter soon, she might find herself in more danger.

"Oh, thank heavens," she murmured with relief as she looked around. She'd run in the right direction. Diana's house was the third one from the other end of the street.

She adjusted her bonnet and smoothed down her skirts, then, with chin up and head high as if it wasn't at all unusual for the sister of a duke to march down Curzon Street with a piece of baggage in her hand, she headed for her friends' house.

As she did, a different kind of euphoria crept through her, different from the feeling of liberation. She'd been able to defend herself. She wasn't completely helpless.

At least against a pair of drunken dandies and provided she was armed with a large bag, her rational mind argued. If the circumstances had been different, the outcome could have been much worse.

So she quickened her steps, and didn't feel safe until she stood on the viscount's doorstep. Setting down the bag, she rapped sharply on the door and waited, feeling rather like a beggar about to make an outrageous request.

The butler, Ruttles, opened the door. There was a momentary flash of surprise in his gray eyes, and another when he saw her bag, but his shock was quickly hidden under his usual stony demeanor. "Good afternoon . . ." He hesitated, glanced at the dusky sky and began again. "Good evening, my lady. Won't you come in?"

She nodded and did so, stepping onto the marble floor of the foyer. The walls were a pale pastel blue, with white trim and cornices beneath an ornate plaster ceiling. Beyond, a hanging staircase led to the upper floors.

"I assume you wish to see Viscount Adderley and his wife?" Ruttles inquired.

"Yes, if I'm not disturbing them," she replied, although she wasn't sure what she'd say if Ruttles told her she was.

"I shall inform Lord and Lady Adderley that they have a visitor," the butler said as he helped her remove her Spencer jacket.

She must look as overheated and unkempt as she felt, but Ruttles gave no indication he saw anything amiss. He'd probably give no indication anything was amiss if she arrived in her nightdress.

She dutifully followed Ruttles to the drawing room. Although this was the principal receiving room in the house, it was quite a contrast to most similar chambers in other London mansions. Diana and Edmond preferred simplicity and ease, and it showed. There was not one chair that didn't look comfortable, or one sofa that didn't invite one to sit and relax. The tables were of a variety of woods, some inlaid, some plain, but all polished to a high gloss. The brightly colored carpet was lovely, yet not so fine one would feel horribly guilty if a crumb strayed from a plate to the floor. The pictures were simple country scenes, many of them from Lady Diana's native Lincolnshire.

After showing her to the drawing room, Ruttles swiftly disappeared, to tell Edmond and Diana she was there, no doubt.

With a weary sigh, Fanny sat on the nearest sofa and leaned against the back—although no proper lady ever did such a thing—and closed her eyes. What a day it had been! She sincerely hoped she never had another one like it.

When the rustle of fabric heralded a woman's arrival, Fanny opened her eyes and found Diana at the door, Edmond right behind her.

Diana rushed anxiously toward her. "Oh, my dear, what's happened?"

"Are you hurt?" Edmond asked, surveying her from head to toe.

"No, just tired. I quarreled with Albert and left the house. I walked here," Fanny explained as she rose. She decided she wouldn't mention the two dandies. "I hope you don't mind that I've come here, and without any warning—"

"Of course we don't mind!" Diana cried as she embraced her. "You're always welcome here, Fanny, anytime. Isn't she, Edmond?"

"Absolutely." The viscount went to the door and called for Ruttles. "Fetch some wine for her ladyship. And tea. And cake. And anything else the cook has handy in the pantry."

Diana sank onto the sofa and pulled Fanny down beside her. "I assume the quarrel was about the wagers."

Twisting her ring, Fanny glanced at Edmond. "Do you know . . . ?"

"I heard all about it, from Brix and the others, and I have to say, Fanny, I was as surprised and disturbed by his behavior as you were," Edmond replied. "Unfortunately, he persists in believing the matter is of no serious consequence."

It sounded as if she wasn't the only one who'd quarreled that afternoon. Fanny felt a moment's guilt, for Brix and Edmond were best friends, or had been . . . but if there was conflict between them, it was far more Brix's fault than hers, and she would not feel responsible. "He can think that way because it's not of serious consequence to him—but it certainly is to me, or I wouldn't be here. Albert heard about Brix's bets at White's and came home angrier than I've ever seen him. He was furious, and he refused to listen to my explanations."

Her anger kindled again. "You'd think *I* was the one who made the original wagers and wrote them up at White's, the way he carried on. Albert didn't care about how I felt or why I did what I did. And then Elizabeth . . ."

She took a moment to rein in her rising temper. "I foolishly thought it would be best to get it all over with at once, so I told them about the bet I made with Brix, too."

"I don't think that was foolish at all," Diana said, patting her hand. "I think you were wise to tell them everything and explain your point of view."

Her husband didn't look quite so sure. "It might have been better to let Albert deal with one thing at a time."

"Or he might have thought she was hiding other things from him if he learned of it later," Diana said. "It was far wiser to tell him all about what happened and why she did what she did."

The last thing Fanny wanted to do was cause a disagreement between her friends. "It doesn't matter now," she said briskly. "What's done is done. And it's not just what happened today that caused our argument. This was only the final straw. I've been planning to leave his home as soon as I possibly could. This situation simply caused me to leave a bit sooner than I expected."

She rose. "I don't want to impose. I can go to a hotel—"

"I won't hear of it!" Diana cried, pulling her back down beside her. "You may stay here for as long as you like, and as long as you need. Isn't that right, Edmond?"

The viscount nodded, and there was sincerity in his brown eyes. "Please don't even think of going to a hotel." He shifted, as if embarrassed by what he had to say next. "I should point out, Fanny, that gossip and rumors are going to run rampant when the *ton* hear about the wagers and the quarrel with your brother, and you leaving home. If you go to a hotel, the gossip will be even worse."

Fanny nodded. "Those wagers are bad enough," she agreed. "I don't want people to think I have no morals at all." Her grateful gaze took in the couple. "Thank you for your help, and your understanding."

Ruttles appeared at the door, leading two maids bearing trays of food and drink.

"Now you must have something to eat," Diana said as the servants entered. "Then we'll get you settled. Ruttles, please take Lady Fanny's bag to the blue bedroom."

As the butler did as he was asked, and Fanny drank a very welcome cup of tea, Diana led her husband a little to one side.

"Tomorrow you must go to Brix and make him see that this wagering business must stop," she whispered, "before things get any worse."

"How much worse could they get?" Edmond replied woefully.

"I don't know, but I don't want to find out," his wife answered.

"Brix may not want to see me. I've never seen him so annoyed."

"You have to try. Fanny's reputation could be at stake. You and I know how vicious the *ton* can be."

"Yes, my love, we do," Edmond grimly agreed, "so I'll go first thing in the morning."

Chapter 3

Letter of the third of May (continued)

So as I close, Aunt Euphenia, Edmond has gone to try to convince Brix to apologize and call off the wagers. I do hope he succeeds, and that Brix realizes the deleterious effect of what he's brought about. But I fear Brix may not appreciate the harm he's done, and not just to Fanny's reputation among the ton. *It seems so difficult for men to understand women's hearts, especially when they've been wounded.*

> *Lady Diana Westover Terrington*

*T*he *Times* unopened at his elbow, a cheroot burning down to a fine-powdered ash in the blue Wedgwood dish beside it, Brix slumped in the upholstered chair beside the hearth in his study and stared at the glowing coals. A clock on the mantel chimed the hour, the sound echoing through the paneled room. Outside, dull gray clouds obscured the morning sky. The rain had stopped a few minutes ago, but it was still chilly, making it a fine sort of day for staying inside beside a cozy fire.

Except that it also led one to contemplate one's mistakes, as Brix had been doing since breakfast.

He shouldn't have lost his temper with his friends. Even if he was right and there really was no need to be so worked up about the wagers, he shouldn't have let his annoyance get the better of him, and he certainly shouldn't have revealed it. He mustn't forget the lessons he'd learned in his childhood when he cried or otherwise demonstrated any weakness. His mother had shooed him away lest his tears stain her gown, his father had told him to show some spirit and his brother had teased him without mercy. No matter how he felt at the time, though, those lessons stood him in good stead with the ever-inquisitive *ton*, who would be even more pitiless if they found a chink in his merry armor.

Of course, it would have been better if he'd kept quiet about the wagers that celebratory night in the club, but that genie had left the bottle, and there was nothing he could do about it. If Fanny had simply remained calm, she would have seen that making a joke of the situation would have solved any potential problems. That was another lesson he'd learned in his youth: that people were generally willing to excuse you if you could make them laugh.

If that also meant people never took you seriously, well, nothing came without a price, and surely that was better than getting everybody's trousers in a twist.

Ah well, he'd simply have to exert himself to

make her see his point of view sooner rather than later. With a little charm and levity, she'd get over her anger and forgive him, too. Eventually.

He wouldn't go today, though. The weather wasn't conducive to visiting, and a little more time would give Fanny more of a chance to calm down and reconsider her outrageous actions, too.

Like that amazing, astonishing, incredibly passionate kiss.

He shifted in his chair, for he could almost feel her lips on his again, and the unexpected—and unexpectedly sensuous—sensation of her tongue thrusting between his lips. How surprisingly wonderful and perfect it had felt to be holding her body against his, her soft, round breasts pressing against his chest as he held her close.

Where on earth had she learned to kiss like that, he wondered yet again. Somebody must have told her, or taught her.

Who could have shown her that kind of kiss? Absolutely nobody came to mind. Given that his mother fairly lived to gossip and that his parents kept telling him he ought to marry Fanny, surely he would have heard of any serious suitor for her heart and hand.

Maybe it hadn't been a suitor. It could have been a servant, some comely young footman or hall boy or groom. Such things had been known to happen.

Maybe one of them had seen a chance for a little clandestine rendezvous with a vulnerable young woman. Maybe Fanny had enjoyed the secrecy, the excitement of a forbidden romance. Maybe Fanny wasn't nearly as demure and innocent as he thought. She certainly hadn't been demure and innocent yesterday.

He flicked what was left of the cheroot into the fireplace and abruptly got to his feet. He had business he should be attending to instead of wasting his time thinking about Fanny Epping and her phantom lovers.

He strode to his pedestal desk and ran his gaze over the correspondence from the foreman of his factory in Yorkshire lying on the dark green leather top. Other local factory owners were complaining that he was paying his employees too much and causing dissension.

With a sardonic little grin, Brix got out his writing materials, chewed meditatively on the end of a quill for a moment, then began to write.

Dear Lord Franklin,

Thank you so much for your charming epistle. I am overwhelmed and touched by the concern you show for my financial well-being, even though we have not yet had the pleasure of being introduced.

The niceties concluded, I shall now address the particulars you were so good as to bring to my attention:

I have no intention of lowering the hourly rate I pay the workers in my factory. I believe that a worker who has adequate means to clothe and feed himself and his family is a more productive worker. Nor do I intend to allow their cottages to fall into rack and ruin. Since I believe it would be an exercise in futility to appeal to your Christian charity, I will simply note that that would not only render the village of Hopburton most unpicturesque, but the subsequent disease and discomfort would not be conducive to maintaining the factory's current excellent level of production, which resulted in a record profit last year, despite what you so delightfully refer to as the addlepated coddling of my workers.

Yours most humbly,
The Honorable Brixton Smythe-Medway

After folding the letter, Brix lit a candle from the coals and melted the end of a stick of red sealing wax. When he had a suitable-sized blob, he pressed his seal into it. "Take that, you greedy varlet," he muttered with grim satisfaction.

"Mr. Smythe-Medway?"

He looked up to see the bewigged first footman standing in the doorway, holding a silver salver and looking rather nervous.

"I wasn't speaking to you, Matthews."

Relieved, the servant approached the desk and held out the salver bearing a white visiting card.

Brix recognized the crest immediately. "Please show the viscount in at once," he ordered.

As the footman dutifully hurried away, Brix thrust his hands in his pockets and strolled toward the marble chimneypiece.

An anxiety he hadn't wanted to acknowledge dissipated. Edmond couldn't be very angry over what had happened yesterday, or he wouldn't come at all. As for his other friends, Buggy was inclined to look on the gloomy side of everything, and Charlie's humble background meant he wasn't familiar with the *ton's* short memory. And Drury . . . Drury was a puzzling, frustrating cipher, and always had been.

A somber Edmond entered the room, and Brix hurried to shake his hand. "I'm glad to see you, my friend," he said, making the first apologetic overture. "I was sitting here in a brown study contemplating my sins, and I must say, that's a horrible way to spend a morning."

"Your sins?" Edmond asked with a significance that didn't escape Brix as he gestured at a chair.

"Well, what happened yesterday. Very unfortunate, and on little D'Arcy Douglas's baptismal day, too. I'm sorry for casting a pall over the proceedings."

Despite his apology, Edmond still didn't relax or resume his usual comfortable manner, or even sit down. He stood before Brix as if delivering a funeral oration over the body of Caesar. "Unfortunately, something has happened that's made the situation rather worse."

It felt as if a rock had landed square in the pit of Brix's stomach. "What?"

"Albert found out about your wagers. He and Fanny quarreled, and Fanny has left her brother's house."

With a horrified gasp, Brix instantly envisioned Fanny lost and wandering alone through the slums of Seven Dials. "When was this?" he demanded as he ran for the door. "Do they know which way she went? Have they sent for the Bow Street Runners?"

"She's not missing," Edmond announced.

Brix halted and swiveled on his heel. "She's not?"

"She's perfectly well. She came to Diana and me."

"Oh, thank God," Brix murmured, catching his breath.

Then, although his heartbeat was still as rapid as the wings of a sparrow in flight, he smiled jovially and returned to his seat. With a theatrical flourish, he laid his hand on his chest. "What a scare you gave me! What were you trying to do, send me to an early grave?"

Edmond studied him a moment before taking a seat and replying. "No. But I thought you ought to know what's happened."

Brix tried not to betray any dismay or remorse as he reached for the box of cheroots at his elbow. After all, Fanny's family business was none of his, except in one way. "I'm glad you told me before I went there and wound up face-to-face with Albert. That would have been damned uncomfortable."

Edmond crossed his arms. "She says she won't go back, and I have to say, Brix, she sounds quite determined."

"This *is* Fanny Epping we're discussing?"

Edmond gave him a look.

"Just making sure," Brix said. "I didn't think Fanny would ever be so presumptuous as to arrive on your doorstep like some sort of orphan and ask to live with you instead of her only family."

"Where else should she go except to her friends?"

Exactly, Brix chided his wayward imagination, which had conjured a vision of Fanny standing in this very room, regarding him with her big blue eyes full of gratitude. She wouldn't be coming to him for help anymore—thank God.

"Fanny says she intends to set up her own establishment."

Brix didn't even try to hide his surprise. "What? Live by herself?"

"With a chaperon and some servants, apparently," Edmond clarified. "She was talking about it at breakfast, and it seems she's been planning to do that for some time."

Brix opened the box of cheroots he'd forgotten he was holding and extracted one. "Surely you and Diana tried to talk her out of it."

Edmond shook his head, refusing the proffered cheroot. "As I said, she's quite adamant, and Diana thinks we shouldn't interfere. She says Fanny's a grown woman fully capable of making her own decisions about her future."

"So Diana agrees with this scheme?" Brix said as he set the box back on the rosewood table beside him and selected a cheroot for himself. "I always thought your wife was a very unique woman."

"This isn't about Diana, Brix. It's Fanny I'm worried about, and you should be, too. It's partly your fault she's in this situation."

"I do realize that, Edmond," Brix said as he lit his cheroot and took a few puffs, hoping it would calm his rattled nerves. "As shocking as it sounds at first, perhaps Fanny's right to want to set up her own establishment. Albert's a tyrant, and his wife is the most useless woman I've ever met. She makes my mother look like a marvel of activity, and that takes some doing—or not doing. Why shouldn't Fanny have her own house, provided she has a companion, some suitably elderly female of impeccable breeding? Mother will likely know a few she could recommend."

"I agree that Fanny might be happier in her own establishment," Edmond replied, "but leaving her brother's protection is going to cause a lot of talk. We both know the damage gossip can do, and it's a lot worse for a woman."

Brix smoked in silence, because Edmond was right, and there wasn't any point trying to deny it.

His elbows on his knees, Edmond clasped his hands together and leaned forward, regarding Brix intently. "And what if the breach with her brother is never mended? I know you don't like Albert, but do you honestly believe Fanny should be estranged from her family?"

"Estranged? No," Brix agreed as he tossed

away his cheroot and rose. He strolled toward the window, then turned to face Edmond. "I hate to think of her nieces and nephews without her around to guide them." He shuddered. "The girls might turn out like their mother and the boys like their father."

"Can't you *ever* be serious?" Edmond demanded, straightening.

"Of course I can, and I meant what I said. I think Fanny's probably the best thing in her nieces' and nephews' lives."

Edmond raised a brow. "So you don't really dislike Fanny?"

"God, no! Who could dislike Fanny?" Brix replied, strolling back to his chair. "I simply disliked the way she followed me around all the time. Damned disconcerting, really. I can't begin to tell you the number of secret rendezvous I've had to forgo fearing that Fanny'd pop out from behind a pillar or a tree. But that's not likely to be a problem ever again," he concluded.

"Then you're willing to do what you can to help mend this rift?"

"Of course," Brix exclaimed as he sank onto his chair. "As long as it doesn't involve having a word with Albert. He hates me, and the feeling is quite mutual."

"I was thinking it would help if the wagers were called off."

He should have guessed. "All of them?"

Edmond nodded. "I've already talked to Drury and Buggy this morning. They're willing, and I'm sure Charlie will be, once I send a letter to him at Portsmouth. He left London too early for me to catch him."

Brix steepled his fingers and laid them against his chin. "I see. What about my wager with Fanny?"

"I think you should rescind that, too, of course."

Brix got to his feet and started to pace as he addressed Edmond. "So what you're suggesting is that in order to allow Fanny to make peace with the odious Albert, I forego the eventual winning of fifteen hundred pounds and apologize to Fanny for causing her to get totally and needlessly overwrought."

Edmond rose and regarded him sternly. "Brix, we both know you weren't serious about the wagers with Drury and the others. I mean, you wouldn't be able to collect until you were fifty, for one thing. And Fanny will probably be glad to forget she made that wager yesterday and eager to accept your apology. You said she would be, and I believe you."

Edmond was starting to sound frustrated. Whatever else happened, Brix didn't want another quarrel with his friend, so he put a raffish smile on his face and reached for the bellpull. "Very well, you've convinced me. I'll go home with you right now and make my humble apologies."

Edmond both sighed and smiled with relief. "I'm glad you're seeing reason."

That wasn't how Brix viewed his capitulation,

but he didn't want any more conflict. Between his parents' squabbles and his brother's bullying, he'd had quite enough of that growing up.

So he once again put on his merry jester's mask and clapped his friend on the shoulder. "We'd better get on our way at once, eh? Otherwise, who knows what Fanny's liable to do next? Throw a tantrum at Almack's? Make a scene in St. James's Park? The mind boggles."

Edmond laughed as they headed for the door, and Brix tried to tell himself things were going to be exactly as they'd been before.

Except that Fanny would probably give him the cut direct for the rest of his life.

"Lady Diana and Lady Francesca are in the morning room, my lord," Ruttles intoned in answer to Edmond's query when he and Brix arrived at Edmond's house.

"Excellent," Brix cried, removing his hat. He tossed it at the elderly retainer, who deftly caught it.

Edmond shot him a critical look, as he did every time Brix threw his hat at Ruttles.

"I told you, he really enjoys it," Brix confided, as he always did. "It makes him feel quite young, doesn't it, Ruttles?"

"If it pleases you to think so, sir," Ruttles replied, standing as stiffly straight as a soldier on parade.

"If you don't enjoy it, and you want to see me humbled, Ruttles, you're more than welcome to come along," Brix said as he sauntered past the butler. "I'm to grovel before Lady Francesca, you see, and I intend to do a very thorough job."

"I beg leave to be excused, sir."

"Come on, Brix, and stop bothering the servants," Edmond chided.

"Oh, very well," Brix said as he hurried to join his friend. "But considering what I'm about to do, you could be a little more lenient, don't you think?"

"You're just going to apologize to Fanny, not offer your head on the block."

"If you'd seen the way she glared at me yesterday, you might not be so sure of that. Really, she looked positively murderous. I can see the headline in *The Times* now: Wastrel Killed by Enraged Spinster."

Edmond cut him a warning look. "I wouldn't call Fanny a spinster to her face."

Brix didn't appreciate being treated like a complete dolt, but in the name of peace, he let that pass, too.

They entered the morning room, a bright chamber painted a pale moss green. Morning rooms were generally used by the mistress of the house as a place to take tea with her friends, to write letters and answer correspondence, and to meet with the upper servants. Diana's morning room seemed to defy that genteel pattern of behavior, however, just as she didn't conform to society's role for the daughter of a duke and wife of a viscount. There weren't a lot of knickknacks or delicate figurines, some of the upholstery on the chairs and sofa bore conspicuous ink stains and the large pedestal desk in the corner was a mess. Papers littered the top and were piled on the floor around it. Books with pictures of mountains, forests and ancient ruined castles lay open on the Pembroke table nearby. A stand bearing a huge dictionary was in the corner, and another stand holding an atlas was over by the window.

She was obviously at work on a new book, although Diana wasn't writing at the moment. Nor was she comforting a sobbing, prostrate Fanny, as Brix had half expected and more than half dreaded.

Instead, Diana and Fanny were sitting on the thick Whitty carpet cooing over little D'Arcy Douglas, who was on a bright blue blanket and, quite oblivious to anybody else, trying to get his toes into his mouth.

Dressed with her usual simplicity, in a slim gown of pale blue muslin, Fanny looked completely at home sitting on the floor, playing with the baby. Her thick brown hair was drawn back into a rather severe knot, as always, yet a few small curls had escaped and danced upon her slightly flushed cheeks and forehead as she bent over the infant and tickled his toes.

What an excellent mother Fanny would be: warm and loving, generous and devoted. Quite unlike his own, who, it was said—and truthfully, too—knew more about the king's offspring than her own.

Edmond announced their presence by clearing his throat.

The charming domestic atmosphere vanished as Fanny looked up, saw Brix and scrambled to her feet, staring at him as if he were an ogre.

He hadn't expected a warm welcome, but he wasn't quite prepared for that, either.

"Good morning, Brixton," Diana said cheerfully, and he was relieved to think she, at least, didn't appear to hold his wagers against him.

Choosing to ignore Fanny for the time being, he addressed Edmond's wife. "Since I've inadvertently grievously sinned, by thought, word and deed, against a virtuous young lady, I've come to make an apology."

"I'm glad to hear it," Diana said as Edmond helped her to her feet. He picked up his son and joined his wife on the nearby sofa, where he dandled the infant on his knee.

So, Brix thought, he would have to grovel with an audience. Well, so be it.

Putting on an extremely remorseful expression, he knelt on one knee in front of Fanny and clasped his hands in an attitude of humble remorse. "Dear Lady Francesca Cecilia Epping," he began, "I've come to beg your forgiveness for my thoughtless, foolish wagers on bended knee, regardless of what my valet may say about ruining my trousers."

As dignified as a queen, Fanny slowly crossed her arms. "Am I supposed to find this amusing, Mr. Smythe-Medway?"

He'd never failed to win a smile from Fanny before, except for yesterday, of course.

He tried again, with a bit more sincerity. "Fanny, I'm sorry that the wagers have caused you some grief. Edmond told me about your quarrel with Albert and subsequent flight. Of course, we both know Albert's a pompous, arrogant bore, and you're better off without him, but society will look askance at what you've done, so let's forgive and forget, shall we? You forgive me for my heedlessness, we both forget the wagers and you go home."

She didn't looked moved in the slightest. "This is still just a joke to you, isn't it, Mr. Smythe-Medway?" she demanded. "However, I assure you, I take those wagers, and what they imply—that I am simply not to be considered marriageable—extremely seriously. So did my brother."

Brix had had enough kneeling. "That's not what I meant when I made them," he said as he got to his feet.

"Really? What exactly did you mean when you said you'd never, ever marry me?"

He spread his hands. "I mean I didn't want to marry you. That's all. I didn't mean that somebody else wouldn't."

"That's a great comfort," Fanny replied with unexpected sarcasm. "But then, you were always so good to comfort me when we were children. Tell me, did you go to your friends and make fun of my woes then, too?"

That stung. "Of course not!"

She regarded him with skeptical scorn. "How can I be sure?"

He straightened his shoulders and replied with a dignity he rarely felt called upon to display. "I give you my word as a gentleman."

"As a gentleman? The same sort of gentleman who will make sport of a woman and her affections? You'll forgive me if I'm less than reassured."

This was getting out of hand.

He took Fanny by the elbow to steer her to the far corner of the room, where he could speak to her without being overheard, but while still in Diana's and Edmond's sight.

Although Fanny came along willingly, she quickly pulled her arm free of his grasp. "I'd prefer it if you didn't touch me."

"Gladly," he said through clenched teeth. "And I'd prefer it if you didn't kiss me again."

"Gladly."

He halted by Diana's desk and faced Fanny, ignoring the vibrant flush to her soft cheeks, and the sparkle in her eyes, and the little curls clinging to her forehead, and the way her breasts pressed against her muslin gown as they rose and fell with her agitated breathing.

"Now listen to me, Fanny," he said, taking no pains to hide his exasperation, "I came here to apologize. I'm sorry I upset you. I regret being the cause of any trouble between you and Albert. I'm willing to erase the wagers in the book at White's, and call off ours, as well. If you can't appreciate that, perhaps I should have stayed at home."

Her chin high, she crossed her arms. "Perhaps you should have."

"Come now, Fanny. Be reasonable. You've always been a sensible girl."

"Oh, yes, I've always been sensible," she replied stiffly. "And dull and boring and what else was it you said? Lacking vitality?"

His jaw clenched, but he gave it another try. If she still wouldn't accept his apology, nobody could say he hadn't done his best to try to undo any damage he'd done. "I was wrong to say those things," he bluntly conceded. "I was even wrong to think them. I'm very sorry. Now will you agree to call off our wager?"

She regarded him with scorn. "You really don't understand, do you, Brix? You think an apology and a few more jokes are going to make everything all right. But they won't. I've been embarrassed and humiliated."

"What more do you want me to do?" he demanded. "Give you a pound of flesh? It's not as if I'll get out of this without some penalty myself. Erasing the wagers won't pass without comment, you know."

"I'm quite sure you'll be able to laugh your way out of any humiliation, the way you laugh your way through life. After all, you're the Honorable Brixton Smythe-Medway, famous for his pranks at Harrow. What a good joke, they'll say! No harm done! What larks!"

She eyed him in a way that made him instantly suspicious that worse was yet to come. "Or perhaps you'd rather not have to go to the trouble of coming up with an amusing explanation."

He frowned and wondered what she was getting at. Whatever it was, he was sure he wasn't going to like it.

With the regal grace of an empress, she turned and walked back toward Diana and Edmond, who was gently extricating the end of his cravat from his son's mouth.

"I don't want you to erase the wagers at White's, Mr. Smythe-Medway," she said as she turned to face him. "In fact, I want the bet we made to be entered in the book at White's."

Brix stared at her, flabbergasted. Had she taken complete leave of her senses?

"Fanny, are you quite sure that's what you want?" Diana asked, looking just as stunned, while Edmond regarded her as if he didn't believe he'd heard correctly.

Fanny smiled like a gambler certain she was going to walk away from the hazard table richer than before. "Yes, I'm sure I want the wagers made official. And then I'm going to do everything in my power to win."

Brix couldn't believe it. He simply could not believe it.

"You can't be serious," he said as he strode toward her.

"Oh, but I am."

She wasn't bluffing. He could see it in her eyes, her very stance. She was going to try to break his heart in six weeks.

Which was impossible, so there was no need for him to be upset.

Nevertheless, the idea was so ridiculous and Fanny so apparently adamant, he appealed to Diana. "Tell Fanny that she ought to let this nonsense drop and be forgotten."

"If I were to agree to let this matter drop," Fanny said, "people may forget the exact circumstances of our wagers, but they'll certainly remember that you didn't want to marry me. If I don't at least try to win, all people will ever see when they look at me is the pitiful, pathetic woman that the amusing Smythe-Medway didn't want. I can't allow that humiliation to follow me for the rest of my life, or I really *will* be mousy little Fanny Epping."

Edmond handed D'Arcy to Diana and rose. "Fanny, I understand you're upset, but I think you ought to reconsider. The gossips will have a festival with this." He looked to his wife for support. "Don't you agree, Diana?"

Diana looked at Fanny, then Brix, then her husband. "Actually, Edmond, I think Fanny has a point. In some ways, it's too late to go back."

Both men stared at her as if she'd announced she was running for political office.

"But people don't know about the wager between Fanny and me!" Brix protested. "Not unless you and the others told anybody. Did you?"

Fanny regarded him steadily. "Are you forgetting Albert? And my sister-in-law?"

"Gad!" Brix cried, appalled. "Elizabeth's a worse gossip than my mother!"

"She knows all about what transpired here yesterday. Soon enough, so will all the *ton*."

Fanny was right, which meant he didn't have much choice now, either, not unless he wanted to be a laughingstock.

"Very well, Fanny," he conceded. "The wagers stand." He forced a smile. "I can't remember the last time I was so sure of winning. I look forward to the battle."

He strolled toward the door with his usual insouciant gait, then paused on the threshold and turned back, flashing them another smile.

"Gad, there's something I never thought I'd say," he observed before he continued out of the room.

Fanny's voice followed him. "I've got six weeks, Brix. We'll see if you're still smiling then."

A short time later, Brix strode up the steps beside the famous bow window of White's and into the entrance hall. He tossed his hat to a footman and continued past the morning room, where the dandies met to see and be seen, accompanied by the aroma of their coffee. He trotted up the stairs leading to the rooms for members only, then through the antechamber and the large subscription room where a group of older gentlemen were heatedly arguing about politics. Another was deep in discussion of the price of cod. He nodded a greeting to a few of the members, but didn't break his determined progress toward the smaller, but no less well appointed, gaming room. A hazard table occupied pride of place, and even at this early hour was surrounded by players, most of whom probably didn't realize it was morning, having played through the night. He brushed past Sir Dickie Clutterbuck and his short friend, Lord Strunk, who were arguing about a boxing match.

A gray haze from the smoking room made him cough, yet he continued straight for the writing desk holding paper, pen and ink for promissory notes, and where the betting book was open on display.

He grabbed a quill, dipped it into the nearest bottle of ink and wrote, with a flourish, *"Lady Francesca Cecilia Epping bets the Honorable Brixton Smythe-Medway that she can break his heart within six weeks from the second of May, 1819."*

His arrival and activity had not passed without notice, and as he wrote, several men who were not involved in card games or hazard wandered over.

Somebody came up too close behind Brix to read over his shoulder. By the scent of pomade and cheroots and whiskey, Brix took a guess as to the man's identity. "Shall I write it larger, Dickie, or can you read it from there?"

"No, I can see it fine," the tall dandy replied. "Who the deuce is Lady Francesca Cecilia Epping and why haven't I heard of her?"

Brix turned around and discovered that the hazard wheel had stopped, and even those players were listening.

He focused his attention on Clutterbuck, who was, as always, dressed with more regard for fashion than what suited him. His crony, Lord Strunk, a squat toad of a man, hovered near his elbow. Rumor had it that Strunk was eagerly assisting Clutterbuck to spend his inheritance at the gaming hells and brothels; it wouldn't be the first time Silas Strunk had been the ruin of a foolish young man.

"I'm not surprised you haven't been introduced to her," Brix replied, his tone deceptively amicable as he put down the quill. "She's is a lady of impeccable breeding and discernment and virtue."

And the thought of these two debauched men anywhere near Fanny was enough to make him sick.

"You're so virtuous yourself," Clutterbuck sneered, his cheeks growing even more red than they were from the wine he'd been imbibing.

"I've never claimed to be virtuous," Brix replied, leaning back against the heavy walnut desk.

"Wait! I know who it is!" Strunk cried, his beady ferret's eyes aglow. "That's the duke of Hetley's sister! A short, homely little thing—the one who's always following you around."

Brix gave the stocky nobleman a cold smile. "Actually, she's just about your height, my lord, and while she may not be as lovely as many ladies of the *ton*, she's hardly homely. And yes, she has been known to seek my company. Which of course, proves that she's discerning."

The card players and others who'd wandered closer laughed or exchanged smiles.

Brix decided to be charitable. "I'd be careful of the company I keep, if I were you, Dickie."

Strunk frowned, looking more like a toad than ever. "Same could be said for your friends, Middling. What do they see in you, anyway?"

"Why, that I'm merry and amusing. You, on the other hand, are neither, and unless Dickie here doesn't start keeping an eye on the purse strings, he's going to find himself penniless one of these days."

"As if anybody with any sense would listen to *you*," Strunk retorted. He grabbed his friend by the elbow. "Come on, Dickie. Let's go where there's some real sport."

"Yes, we'll go where there's some real sport," Clutterbuck echoed, allowing himself to be led away, and astray.

The hazard wheel turned again, summoning the players back to their game, and others, their curiosity satisfied, returned to the smoking room or their drinks or conversations.

"The duke of Hetley's sister, eh?" the elderly earl of Clydesbrook noted from his place at the *vingt-et-un* table. "She's been on the shelf for years. Seems an odd way to try to get off it."

The middle-aged marquis of Maryberry, also at the card table, started to laugh, a horsey whinny of a sound that exposed his stained teeth. "She must be mad. Or desperate."

Brix bristled at their condescending tone. To be

sure, he wasn't happy about what had happened with Fanny, but that didn't mean he liked hearing her disparaged by men who hardly made exemplary spouses themselves. The earl of Clydesbrook's first wife had run off with his valet after hinting darkly of violent rages, and the marquis of Maryberry had made no secret of the fact he'd married the daughter of a wealthy colonialist for her dowry.

"Actually, she was extremely angry at the time," he blithely explained. "She'd just found out about my other wagers regarding matrimony. I must say it's a good thing she wasn't armed, or I might not be here now."

The earl, marquis and other players chuckled.

"The duke was nearly apoplectic when he heard about those wagers," another nobleman remarked. "You'll be lucky if he doesn't call you out."

Brix hadn't thought of that. But Albert hadn't come to him and complained or issued a challenge to duel; he'd taken out his anger on Fanny.

He should have realized that might happen, too.

In spite of the dismay and regret those thoughts engendered, Brix smiled and told himself he couldn't allow this minor bit of trouble to assume greater importance than it merited, as Fanny had. "I agree Lady Francesca's wager seems ludicrous. Nevertheless, I've decided to indulge her little whim."

"Ah, I know!" the marquis cried as if he'd solved a great mystery, his voice carrying to the far corners of the room. "You're trying to seduce her. Interesting way to go about it, making her do all the work."

Brix nearly choked. This was even more ludicrous than Fanny's wager. "I'm not trying to seduce Fan—Lady Francesca," he protested just as loudly.

Remembering he had an audience, he forced another grin. "Why, good God, gentlemen, you know seduction is quite beyond me. Too much effort. No, I simply make it known I'm in the market for a lover, and the ladies of the theater seem to find me."

The men around him laughed. For a moment, Brix felt normality had been restored, until the earl spoke up again. "So what's the penalty if you lose?"

Brix hadn't thought about that, either. Fortunately, an answer quickly came to him. "Why, the shame of losing, of course, and having people know you've lost."

"Not so bad for you, is it, Smythe-Medway?" the marquis remarked. "You don't mind losing. Why, I've seen you lose at cards all night and never break a sweat."

Several men nodded their agreement.

"Accepting a loss with good grace doesn't mean I enjoy the prospect," Brix replied.

And this wager with Fanny was very different from a card game.

"I daresay you'll come up with some sort of payment if *she* loses," the earl said, leering.

Brix regarded him with undisguised disgust. "It may be that some men have to resort to such measures, but I don't. A lady either comes to my bed willingly, or not at all."

Deciding to leave before he said something scathing, however deserved, to the earl and marquis, he once again assumed his mask of merry levity and bowed to the men around him. "Now if you gentlemen will excuse me, I have an appointment with Miss Nellie Teasdale, of the King's Theater who, I assure you, does come to my bed willingly." He winked. "Very willingly."

He strolled toward the door. "Feel free to talk about me and my astonishing wager once I'm out of the room, gentlemen. I fully expect that you'll tell your wives, sisters, sweethearts and lovers about this, too. All I ask is that you also tell them that there's about as much chance of Lady Francesca Cecilia Epping breaking my heart as there is of a man walking on the moon."

Chapter 4

London, the seventh of May, 1819

Dear Aunt Euphenia,

I'm sorry that I haven't written sooner, but it's a whirlwind of activity here. Because of all the invitations we've been receiving, Fanny and I went shopping today—the first time I've been away from D'Arcy for a few hours. The little darling was very good, and we could have stayed longer, but I think something happened when Fanny was buying some silk. I went off to purchase some flannel for the baby, and when I returned, Fanny was very anxious to leave. I didn't want to press the poor girl for an explanation after all that's happened lately, and especially since I noticed Lady Emeline St. James and Lady Mary Bredbone in the shop when we arrived. I do hope they didn't say anything upsetting to her. You know how they can be.

Lady Diana Westover Terrington

As Fanny stood in the linendraper's shop surrounded by bolts of beautiful silks, satins and velvets, lace and trims, she felt like a little girl who had a bakery all to herself and permission to eat whatever she pleased. She also felt that her simple brown wool pelisse and straw bonnet were woefully plain and ugly.

From now on, when she ventured into society—and into Brix's social orbit—she intended to be as fashionably turned out as anybody. No more demure modesty for her! After all, what had it brought her but condescension and pain and being called mousy? She wouldn't go completely wild in the shops, but she wouldn't be as parsimonious as she had in the past.

Turning her attention to the matter at hand, she ran her hand over a bolt of pale pink silk. It was soft, smooth and pretty, and based on several observations Elizabeth had made over the years, Fanny was fairly sure it would flatter her complexion.

Poor Elizabeth—how many times had she tried to talk her into buying something like this? She'd be sorry she'd missed this expedition and the chance to repeat her various strong opinions about fashionable fabric and patterns.

"How much is this silk, Mr. Griswold?" Fanny asked, giving the clerk a bright smile.

When he told her, and in spite of her resolution to spend freely, she nearly choked.

"It's worth every penny, my lady," Mr. Griswold assured her. "It's the very finest quality."

"I'm sure it is," she murmured, caressing it

again, and imagining herself in a pretty gown of such material, and Brix's reaction to it.

He'd probably be shocked—and that was good enough for her. "I'll take it. Now, what about that royal blue velvet?" she asked, nodding at the huge roll on the shelf above his head. "I've always longed to have a velvet riding habit."

As Mr. Griswold began to unwind some of the fabric from the bolt to show her, out of the corner of her eye Fanny spotted two ladies watching her. Lady Emeline St. James, tall, slender and stylish, had been the belle of the season five years ago, and married very well. Lady Mary Bredbone, her sister, was slightly shorter, plumper and a little less stylish. Fanny knew them only slightly, from a few encounters at parties. Whenever they came to take tea with Elizabeth, she'd excused herself, preferring not to listen to their acidic comments on other ladies, or what they considered the latest news of court. They were said to have two of the most waspish tongues in London.

No doubt she would be the subject of their next conversation at tea, for they were surreptitiously watching her, then exchanging whispered comments behind their hands.

She reminded herself that most ladies of the *ton* hadn't gone out of their way to be nice to her before, and she tried to pretend their insolent scrutiny and rude whispering didn't bother her.

"I think this will make a lovely riding habit, my lady," Mr. Griswold offered, smiling and bowing.

"We have some very fine silk for a veil that matches perfectly. If you'll excuse me, I'll just go fetch it, and you can see for yourself."

As Mr. Griswold bustled to another area of the shop, Lady Emeline and Lady Mary came even closer. They were probably curious to find out how much she was spending or—worse— preparing to make some nasty comment.

Ignoring them as best she could, Fanny toyed with the chain of her reticule, tapped her foot and studied the bolts above as if seeking the answer to the meaning of life.

Lady Emeline came into her line of sight. She was going to say something. Fanny could feel it in her bones, and she prepared for the onslaught.

"I hope you don't mind the intrusion, Lady Francesca," Lady Emeline said, with a timid, yet friendly, smile, "but I wanted to tell you that that silk is an excellent purchase. I had a gown made of it myself, and it wears beautifully."

Fanny couldn't have been more surprised if Lady Emeline had offered to pay for it.

"And that color is so pretty," Lady Mary offered, likewise unexpectedly friendly, as she smiled and nodded so that the ostrich feather in her hat danced. "I'm sure you'll look very pretty in it."

Fanny didn't know quite what to make of their behavior, except that it was infinitely better than the reception she'd been dreading.

"Since your taste is well-known," Fanny said,

her comments and her smile encompassing them both, "I'm glad I decided to take it."

"I'm sorry we didn't speak to you right away," Lady Emeline said apologetically. "We weren't quite sure it was you at first, you see. We've seen so little of you lately."

They'd seen little of her ever, since she'd rarely attended social functions in the past, and only if she was sure Brix was going to be there.

"And there's that troubling business with Mr. Smythe-Medway," Lady Mary added. "Is it true you've bet you can break his heart in six weeks?"

Fanny's teeth clenched. Perhaps the ordeal had just been postponed. But there was no point denying what she'd done. Obviously, the news was wending its way among the *ton*. "Yes, it's true."

Lady Emeline cut a censorious glance at her sister, as if condemning her for mentioning it. Then, to Fanny's further shock and amazement, Lady Emeline patted her hand and gave her a sympathetic smile. "Then I hope you win, my dear. Frankly, I think it's about time Smythe-Medway had a setdown. Why, when he was at Harrow with my brother Harry, he told Harry he was a foundling that had been left on our doorstep. Can you imagine? The poor fellow had nightmares for months."

They were taking her side? They weren't condemning her or thinking she had committed a shocking breach of protocol? They didn't think she was immoral or wicked or wanton?

Nearly giddy with relief, Fanny felt as if she'd been spared six weeks in the stocks. "Yes, he does deserve to be hoist on his petard, doesn't he?" she agreed. "I was so incensed when I discovered his wager with his friends, I simply couldn't overlook it. I admit I was rather impetuous making my own wager, but I couldn't let the matter stand without retaliating somehow."

"We understand completely," Lady Emeline said, smiling. "Good for you, I say. And I'm not the only one who thinks so, I assure you."

"Yes, it's about time he paid for his thoughtlessness," Lady Mary said, her feather bouncing again. "I well remember the incident at Harrow when Lord Fallston nearly drowned. *Some* people were sure it was all Viscount Adderley's doing. *I* knew better. That sort of scheme could only come from Brixton Smythe-Medway, and I said so at the time."

That anybody had ever blamed Brix for that particular prank gone awry was news to Fanny. Edmond had been held to account by everyone, including Crispin Fallston, who'd accused the viscount of trying to kill him even though the river had been only two and a half feet deep where the punt sank.

"I don't know why he wasn't sent down," Lady Mary concluded.

Fanny could guess why. Brix had been a roguishly charming boy, with freckles, an infectious grin and persuasive manner. A headmaster would have had to have a heart of stone to resist his explanations, which were sure to be colorful and entertaining.

"My word, what have we here? A veritable orgy of feminine extravagance?"

At the sound of Brix's voice from the other side of the shop, Fanny turned and watched him stroll toward them. In spite of her resolution to win the wagers, her heart did that little flutter it always did when she saw him.

How could she still feel that way about a man who'd hurt and humiliated her?

Perhaps it was the fact that she still found him a very attractive man, from his boyish mop of untamable blond hair to his gleaming Hessian boots.

As always, Brix was impeccably dressed. His clothes were well tailored, accentuating his broad shoulders. His vests tended to be on the extravagant side in terms of color, but never outrageously so, and today's was in keeping. It was scarlet brocade, which looked quite well with his dark blue jacket. His fawn-colored breeches were tight enough to suggest muscular limbs without being offensive.

That might explain why she couldn't hate him on sight, but it was obvious Lady Emeline and Lady Mary didn't share her sentiments. They regarded Brix with blatant animosity and disdain, yet he didn't seem bothered a bit.

What was he up to anyway? Given the wager and those looks from Lady Emeline and Lady Mary, he should be avoiding them, not sauntering up to them as if nothing was amiss.

"Good day, ladies," he said cheerfully as he swept off his hat, releasing his hair, and bowed.

He must be completely certain he was going to win—or else he thought the wager so inconsequential, he didn't care whether he won or not.

Well, she cared. And by God, she'd make *him* care, too. He had to be made to see that what he'd done was no joke to be lightly brushed aside, or ignored.

But she wouldn't be angry or irate today; she'd tried that to no avail. Today, she would take her cue from the Honorable Brixton Smythe-Medway himself, as well as the other young ladies of the *ton*. She'd had several opportunities to witness how they acted when they were around Brix, or any other attractive young gentleman. She'd emulate their coquettish behavior and see if that disturbed Brix's infuriating equanimity.

So she smiled at him as if he were the light of her life and clasped her hands together as if enraptured. "Good day to you, Mr. Smythe-Medway. What a delightful surprise."

His grin faded for an instant. Although it quickly returned, he obviously hadn't expected her effusive greeting.

Thrilled with this bit of success, she continued just as brightly. "I trust you know Lady Emeline and Lady Mary. They certainly know you."

Although he'd been taken aback before, he didn't bat an eye as he tucked his hat under his arm and smiled at the ladies. "Yes, I've had the pleasure of making their acquaintance," he said, as affable as always in spite of their dark looks.

"If you'll excuse us, Mr. Smythe-Medway," Lady Emeline snapped, her lips puckering as if she'd just sucked on a lemon, "my sister and I should be on our way." She turned to Fanny. "I hope to see you soon, my dear." She ran another derogatory gaze over Brix before heading toward the door. "Come along, Mary!"

Lady Mary murmured a farewell, then dutifully followed her sister. Mr. Griswold, returning with the blue silk, watched them depart with regret—no doubt seeing potential sales go out the door with them—then hovered a short distance away.

"Well, well, well, I seem to have cast a pall over things," Brix said, his cavalier tone at odds with his apologetic words. He gave her a smug smile. "Yet you're still here."

"Did you think I'd scurry away like a timid little mouse?" she asked, still smiling. "Why, how could I win our wager if I did that?"

She didn't give him a chance to answer. "Now, since you're here, and I understand you have excellent taste, and because you've sent Lady Emeline and Lady Mary off, you can help me decide about the fabric for my new ball gown."

His brow furrowed slightly as he did a quick survey of the main floor of the shop. "Isn't Diana here? Surely you didn't come by yourself."

She laughed. "I may be willing to take some

risks when it comes to my reputation, Mr. Smythe-Medway, but I'm not foolish enough to disregard *all* of society's conventions." She gestured at the double doors leading to another section of the shop. "Diana's getting some flannel for little D'Arcy."

His gaze swept over the bolts of fabric on the counter table in front of them. "While you seem to be indulging yourself a great deal here."

"Why, so I am," she cheerfully confessed. "It's about time I did, don't you think? After all, dressing plainly didn't do me any good. You know, I never should have listened so much to Miss Stamford. You remember my governess, don't you?"

"A very grim lady, I recall."

"Very grim and very proper. I shudder to think what she would have made of my fancy for *you*. I don't think she would have approved. It's a good thing she went to live with her sister in Jamaica when I came of age. As for our wager . . ." She shuddered. "I daresay she's better off not knowing."

Brix's smile was getting rather strained. "I daresay she's better off not witnessing your extravagance."

"Probably not," Fanny agreed. "She always told me that genteel young ladies didn't indulge in lavish trimmings, expensive fabrics and other fripperies. I might have been tempted nonetheless, except that I thought such things made me look too young. And lately, I've been trying to save my pin money." She waved her hand as if brushing away such concerns. "Now that we've made our wager, though, that's all in the past."

His smile completely disappeared, replaced by a frown. "You might as well spare yourself the effort and the expense of new clothes, Fanny. It will take more than some new gowns to win our wager."

"Well, if I fail, at least I'll have some pretty new dresses," she replied, "and I need them. It's amazing how many invitations I've received since I left Albert's. Dinner parties, balls, fetes. Why, Lord and Lady Cheswick invited me to dinner next week, and they've never asked me before."

She tilted her head to regard Brix. "And I do believe I owe that all to *you*, Mr. Smythe-Medway. People are no doubt dying of curiosity to hear about my recent adventures. Why, if it weren't for those wagers, I'd likely be sitting at home every evening sewing and feeling sorry for myself, just as I used to do, while you were out enjoying all that London has to offer."

His smile returned, but it wasn't good-natured. It was as sardonic as any smile she'd ever seen. "Naturally, I'm delighted I could be of service, my lady."

"And you *are* of service!" she cried, patting his chest.

He took a step back.

"There's no need to back away, Mr. Smythe-Medway," she exclaimed. "I haven't taken leave of my senses. I've decided to enjoy our little competition, that's all."

"Do you also intend to bankrupt yourself in the

process?" he asked without looking at her as he adjusted the cuff of his pristine white shirt.

"Oh, I'm not going to spend with *complete* abandon," she assured him. "I wouldn't put myself into debt for a man, not even you. Still, I'm determined to have some new ball gowns, ones that make the most of my figure. Oh, and a new riding habit, in lovely soft velvet, like this royal blue."

Prompted by some impish impulse, she slowly caressed the material.

His eyes strayed toward the fabric.

She gave him a coy smile as she turned her attention to the pale pink silk, brushing her fingers lightly over it, as she had the velvet. "I've already decided to have a ball gown made out of this, something that will make it very clear I'm not a little girl any longer. What do you think?"

His gaze was still focused on her fingertips making their leisurely progress. "It's expensive, isn't it?"

"Yes, it is," she replied. "But I can afford it." She picked up the end of the fabric and draped it across her bodice. "Don't you like it?" she asked, batting her eyelashes.

He glanced at her face for the briefest of moments, and she was sure his cheeks colored a bit. "No."

Liar! He wasn't nearly as unaffected as he was pretending, and a surge of triumph flooded through her as she gave him a fraudulently woeful smile.

"Oh, dear," she said, putting the fabric back on

the counter table. "It's too late, I'm afraid. I'll have to make the best of it, I suppose."

Brix looked at her, his green eyes glittering. Then he smiled indulgently, as if she were only a little girl pretending to be grown-up. "If it makes you happy, Fanny, go ahead."

"I shall. Now that you've helped me, perhaps I can help you."

His brow furrowed slightly.

"You surely aren't here to purchase something for yourself."

His smile returned. "As a matter of fact, I've come to buy a gift."

"Oh, really? Your mother's birthday isn't for another month."

"It's not for my mother."

Fanny raised her brows. "Indeed? Are you thinking of getting engaged?"

He gave her a cynical smile and shook his head. "Not for several years, as you well know."

Fanny raised her brows even more. "Oh, so it's for your paramour." She frowned as if trying to remember something. "What's her name?"

She ignored his shocked expression as she tapped her chin with her fingertip. "Don't tell me, I'll think of it in a moment."

"Fanny, you're being—"

"Nellie Teasdale!" she cried, cutting off whatever observation he was about to make. "At least, I think that's the name of your current mistress, isn't it? The travesty dancer at the opera who wears male clothes onstage?"

Brix leaned back against the counter with his usual casual aplomb. "You seem very well informed, Fanny."

"Oh, I am. I always have been," she said as she toyed with a loose thread from the velvet. "Albert and Elizabeth and several other people all seemed to feel it their task to tell me everything they heard about you, in great salacious detail. They were trying to make me see why I shouldn't like you."

His hat dangling from his long, slender fingers, he crossed his arms. "How very kind of them."

"Just think—if only you'd made those wagers and I'd heard about them sooner, their efforts could have been spared."

Brix's expression became mildly curious. "I must say you're very lively this morning, my lady. If I didn't know you better, I'd be afraid you'd been into the viscount's wine. Either that, or you're turning into an outrageous flirt. I'd cease and desist, Fanny, if I were you."

As he uncrossed his arms, the placid look in his eyes changed, to one seriously uneasy. "You could be doing more damage to your character than my wagers ever could."

She wouldn't let his apparently genuine concern touch her. If he was so sincerely worried about her fate, why had he made those wagers?

She regarded him with bogus dismay. "But Lady Emeline and Lady Mary were the very soul of kindness and sympathy!" She dropped her voice to a confidential whisper. "Did you really tell Lady Emeline's brother that he was a foundling who'd been left on the doorstep?"

"He said some terrible things to Charlie Grendon about his lack of breeding, so yes," Brix replied, "I told Harry that he was a foundling, although if he had the brain of a flea, he'd have realized he looked far too much like his mother to be a foundling."

Now that she thought of it, Harry St. James was indeed the image of his mother. "It still wasn't very nice."

"I'm not always nice, Fanny."

She couldn't look directly at him for a moment, and her throat went a little dry. "Yes, I've found that out."

He ran another gaze over her, one that was cold and disapproving. "What do you think you're doing, Fanny, acting like the most silly, addlepated chit during her first season in London?"

She wouldn't let him upset her, or disturb her, or make her warm, or blush . . .

"I don't think I'm being silly and addlepated," she replied with a forced laugh. "I'm simply saying what I think, something I was always too afraid to do before, in case I upset my parents or Miss Stamford or the *ton*. Now that I'm somewhat notorious anyway, I feel quite free to be myself and voice what's on my mind. It's very refreshing."

"It's dangerous."

"Oh, and you don't say things that upset people?" she countered.

"You know what I mean."

Determined not to let him distress her, inspired by his reaction to her hand on the silk, she decided to return to her original course. She sidled closer and gave him a coquettish smile. "What's the matter, Brix? I thought you liked bold and brazen women. And it's not as if I'm about to start seducing every man in sight." She lowered her voice so that only he could hear. "Just you."

His green eyes seemed to reach right into her heart and make its rhythm erratic. "If you're going to try to seduce me, Fanny, you've got a lot to learn."

She struggled to remain cool and calm. This was Brix, after all, not some seductive Don Juan she'd only just met. "Do I? Will you teach me?"

"If you'd like."

She could easily believe this was the way he sounded when he was alone in bed with a woman. After they'd made love.

Her throat constricted. Breathing wasn't easy. Yet she mustn't give him the satisfaction of thinking he could affect her in any way. "Perhaps not."

He looked down at her with a look in his eyes that was even more potent than his voice. "Why don't you ask the man who taught you how to kiss for lessons in seduction?"

She instinctively moved back against the counter table, seeking out its solid support. "I can't."

His lips curved up in a victorious smile. "Why not?"

"Because that would be you."

He frowned. "I should think I'd remember teaching you how to kiss, Fanny."

"You're the only man I've ever kissed in my life—so far," she added hastily.

He moved a little closer, effectively trapping her against the wide, heavy table. "As relieved as I am to hear you aren't kissing men indiscriminately, I'm not talking about that kiss in the rose garden, Fanny. It's the one you gave me in Edmond's study the other day. The French kiss."

Putting his hands on either side of her, so that she was trapped by his body, he dropped his voice to an inviting purr. "You do know that's what it's called, don't you, when you use your tongue that way?"

She swallowed hard and forced herself to sound only slightly impressed. "As a matter of fact, I didn't. I should have realized I could count on your expertise to provide the term, should I require it."

"Are you curious about the rest of my expertise, as you call it?"

A host of incredible images burst into her mind, more graphic and sensual than any of the several daydreams she'd harbored featuring Brix in the past.

She cleared her throat. "Are you sure you're an expert, or is that only the opinion of the women who are paid to enjoy your talents? If so, I should point out that they have a vested interest in praising your skills. An impartial observer might have a different opinion."

An expression flitted across his face, one she'd seen only once before, when he'd flown into a fit of temper over her brother's teasing of her. He'd tackled Albert like an enraged bear and pummeled the older, considerably larger Albert until her brother cried for mercy.

Perhaps she'd gone too far, she thought . . . until his expression changed. His full lips curved up into what could only be called a seductive smile. "I don't think you're impartial, Fanny."

Mr. Griswold appeared on the periphery of Fanny's vision, flitting about like an agitated sparrow. "Mr. Smythe-Medway!" he exclaimed in a loud whisper. "Mr. Smythe-Medway, please! This is a respectable shop."

Brix glanced at the little man over his shoulder, then pushed himself away from the table. "I seem to be upsetting the clerk."

Fanny felt as if she'd just taken off a very tight corset and was free to breathe—and think clearly—again.

"What a pity," Brix continued as he smiled that smug, unendurable smile of his, as if he had won a great victory. "I was just beginning to enjoy myself."

Because he'd entrapped her against the counter table like a lascivious cad?

She'd set him right about who had triumphed today.

Regardless of Mr. Griswold dancing about in their vicinity, she took hold of Brix's lapels and drew him close enough to kiss. She could feel his chest moving against hers as he breathed.

"I'm quite willing to believe that your paramours are right, and you're very talented in that regard, Brix," she said softly. "It's a pity I'll never find out. But then, you'll never find out what talents *I* might possess, either."

His eyes flared wide for an instant as she let go and stepped back.

"Now if you don't mind, Mr. Smythe-Medway," she continued in a conversational tone, "Diana can't be away from little D'Arcy for the whole morning, and I fear Mr. Griswold is going to fall into a fit unless you leave me alone."

The muscle of Brix's jaw twitched before he spoke. "So I'm dismissed, am I? Very well. After all, it wouldn't do to make a scene in a linen-draper's shop, would it, Lady Francesca? It's tempting, though."

He took a step toward her.

"Mr. Smythe-Medway!" Mr. Griswold cried. "What will people say?"

Brix ignored the clerk's plea and kept his gaze firmly on Fanny as he whispered, "As a matter of fact, Fanny, I'm very tempted to take you in my arms and teach you a great deal more about kissing. You could use some instruction. Your effort the other day was interesting, but definitely needed some work."

As Fanny gasped at his insolence, Brix merely grinned. "But another time, perhaps, when we aren't in so public a place." He set his hat on his head and gave it a pat. "Now good day, my lady. Give my best to Lady Diana, and Edmond, too. I do hope I'll see you soon—in a gown of pale pink silk, perhaps?"

With that, he turned and sauntered out of the shop as casually as when he'd first approached her.

Fanny leaned back against the table and slowly let out her breath. She felt as if she'd had a very narrow escape.

She realized Mr. Griswold was still nearby, shifting impatiently from foot to foot. "Will you be so good as to tell Lady Diana I'm ready to leave?" she asked.

"At once, my lady," he replied, mopping his brow with a large silk handkerchief.

As he hurried off to do as he was bidden, Fanny could hear him muttering, "Such goings-on in a respectable shop!"

She couldn't blame him for being upset. Such goings-on, indeed!

Chapter 5

London, the twelfth of May, 1819

I think you'd be as surprised as I am, Aunt Euphenia, at the way Fanny's blossomed in a few short days. She seems quite a different woman—happy and carefree in a way I've never seen. Perhaps, despite all my worries, these wagers are the best thing that could have happened to her.

As for Brix, Edmond doesn't think he's as unaffected by the wagers as he's letting on. I'll have to take Edmond's word for it, since he knows Brix better than I.

Lady Diana Westover Terrington

Brix disembarked from his barouche in front of Lord and Lady Cheswick's mansion and headed for the steps, whistling a jaunty little tune. There was another gentleman at the bottom of the stairs, and Brix fell silent when he saw who it was: Buggy Bromwell, and in full evening dress, too.

Usually it took a major social occasion to get Buggy away from his spiders.

"Good evening, Brix!" Buggy cried, breaking

into a smile. "What a relief you're going to be here. I'll have somebody to talk to now, other than the host and his wife, of course."

"I'm delighted to see you, too," Brix said, likewise relieved, because Buggy was clearly no longer upset with him, in spite of what had happened at Edmond's. "But I must say, I'm surprised to find you at a dinner party."

"I confess my motive is purely mercenary," Buggy admitted as they went up the steps together. "I'm hoping Lord Cheswick will agree to help fund my next expedition. I've called upon you and Edmond and the others quite enough."

Brix knew better than to ask if Buggy's father was going to contribute anything. Lord Bromwell was extremely wealthy, but he'd never approved of his son's scientific studies. He'd been pleased by the success of Buggy's book, yet he still drew the line when it came to actually contributing money toward his son's efforts.

"I'm sure you'll be able to convince his lordship," Brix said as one of Lord Cheswick's footmen opened the door, and they walked into the lavishly decorated foyer.

Lord Cheswick and his wife simply didn't know the meaning of restraint. There wasn't a flat surface that didn't have some kind of plasterwork—garlands, festoons, medallions, heads of dead Romans. Statues collected from all over Italy filled the vast space, and portraits of generations of Cheswicks looked down from the walls. There were five pier tables topped with mirrors. Vases of hothouse flowers whose heavy, exotic scent filled the air stood on gleaming satinwood tables.

"I confess I didn't expect to find you here, either," Buggy said, while another footman took their hats and cloaks.

He suddenly started and stared at Brix as if he'd committed a tremendous faux pas. "You do know Fanny's going to be here, don't you? Edmond did tell you, didn't he?"

Brix wasn't about to let the possibility of Fanny's presence determine what he did, especially after her shocking, outrageous, flirtatious behavior, so he gave his friend another grin and clapped him on the shoulder. "As a matter of fact, Fanny herself told me. We had a very interesting chat at a shop the other day."

"Yes, I heard something about that," Buggy murmured as he regarded his reflection in one of the pier glasses and adjusted his cravat.

Brix was extremely curious to know exactly what Buggy had heard, but he wasn't going to ask. He didn't want anybody to think he was at all bothered by what had happened in the linendraper's, even if he'd been so annoyed and frustrated, he'd forgotten to buy Nellie a birthday gift. He'd then gone straight to his club for some drinks and some cards, and forgotten Nellie's birthday entirely.

She had not been pleased, and that had been the end of the that.

"I thought perhaps it would be rather awkward for you, that's all," Buggy said.

Brix pretended he'd been preoccupied with trying to fix his wayward hair in another of the pier glasses before he turned to Buggy with a mischievous gleam in his eye. "I think I can manage to get along with Fanny for one evening."

Provided she behaved herself. And he kept his distance.

Fanny's words and actions that day in the shop had caused the most incredible images to flash unbidden into his head then, and several times since, whether awake or sleeping. Simply standing in a linendraper's stroking some fabric, she'd managed to tantalize and tempt him in a way no woman ever had, not even Nellie.

Perhaps that explained why he'd acted the way he had in the shop, as if he were some sort of Don Juan. He'd never behaved that way with a woman . . . although he had to admit, it had been undeniably exciting. It was like letting some secret part of him—his most primitive passions, his deepest desires—come out into the light of day and play.

Since then, though, he'd been virtually haunted by visions of Fanny—*Fanny*, of all women!—in his arms, sometimes naked, sometimes not. Making love with Fanny in his bed. In his carriage. In the woods. In one of the small salons of his club.

"I've been hearing some strange stories, Brix, about you and Fanny. I'm sure they're exaggerations and rumors run wild," Buggy said as they followed another liveried footman to the drawing room. "You couldn't possibly have behaved in the manner that's been described to me, like some sort of loathsome lothario."

"Loathsome lothario?" Brix exclaimed as he came to a halt on the threshold of the extravagantly decorated drawing room. "It was Fanny who—"

He fell silent as more than fifty pairs of eyes turned to look at him and a hush fell over the room.

Feeling like an exhibit or some freak of nature, Brix's gaze swept over the gathering of well-dressed men and women. Buggy stood blushing nearby, as if he'd been caught acting like a loathsome lothario.

Diana and Edmond were at the far end of the room, standing shoulder to shoulder like sentries, and apparently not particularly pleased to see him.

So much for his best friend.

Drury wasn't there. Thank God. He didn't want to have to deal with what he secretly thought of as Drury's Death Stare, which was so effective when examining witnesses.

Fanny was most definitely present, sitting on a sofa surrounded by a group of women as if she were holding court. Or telling them some fascinating gossip.

She'd done something different with her hair. Little ringlets danced about her cheeks and small curls clustered on her forehead. Ribbons that matched her dress—a simple gown of blue sprigged muslin, dressed up with some trim—were wound through her thick chestnut hair. Even with the lace, her gown looked rather countrified compared to the silks, satins and velvets the other ladies wore. That must explain why she seemed so fresh and innocent and pretty, like a milkmaid who'd wandered into a cyprians' ball.

Until he saw the smug look she cast his way.

So, she thought she had the upper hand, did she? He'd show her how mistaken she was, no matter what she was saying about him. After all, he was the amusing Brixton Smythe-Medway, and he could triumph over mousy little Fanny Epping.

Putting on his usual jovial expression, he strolled toward Lord Cheswick, a robust man of fifty with snow-white hair. "Good evening, my lord. Charming night for a dinner party. I hope you had your cook do that roast mutton again. I've been practically salivating in anticipation all day."

"Ah, Smythe-Medway!" Lord Cheswick cried, shaking Brix's hand with enthusiasm. "Delighted to see you. My wife was sure you weren't going to come."

Brix's jaw clenched. Did she think he'd be afraid to show his face because of a wager?

"Why not?" he calmly inquired, forcing himself to relax and pretending to be baffled. "I'm in perfect health."

Lord Cheswick lowered his voice and nodded

at the bevy of ladies around Fanny. "Seems to be a bit of a furor over that wager you made. Turns out the women are rather on Fanny's side, you see."

Brix laughed as if this news didn't bother him a bit. "Even if they are, you don't expect the ladies to attack me, do you?" He stroked his chin as he reflected. "That might be rather enjoyable, come to think of it."

Lord Cheswick chortled. "Just thought you ought to be warned there might be some rocky roads ahead tonight."

If most of the *ton* wanted to snub him, he didn't care. Several of them had no use for him already, because they had no sense of humor, or agreed with his brother that his business methods were foolhardy. He could always go to his club, that male sanctuary where a man with a ready wit and generous nature was always welcome.

"Have no fear, my lord," he replied. "I'll have no trouble with Lady Francesca. In fact, to ease your dread, I'll demonstrate."

Determined to prove to Fanny and everybody else that she wasn't going to intimidate him in any way ever, Brix headed directly for Fanny.

In spite of his resolve, he was glad she wasn't wearing that pale pink silk she'd been caressing as if it were her lover's naked skin.

When the ladies around Fanny realized who was coming their way, most of them scattered like a flock of startled birds, albeit to land within hearing range. Their hostess, a substantial woman in pearl gray silk, with diamonds hanging from her ears, was seated beside Fanny, and she looked as if she feared he was about to try to take a bite out of her.

Her hands folded demurely in her lap, a little smile on her face, Fanny didn't look nonplused in the least.

For the moment, Brix ignored her as he bowed to his hostess and gave her his most charming and merry smile. "Good evening, my lady."

He took Lady Cheswick's gloved hand and pressed a kiss on the back of it.

Then he turned to Fanny and bestowed a wolfish grin upon her. "Good evening, Lady Francesca. You look lovely tonight."

"You're looking very dashing yourself," she pertly replied, apparently not the least troubled by his expression as she studied the top of his head. "What a pity your valet can't do something about your hair, though."

If she was going to insult him so blatantly, this was no little skirmish. This was going to be outright war.

In spite of that realization—and because of it— Brix continued to smile as he reached out and rather forcibly took her right hand in his. Short of yanking her hand back, she was helpless to prevent him from kissing it.

He lifted her fingers to his lips. Although she, too, wore gloves, he could feel the warmth of her skin as he pressed his mouth on the back of her hand.

If they'd been alone, and she wasn't wearing gloves, he would have turned her hand over and kissed her palm. He would have let his mouth glide toward her wrist, his lips linger on her throbbing pulse.

Another vision burst into his head, of Fanny's hand stroking not that fabric, but his naked chest. Fanny's fingers on his body, caressing and arousing him.

Heat unfurled within him, and his traitorous body began to respond.

She was the one who was supposed to be discomfited, not him!

He immediately drew back and raised his eyes to look at her face. Even though her eyes sparkled with anger, she was blushing, her cheeks tinged with the pale pink flush of a rosebud.

Despite his body's unwelcome response, now once more under control, he felt a surge of triumph. She could say what she liked and act as coy as she pleased, but she couldn't fool him. He *did* affect her.

Nevertheless, her blush didn't last long, and she again folded her hands in her lap as she regarded him steadily.

Did she expect him to just walk away?

"If I may, Lady Cheswick," he said, insinuating himself on the sofa between his hostess and Fanny. "I'm rather tired. I've had a very fatiguing day. I hope you don't mind if I join you."

Lady Cheswick extricated herself from the sofa. "I should greet some of my other guests," she murmured, hurrying over to another group of ladies close by who were watching them with avid interest.

Brix turned to Fanny and gave her another smile. "I'm sorry you don't approve of my hair, my lady. However, I believe I'll refrain from suggesting to Ramsbottom that he quit his efforts to make my hair look like that of every other gentleman in London. It would be robbing the dear fellow of the goal of his life."

"I certainly wouldn't want to do that," Fanny agreed, regarding him complacently. "A man without a goal in life is rather pitiable, don't you think?"

He dropped his voice to that low, sultry tone he was beginning to consider his Don Juan voice and slid his arm along the back of the sofa behind her. "Oh, I have a goal, my lady."

Out of the corner of his eyes, he noticed a few of the younger ladies drifting a little closer. Obviously, that tone was quite effective—except upon Fanny, whose expression didn't change at all.

"I hardly consider amusing oneself a goal," she replied, "or at least, not a worthy one."

"That isn't my only goal, my lady," he said, gazing into her bright blue eyes and moving closer to her.

A few of the younger ladies sidled nearer, distracting him, and it was all he could do not to tell them to quit listening and go away.

"Are you talking about seduction?" Fanny

asked, so bluntly, he gasped, and so did some of the young ladies.

Fanny carried on as if completely unaware she was scandalizing her listeners—Brix included. "I consider *that* amusing oneself, since I equate seduction with a man of no morals attempting to entice a lady to forget *her* morals for his own selfish satisfaction."

"I have morals!" Brix retorted. "And I don't set out to seduce women."

"No," she agreed, "from what I hear, you don't."

She made it sound as if a successful seduction on his part would be impossible, even if he set his mind to it. But if he replied to that effect, she would probably say something that made him sound like a loathsome lothario.

She tilted her head to study him. "You look very handsome in evening dress, so I can understand how a woman of loose morality would be tempted by you."

Gad, she could turn a compliment into a condemnation! He opened his mouth to say something, *anything*, but she blithely carried on, robbing him of the chance.

"It's really no wonder you always look so comfortable in such clothes, since you spend so much time out and about in the evenings at the gaming tables and theater."

"I don't spend *all* my time in such pursuits," he said, finally getting a word in.

"No, that's true," she replied. "You enjoy playing billiards, too, as well as spending time with singers and fruitsellers and dancers. You gamble, too, of course, and spend a great deal of time at your club, presumably talking as well, which is what you seem to do best."

She seemed determined to embarrass and upset him, but he'd be damned before he let her. "Yes, I have a lot of interests. How about you? Read any good books lately?"

"A few. And you?"

"As a matter of fact," he answered honestly, "I've been reading *The Reports of the Society for Bettering the Condition and Increasing the Comforts of the Poor*."

Fanny didn't look impressed. "Really? Picked that up by mistake, did you?"

"I have serious interests, Fanny. I just prefer not to bore people with them."

"I should think a man like you could make even the most serious subject interesting."

His eyes narrowed, because this sounded suspiciously like a genuine compliment. But no matter what she said, or how she tried to goad him, he wasn't about to explain that he didn't discuss his goals or interests because he'd already endured enough ridicule for his ideas about manufacturing and labor from his family.

"Ladies and gentlemen, dinner is served," Lord Cheswick's rotund butler, who looked like a formally attired gnome, announced from the doorway.

Brix had forgotten about dinner, and everything else. Startled, he rose and instinctively held out his hand to lead Fanny in to dinner, as he had in the past, and whether she liked it or not.

"Oh, no, Mr. Smythe-Medway," Lady Cheswick cried, blushing and bustling up to him with a look on her face that seemed to suggest he'd just done something unforgivably rude. "There's obviously been a misunderstanding. You must take in Lady Annabelle Dalyrimple. Lord Strunk will take Lady Francesca in to dinner."

Brix froze. Strunk was here, and he was to take Fanny in?

Fanny gave him a pitying look. "Perhaps I should have told you that for some time before little D'Arcy's baptism, I've been secretly requesting that you be allowed to escort me to the dinner table, although I am of higher rank than you."

Brix stared at her, dumbfounded, as the heat of shame and embarrassment flooded though him. Fanny had arranged . . . ? He didn't want to believe it, but he couldn't deny that she was right. She did outrank him socially.

To make matters worse, the toadlike Silas Strunk came striding up to them as fast as his short, fat legs could carry him.

"Bless my soul!" Strunk cried—something Brix was quite sure he'd never heard the man say before—"Don't tell me this beauty is Fanny Epping!" He darted a nasty glance at Brix. "And to think I'd heard you were homely."

Brix wished Strunk was at the bottom of the Thames.

But then Fanny retorted with such surprising venom, Brix could hardly believe his ears. "And to think you're supposed to be a gentleman. You certainly didn't act like one the first time I met you."

Strunk, not normally easily embarrassed, colored and stepped back as if she'd slapped him. "Have we met before, my lady?" he asked, echoing Brix's silent question.

"Once. You were rather foxed at the time, although that doesn't excuse your deplorable behavior, or that of your friend. No true gentlemen would accost any woman walking along the street the way you did."

Stunk had accosted Fanny on the street? When? No young lady ever went anywhere unescorted—unless, perhaps, she was fleeing her brother's house.

Good God, she'd taken a risk. She could have been in serious danger. Yet somehow, she'd managed to get the better of Strunk and some other man—Dickie Clutterbuck, probably—and with her pride intact, too. He couldn't help but be impressed.

As a look of incredulous understanding was dawning on Strunk's reddening face, Fanny turned to their hostess. "If you don't mind, Lady Cheswick, I believe I'd prefer to have another escort to the table."

Brix couldn't help it. He wanted Lady Cheswick

to suggest him—but only to find out more about what had happened between the despicable Strunk and Fanny.

Instead, the hostess motioned for . . . Buggy. He eagerly came forward, looking like a sleek greyhound with his lean, sharp features. "Yes, my lady?" he said to Lady Cheswick.

"Do be so good as to take Lady Francesca in to dinner, my lord."

Baffled, Buggy looked from the hostess, to Brix, to Fanny, to Lord Strunk, who was glaring at all of them.

He seemed to realize there was only one thing for him to do. "Delighted," he murmured, holding out his arm.

With a gracious smile, Fanny accepted, and they headed toward the dining room.

Avoiding his gaze, Lady Cheswick bustled off to sort out the other guests, while Brix turned toward Lady Annabelle, giggling in the corner.

"You've been put in your place, eh?" Strunk sneered.

Brix continued toward Lady Annabelle as if he hadn't heard a word.

Even though she wasn't sitting near the disgusting Lord Strunk, the dinner was far from enjoyable for Fanny. She was seated between Lord Cheswick, at the head of the table covered in a blindingly white damask cloth, and Buggy Bromwell on her right. Although the room was illuminated by several candelabra on the table and mantel and side-

board, and candles in sconces on the wall, she
might as well have been invisible, except to the
footman responsible for serving her. He was one of
a veritable army of servants standing stiffly at attention behind the Hepplewhite mahogany chairs.
They were all presided over by the plump, but
definitely commanding, butler, who watched
everyone—including the guests—so sternly, she
couldn't help wondering if he was afraid they'd
try to steal the silver.

There was certainly plenty of plate, with a daz-
zling array of cutlery and serving dishes. The
bone china was, of course, decorated with an oriental design, as Lady Cheswick was sure to have
the most fashionable dinnerware. The Waterford
crystal sparkled like diamonds, and white roses
beautifully arranged in low silver dishes scented
the room, until the soup was served.

Buggy was clearly trying to garner financial
support for his next expedition, and she didn't
have the heart to interrupt him or change the
subject from one that roused him to such passionate enthusiasm. He really did like spiders, including the poisonous ones, and everything
about them.

On the other side of the table, the earl of
Clydesbrook and the marquis of Maryberry were
discussing the current problems of government at
great, interminable length, when they weren't
casting leering looks in her direction. They must
have overheard some of the things she'd said to
Brix in the drawing room.

She never should have tried to render Brix's incredibly seductive looks and innuendoes ineffective by countering with such blunt responses. She should have remembered they weren't alone instead of rising to Brix's bait, getting in over her head, then having to beat a hasty retreat to the subject of his appearance.

"Poor Dickie took a punch right in the nose," Lord Strunk declared from farther down the table, his voice too loud and slurred from drinking.

He was already so foxed that his eyes were little more than slits above his plump, scarlet cheeks as he continued to slur his way though a description of what had happened to his friend during a recent encounter with a renowned bare-knuckle fistfighter, which had resulted in a broken nose for the nobleman.

Fanny suspected "Dickie" was the other man who'd accosted her that memorable day. She was relieved he wasn't here, too.

As she took a bite of asparagus, she wondered what Brix made of her response to Lord Strunk. He hadn't seemed at all curious about how she knew Lord Strunk or her reaction to him, but perhaps that was because he'd been so shocked by the discovery of her covert schemes to have him escort her at dinner parties.

Poor Brix. That little public humiliation had stung—yet it was nothing compared to the humiliation he'd caused her.

She slid a surreptitious glance down the table, to where Brix was regaling a giggling Lady Annabelle Dalyrimple with the tale of the Royal Opera manager's latest attempts to hire a noted soprano.

She reached for her wine and took a sip of the cool, rich liquid. She shouldn't let his appearance continue to affect her as it did. She shouldn't still feel that little thrill of happiness whenever he walked into a room.

"And I said, 'Hit him again, Dickie!'" Strunk cried.

At a signal from her ladyship, a footman moved in and removed Strunk's wineglass. He didn't immediately notice.

Stifling a sigh, Fanny listened for a moment as Buggy described what he needed to equip his ship for a scientific voyage to South America. She tried not to look at Brix again, or strain to hear what he was saying about the latest problem at the King's Theater. Brix had a subscription to the opera and ballet there, which meant he had his own box and was privy to the management's machinations and tribulations. He made the theatrical dilemmas into very funny stories, imitating voices and accents as if he were a performer himself.

Naturally, he didn't sympathize with the management's problems. He only made fun of them. No doubt they wouldn't be any more amused by his anecdotes than she was amused by those wagers. Now she wished she hadn't laughed so much when she heard Brix talk about theatrical rivalries and jealousies and the maneuvering for starring roles.

"The mating ritual of that particular species is quite fascinating," Buggy declared, catching Fanny's wayward attention. "But I shouldn't discuss such subjects when there are ladies present."

"No, no, I suppose not," Lord Cheswick agreed. "Now, about that ship . . ."

As Fanny chewed some delicious, excellently cooked roast mutton, she glanced at Brix again. He was still talking about one of the dancers. Nellie Teasdale, perhaps?

Being a subscription holder gave Brix easy access to all areas of the theater, which no doubt came in handy when he was wooing the dancers and singers into his bed, probably using that low, bewitching tone of voice, subtly sliding his arm around them, kissing their hands, making them fall in love with him. . . .

She *had* to learn to control her responses where Brix was concerned, or she'd never win that wager and assuage her wounded pride. She had to make Brix fall in love with her and not be in love with him herself.

Surely she was already out of love with him. How could she care about him after what he'd done? He was nothing but a shallow, immoral jokester who thought it was amusing to make fun of her and her feelings.

She wouldn't believe he ever considered serious subjects, even though he'd known the exact title of that pamphlet about the poor. Maybe somebody at his club had mentioned it. Or he'd taken a lucky guess.

"And that's only the ones we've found, my lord," Buggy went on. "There are sure to be several more species. Nor will we confine ourselves to spiders."

"So there he was, flat on his back. Damn good thing I'd bet on the other chap," Strunk confided with a sodden chuckle.

Lady Annabelle giggled.

Fanny speared a piece of roast mutton with her fork and wondered if she was having any success at all making Brix love her.

She'd managed to get his attention, at any rate. He wasn't ignoring her, or avoiding her, as he had in the past. Although he was trying to act as if he wasn't affected by her or what she did, she knew him well enough to believe otherwise.

But did that mean there was a possibility he would fall in love with her, or was he merely teasing and toying with her, playing another sort of game? Unfortunately, she didn't know what sort of thing really appealed to Brix when it came to women, or how he behaved when he was in love.

The more time she spent in Brixton Smythe-Medway's company, the more she realized she didn't really know him. She couldn't get past that merry mask he wore, and she didn't know how to make it slip.

As the footman removed her dinner plate, she glanced down the table again. Brix was telling

Lady Annabelle about a dispute over a wig between two dancers in the *corps de ballet*.

Fanny quickly turned away as a bold, brazen idea flashed into her head.

But first, she'd have to persuade Diana and Edmond to take her to the King's Theater.

Chapter 6

London, the nineteenth of May, 1819

Dear Aunt Euphenia,

I fear you may indeed prove to be more correct than I've been about Fanny. I've been reluctant to see her behavior in a critical light, but after what happened last night at the King's Theater, I can't deny that I may have been mistaken. Fanny disappeared for a considerable length of time. She claims she was lost in the crowd, but I fear, dear aunt, that this is simply not true.

Lady Diana Westover Terrington

"That was quite a dinner, Brix," Drury noted as they rode in Brix's barouche to the King's Theater in Haymarket the following week. "I hate to think how much it set you back."

"Money was no object tonight, my friend," Brix jovially replied as he relaxed against the squabs. "Surely winning your one hundredth case is worthy of celebrating with a fine meal, fine wine and the theater. I'm just glad you accepted. I wasn't sure you would, because of that business with Fanny."

He should have kept quiet, because Drury suddenly regarded him with the Death Stare. Drury's eyes were second only to his voice when it came to persuading a witness to reveal all, or sway a judge or jury.

"Edmond came to my chambers last week and told me about her quarrel with her brother," Drury replied. "I gather you were at a dinner party with them recently, as well."

Brix didn't frown, although he was far from happy to think Edmond and Drury had been talking about him behind his back. "Yes, I was at Lord and Lady Cheswick's dinner party, having been invited. Buggy was there, too, trying to get some money for his expedition. I must say, it's rather amusing to think of you and Edmond—two of the most notoriously attractive gentlemen in London—gossiping like two old ladies over their tea and crumpets."

Drury didn't look amused, but then, he rarely did anyway.

"What else did Edmond say?" Brix inquired as if it didn't particularly concern him.

"Very little, except that you now seem determined to flirt with Fanny," Drury replied as the carriage lurched over a bump in the cobbled street.

Outside, the street sellers still plied their trade, although their voices were weary from calling out to passersby all day. It had rained earlier, and the damp scent of mud and stone lingered in the air, mingling with the smoke from hundreds of coal fires.

"It's not as if I was doing all the flirting, you know," Brix explained. "You wouldn't believe some of the things Fanny's said to me lately. Honestly, I can't remember when I've been more shocked and appalled."

Well, he'd been shocked, anyway. And titillated, but he wasn't going to say that to Drury.

"I find Fanny flirting with anybody rather difficult to believe, although Buggy told me that she was behaving oddly," Drury said, his expression as inscrutable as always. "And last Friday I heard something surprising from a linendraper's clerk who happened to be in a tavern I frequent."

Brix knew better than to ask what Drury was doing in a tavern. The lawyer had acquired a number of odd habits over the years, including preferring the company of a certain class of people to his own.

"What exactly did this linendraper's clerk say?" Brix asked, quite sure it must be the fellow from the shop where he'd encountered Fanny and resolving never to go there again.

"Did you get Fanny up against a counter table and kiss her?"

Gad, that made it sound as if he'd tried to take her then and there. "I most certainly did not!"

"You didn't meet her in a linendraper's shop?"

"Well, yes, I did, and I spoke to her, but I didn't . . . well, I didn't do *that*."

Drury's unnerving gaze didn't waver. "What exactly *did* you do?"

"I simply talked to her. Gad, if seeing a man and a woman having a quiet conversation was so upsetting to that clerk, I think he should find himself another line of work."

When he saw the look on Drury's face, Brix took a deep breath and commanded himself to be calm. "He's obviously starved for excitement, poor fellow," he continued with a grin, "exaggerating things like that. I mean, I did speak to Fanny, and we weren't talking very loudly, but it wasn't as if I was trying to have my lascivious way with her. And that clerk didn't hear what she said to me, or see what . . ."

Brix discovered he didn't want to describe Fanny's stroking of silk in the linendraper's.

Drury crossed his legs. "I confess I'm surprised you spoke to her at all, after claiming you don't want anything to do with her, ever."

"Perhaps I shouldn't have, especially if clerks are going to gossip about me all over town," Brix agreed with a slightly strained laugh.

Drury took his gaze off Brix to look at the passing shops and the people hurrying home, or to other activities.

Brix tensed, because that didn't mean the discussion was over. Drury often did the same thing in court. It was more likely he was planning to deliver the *coup de grâce*.

And he did.

Drury fixed a steely gaze on him and said,

"Perhaps you can clarify something for me, Brix. You claim that you want to be rid of Fanny Epping, yet instead of ignoring her, you speak to her in a shop in a manner that has the clerk convinced you were about to kiss her. At a dinner party, you don't content yourself with conversing with other people, but immediately sit beside her on a sofa in the drawing room and all but embrace her."

Brix didn't appreciate Drury's courtroom tactics. "I didn't *all but embrace her* at Lord Cheswick's," he protested. "I simply rested my arm along the back of the sofa. Good God, can't a man even do that without being accused of lechery? She's not the naive innocent you all think, either, as that kiss in Edmond's study should have told you. If you think I'm behaving outrageously, you ought to spend time with Fanny these days. I tell you, *she's* the flirtatious one."

"There's no need to get angry with me," Drury replied, his tone as calm and reasonable as ever. "I'm simply trying to understand what's going on between you. I had only Edmond's views of events, and some bits of gossip. From what you're telling me, though, I believe Fanny may be guilty of some questionable behavior."

Brix took off his hat and ran his hand through his hair as he tried to regain some semblance of calm. "I'm glad somebody's at least willing to concede the possibility that Fanny isn't virtue personified."

"I'm really trying to remain neutral, Brix, but in

all honestly, I have to say I think you and Fanny are both acting like children."

Children? He wouldn't think that if he'd seen Fanny stroking that silk, or heard some of things she'd said, or kissed her.

But he wasn't going to enlighten Drury about those things.

Instead, he managed a self-deprecating chortle. "I should have known I'd get brutal honesty from you," he said. He bowed his head in acquiescence. "Very well. Guilty as charged, m'lud, since you accuse her of childish behavior, too."

"I begin to despair that you'll ever grow up, Brix," Drury said as the barouche rolled to a stop outside the large theater that took up a whole city block and was over three stories tall.

"I came into my majority years ago."

"You know what I mean."

"Get all serious and grim?" Brix shivered dramatically. "I hope I never do."

To Brix's surprise, Drury actually smiled. "I don't want you to, either. My life is dull enough as it is."

Brix wished Fanny could hear that.

"You would have made a good barrister yourself, Brix. You certainly talk enough."

Brix ignored the painful little sting of being told—again—that he was loquacious. "That's quite a compliment, coming from the most famous barrister in London."

"I mean it, Brix."

The driver let down the steps and opened the

door. Glad to get out of the confines of the carriage, Brix exited first and waited for Drury by the curb. The night was warm and the sky clear, or as clear as a London sky ever got, even in the spring.

The theater's upper windows were ablaze with light. A crowd had gathered beneath the arched portico where Brix and Drury disembarked, another under the columned one at the other end of the building.

The dark-haired lawyer probably couldn't help looking like a conquering hero as he alighted from the carriage into the lamplight, and a Roman general leaving his chariot after a triumphal parade could hardly cause less of a stir.

Obviously, he wasn't the only person aware of who Drury was, and as they made their way to the entrance of the King's Theater, excited, hushed voices followed their progress. More than a few among the fashionably well-dressed crowd blatantly stared.

Drury scowled.

"What's the matter?" Brix asked as they walked under the portico. "You should be used to people looking at you. You make speeches in court all the time."

"I make arguments and examine witnesses. This is distinctly different," Drury muttered, staring straight ahead as they entered the foyer.

"The price of fame and success, I suppose," Brix mused aloud. "Thank God I'm spared."

He realized Drury wasn't listening. His friend's attention was completely focused on a group of lively young women who were clustered on the steps of one of the massive staircases leading to the five tiers of boxes and the gallery. Their silk gowns were cut very low, and their corsets had to be extremely tight, to judge from the way their breasts almost overflowed their bodices. And unless Brix was very much mistaken, they were wearing cosmetics.

It wasn't only their dress and faces that told Brix these young women were not there to watch the opera or the ballet; the way they laughed and eyed the men in the foyer told him what their primary purpose must be.

As if to confirm it, one of them smiled boldly at Brix, then nudged her companion. They started to whisper and laugh behind their fans. A third, seeing them, followed their gaze and winked at Drury.

If Brix had had any doubt as to their livelihood, that wink erased it.

"You do realize they're cyprians?" he asked his friend as one amply endowed young woman in a shockingly thin white gown leaned over the balustrade in such a way that one could likely see down her bodice all the way to her toes if one were close enough.

"I know what they are," Drury replied, turning to look at Brix with what might have been a momentary twinkle of amusement in his dark eyes. "I also know they're trying to get our attention."

"Yours, at any rate," Brix replied as they started

up another staircase leading to the first row of boxes.

"Or yours, if it's true that you've ended your liaison with Nellie Teasdale."

Brix eyed him, and the wariness wasn't completely bogus. "Good God, I haven't told anyone we've called an end to it. I dare say Nellie hasn't kept it a secret, but I didn't realize you had informants in the theatrical world, too. Is there *anything* going on in London you don't know?"

"A few things," his friend replied with a sardonic little smile. "That's why I have to ask if it's true that it's finished between you."

"Nellie and I parted ways after an argument the other day," Brix genially admitted. "It was inevitable anyway. She wanted a more formal arrangement, with a legal contract. I'm not anxious to play at being a husband."

"You gave her a substantial sum in recompense, I don't doubt."

"Of course."

And despite what Fanny might think, Nellie and his two previous mistresses had liked him in a way that had nothing to do with their financial arrangements.

"This is still a vastly more respectable place than Drury Lane or Covent Garden," Brix went on. "It's impossible to keep cyprians away from any place well-to-do men congregate."

"And men with money to spend away from them," Drury noted.

"Exactly," Brix agreed as they reached his box. As one of the principal subscribers, he had a *loges infernales*, a double box abutting the left side of the stage. It was as close to the stage as one could get, barring being on it, and gave an excellent view of the performers.

Brix had seen to it that the chairs were thickly upholstered for comfort and that it was kept scrupulously clean. Smoke from the enormous chandeliers and stage candles quickly ruined walls and furniture otherwise.

The bucks and dandies, with their expensive clothes and raucous voices, sauntered along Fop's Alley, a wide aisle down the center of the house where they loitered before, during and after the performances. All sorts of other people, from the highest ranking to the fruitsellers, took their places in the rest of the theater, filling the pit, the five tiers of boxes and the gallery.

As they took their seats, Brix noted two familiar faces in Fop's Alley: Clutterbuck, whose nose was grotesquely swollen, and Strunk. As was usually the case when they were at the theater, they were drunk.

Brix was so focused on Clutterbuck and Strunk and their equally drunken cronies, it took him a moment to realize other people already in their boxes or the pit were looking toward his box.

"You seem to be causing a bit of a stir," Drury observed as if he'd just read Brix's mind.

"Oh, it couldn't be me," Brix said with a self-deprecating laugh. "It's you. Sir Douglas Drury on a rare visit to the opera. There's likely to be something about it in the papers tomorrow."

Drury shook his head. "No, it's not me they're looking at. It's *you*."

Brix refused to believe it. "Don't be ridiculous."

"I'm not being ridiculous. I'm basing it on the evidence before my eyes, and the fact that you've become rather infamous."

"*Infamous?*" Brix cried, genuinely taken aback by that word.

To his dismay, Drury nodded. "It seems, my friend, that all of London's heard about those wagers, and is speculating who'll win. Even my clerk told me yesterday he's made a bet on the outcome."

Good God. He'd expected the *ton* to gossip about the bets, especially given Fanny's recent behavior, but a barrister's clerk was wagering on his wager? What was next? Odds at a bookmaker?

Hiding his dismay, he put on a jovial expression. "Well, I hope your clerk bet on me and not Fanny."

"I didn't ask him. I suggested he spend both his time and his money more wisely."

Typical Drury. "I don't suppose your clerk mentioned any odds?"

"Five to one."

There really were odds? He'd only been joking. "On Fanny."

Brix struggled to remain calm. He mustn't show his anger, or imply that he cared about a clerk's wager. "Poor fellow's going to lose his money," he said as he turned away to survey the rapidly filling house.

Five to one? Five to one in Fanny's *favor?* He couldn't believe it. He *wouldn't* believe it. Drury must be having him on... except that Drury never joked.

"I had no idea this place could hold so many people," the lawyer remarked.

"Twenty-five hundred," Brix muttered absently. Wagers on his wagers. Clerks betting on his love life. Fanny had a lot to answer for...

"And the theater makes a profit, does it?"

"Enough to keep it going."

"Just curious," Drury replied.

With a twinge of guilt, Brix realized he was being a very poor host. This was supposed to be a night of celebration over Drury's latest victory at court.

He turned toward his friend. "Forgive me, Drury. It's just that those odds are ridiculous."

Drury didn't answer. He was staring across the stage as Brix had never seen Sir Douglas Drury stare before.

He followed his gaze to Lady Jersey's *loges infernales* opposite—and Fanny now taking her seat, wearing a gown of that pale pink silk.

His breath caught in his throat. He stared at Fanny, laughing gaily and speaking to Diana and Edmond, who had entered the box with her. Her flowing, high-waisted dress made no secret of her trim figure and was cut low enough to reveal the swell of her breasts. With her hair dressed very stylishly *à la grecque*, she looked, quite simply and unequivocally, the equal of any beauty in London. Or anywhere else, for that matter.

Drury shifted in his seat, immediately drawing Brix's attention.

The man was regarding Fanny as if mesmerized.

To Brix's further dismay, a quick survey of the house proved that most of the young men in Fop's Alley were watching Fanny, too, including Clutterbuck and Strunk.

What was Edmond thinking, bringing Fanny here dressed like that? He was as good as her guardian these days. He shouldn't be exposing her to the insolent, lustful stares of the young men in Fop's Alley, most of whom were blatantly ogling her and even trying to catch her eye. And what was Diana about, allowing her to have a gown like that? Didn't she have better sense? Didn't Fanny?

"I almost didn't recognize her," Drury murmured, his eyes still focused on the box opposite.

Brix didn't bother to ask who he meant. "That *is* a nice dress," he said in an offhand manner, as if it was only the dress that made a difference. "Rather skimpy, though. And her hair looks like a particularly complicated sort of bird's nest, don't you think?"

Drury faced Brix, and when he did, it was with an expression Brix had never seen on the man's face before. "I never realized how pretty Fanny is. She's always been so quiet and shy. But there's certainly something about her tonight . . ." He drifted into silence and looked back across the stage.

Brix had never heard quite that tone in his friend's voice, either. "If I didn't know you better, Drury, I'd say you were fascinated," he remarked.

"I am."

Brix refused to allow himself to be upset, or annoyed, or anything but mildly amused. "Pity she didn't kiss you in Edmond's study, then."

"Yes, I've been thinking about that kiss," Drury muttered.

Brix immediately envisioned Drury kissing Fanny. Deeply. Passionately. And Fanny kissing him. Deeply, passionately.

Drury swiveled around and subjected him to the full force of his Death Stare. "You really don't care for Fanny in that way?"

Brix feigned ignorance. "What way?"

"As a potential wife?"

What the devil—? Since when had Sir Douglas Drury ever considered Fanny a suitable candidate for his wife? When had Sir Douglas Drury ever considered marriage at all, for that matter?

He realized Drury was waiting for an answer. "No, I really don't want to marry Fanny. I never have, and I never will."

Drury's stare grew even more penetrating, as if the man's eyes were directing some sort of savage energy at him in an effort to make him reveal his deepest feelings. "Do you think Fanny could be persuaded to care for somebody else?"

"Yourself, perhaps?" Brix forced a smile. "Don't tell me some doubt of his attractiveness to the fairer sex has entered Sir Douglas Drury's mind? How can this be? Women flock about you like birds over bread crumbs, and she's a woman, isn't she?"

"She's a woman who's been in love with *you* most of her life, despite very little encouragement. That sort of devotion is very hard to overcome."

"Devotion?" Brix exclaimed, refusing to accept Drury's definition of Fanny's previous feelings for him. "I wouldn't call it that."

"What would you call it?" Drury inquired.

"I'd call it an inability to realize when she's being a nuisance." Brix realized his shirt was sticking to his back and fought to ignore his discomfort. "Gad, people still seem to assume I have some sort of monopoly on her affections. I assure you, I don't, and if I ever did, I didn't want it. So by all means, Drury, you're welcome to pursue her, and I wish you success."

"So I would have your blessing to try?"

Had the man lost his hearing? "My blessing? Good God, man, it would be blessed relief." He forced another smile. "So, you'd actually consider marrying Fanny?"

His friend's expression hardened. "What else would I be referring to when the woman in question is Lady Francesca Epping?"

Brix kept smiling. "Just wanted to be clear." He looked down at the pit. "The orchestra are taking their places," he noted.

Thank God. He didn't want to discuss Fanny and marriage anymore, even if he should welcome the idea of Fanny being pursued by another man, especially Drury. If Drury expressed an interest, the other bucks and dandies of the *ton* would soon be buzzing around Fanny like bees to honey, and he'd have more cause to believe he'd win the wagers.

But what if she chose one of them? What if she married some charming rakehell who'd make her miserable?

That wouldn't happen. Fanny had a good head on her shoulders; she could be counted on not to make a foolish mistake . . . but then, that wouldn't explain her previous fascination with *him*. Or her recent conduct.

Her actions and behavior were not his concern. Yes, he'd made the wagers, but anything beyond that was Fanny's responsibility. He certainly hadn't told her to get a dress like that pink creation that so displayed her figure to advantage, or wear her hair in that becoming style, or smile so brightly, or kiss him in a way that had him dreaming about her in his bed, naked, kissing and caressing him and whispering such tantalizing things . . .

His thoughts were interrupted by the overture to *The Marriage of Figaro*.

Never in his life had the distraction of music been more welcome.

Holding the hood of her light evening cloak close about her face, Fanny headed down the pit passage toward the dressing rooms. Getting sepa-

rated from Diana and Edmond on purpose in the
exiting crowd had been even easier than she had
hoped. When they had retrieved their wraps, she
had simply hung back while Diana went to join
Edmond at the main entrance where their carriage was waiting.

Then she'd headed back into the theater and
made her way toward the door leading to the area
behind the stage, where Nellie Teasdale's dressing room would be.

Once in the dimly lit passage, though, it was as
if she'd entered a foreign country. A babble of
voices talking and issuing orders, with accents
from all over Britain, assailed her ears. The scent
of sawdust was very strong, coupled with sweat
and another smell she couldn't name.

One of the dancers in heavy face paint hurried
past her. Seen from this proximity, her face looked
grotesque, with exaggerated lips and rouged
cheeks, and either she wore a most unusual perfume, or the smell Fanny hadn't recognized came
from her heavily applied cosmetics.

Perhaps Nellie Teasdale wore a lot of cosmetics,
too. She certainly didn't wear much in the way of
a costume, but that was to be expected, Fanny
supposed, since she was a travesty dancer. They
were women who specialized in men's roles, and
so wore men's clothing, which incidentally revealed their legs to a shocking degree.

She could never expose her limbs in such an
outrageous fashion, she was sure—unless absolute necessity drove her to consider a career

upon the stage. Even then, she'd never take a lover or "protector," as such men were pleased to call themselves.

In spite of that belief, as she crept farther back into the dim recesses of the theater, she began to imagine herself in Nellie's costume, with her hair cropped short. She wondered if Brix would approve, his eyes flaring with interest just as they had when she'd caressed the silk now flowing over her body, or if he would only think she looked ridiculous.

Did he think she looked ridiculous tonight? Or did he think that she had deluded herself into believing she was a beauty? Whatever he thought, in her new silk gown she'd felt beautiful and the equal of any young lady.

Brix had to have noticed her, given the way Sir Douglas Drury was watching her with his dark, intense, disturbing gaze, as if he was about to accuse her of murder or some other dastardly deed.

She froze and watched as two familiar and drunken men careered into the passageway from a door at the end—Lord Strunk and his equally disgusting crony with the broken nose, Sir Richard Clutterbuck.

In spite of her little victory on the street and her subsequent silencing of Lord Strunk, panic seized her, for she was alone, and where no lady ought to be.

She was also beside a door. She had no idea where it went, except away from them, so she put her hand on the latch just as two brawny laborers carrying a large piece of scenery appeared behind Clutterbuck and Strunk and shouted for them to get out of the way.

As they pressed back against the wall, she eased the door open. She saw fusty draperies and dusty bits of furniture. A storeroom, obviously.

She immediately slipped inside. A small, dirt-encrusted window allowed in a little moonlight to illuminate the cluttered room. The draperies—heavy velvet, with the nap rubbed off in some places, the tasseled trim torn and dangling—were suspended from the rafters overhead. The furniture included what appeared to be a throne, a chest, some tables, a few spindly chairs piled on top of each other, and several round, gray shapes she assumed were supposed to be rocks. A full suit of armor stood in the corner and a few spears leaned against the wall nearby. There was an oriental gong under the window, and an armoire missing a door beside it. Everything was covered with a layer of dust, so she hoped that meant nobody would be entering before those men went on their way.

Pressing her ear to the door, she heard another familiar voice, one that made her breath catch.

"Well, gentlemen, and I use the word only in the broadest sense, what brings you here this evening?" Brix said, his voice slightly muffled by the wood.

"Just been chatting with Nellie," Clutterbuck replied, his words slurring.

"I take it you're referring to Miss Teasdale,

Dickie. If so, I suggest you use a more appropriate means of address."

Fanny'd never heard Brix sound like that, as formidable as the commanding officer of an army.

"I mean your little friend who's not your little friend anymore," the odious Strunk retorted. "Since you've cut her loose, she's fair game."

So, the rumors were true. Relief filled Fanny, until she remembered why she was here in the first place: to find out how to break Brix's heart.

"Although Miss Teasdale is no longer under my protection," Brix replied with haughty majesty, "we are still friends, so I shall certainly make it my business to see that she's not bothered by anybody she'd rather not know."

"Well, pardon me," Clutterbuck said sarcastically, "but I'm sure she won't mind being bothered if I make it worth her while."

"You obviously don't know Miss Teasdale."

"Not the way you do, eh?" Strunk sneered. "Not yet, anyway. How much do you think it'll take? Fifty pounds? Ten?"

Fanny jumped back as the door rattled from a weight thrown against it.

"You don't have enough money to make any woman want you, you little toad," Brix growled, "unless she's absolutely desperate." The door rattled again, as if he'd pushed Strunk against it. "Now, since Dickie's taken off like the coward he is, I'd like you to answer some questions for me, Strunk."

The nobleman's answer was a strangled gulp.

"What the devil have you had to do with Lady Francesca Epping?"

Holding her breath, Fanny strained to hear.

"W-we met her on the street and thought she was a maid running away from her place," Strunk stammered. "We didn't know who she was."

"So you tried to charm her in your own inimitable way, is that it?"

"Clutterbuck invited her to his house, that's all."

"I can imagine how he did it, too."

"We didn't hurt her," Strunk whined. "*She* attacked *us*."

Brix laughed with sarcastic scorn. "You expect me to believe Fanny Epping attacked you?"

"With her bag. Then she ran away."

"She's a smart woman. Now get out of my sight, Strunk, and stay away from here, and Fanny, too. If I ever see you so much as breathing in her direction, you'll be sorry."

The door rattled again, although not as much. Brix must have released Strunk.

Holding her breath, Fanny continued to listen, but she heard nothing more. Brix must have gone, too. She turned and relaxed against the door, and wondered what Brix thought of her attack upon Strunk and his friend.

The latch moved.

In two quick steps, she was behind the dusty velvet draperies, although they smelled of mold and the slightest movement unleashed a cloud of dust.

The door creaked open and a shaft of light penetrated the gloom.

She didn't dare move a muscle, even as dust tickled her nostrils. Her eyes started to water.

Just when she thought she must draw breath, or sneeze, the door began to close.

Safe at last.

She stepped out from behind the drapery—right into the arms of the Honorable Brixton Smythe-Medway, who took hold of her shoulders while his lips curved up in a mocking little smile. "Why, Lady Francesca, what an unexpected pleasure."

Feeling like some sort of criminal—although of course she wasn't—she wrenched herself free and stepped back, colliding with the dusty draperies.

"What are you doing here?" she demanded as if she had every right to be in this room. Then she sneezed.

Brix reached into his pocket and produced a silk handkerchief. "Since I subscribe, my presence doesn't require an explanation," Brix said as he offered it to her. "The question is, what are you doing back here?" He surveyed the cluttered area. "And in the property room, too."

She took her own handkerchief from the reticule dangling from her wrist, wiped her nose, then put it back and snapped the reticule shut. That gave her time to collect herself and decide what to do.

"I wanted to tell Miss Teasdale how much I admired her performance tonight," she lied, giving him a bright and bogus smile. "Is that why you've come back here, too?"

His expression unexpectedly serious, he shook his head, making a lock of hair tumble over his forehead. "As a matter of fact, I came looking for you. Diana and Edmond are quite frantic over your disappearance. Edmond's dashing about making a nuisance of himself. Drury's gone for the Bow Street Runners, in case you've been kidnapped."

Fanny gasped. She thought she'd been gone only a short time, not nearly long enough for Edmond and Diana to worry about her. Clearly, she was wrong.

She went to go past Brix, but he deftly stepped in front of her. "That's a slight exaggeration, although they *are* looking for you," he said. "They assume you got lost in the crowd. I didn't think you could ever be so thoughtless as to make them worry about you, Fanny."

How dare he accuse *her* of being thoughtless! And how dare he upset her even more! Hadn't he done that enough?

Her hands balled into fists as she glared at him. "I'm sure this is just another of your attempts to be amusing, Mr. Smythe-Medway. I suspect they haven't even noticed I'm gone."

Brix raised a brow in that infuriating way of his. "My, my, Fanny, what has come over you lately? Such fire, such spirit, such strange behavior. Such a low-cut bodice." His gaze flicked down her pretty gown, making her blush in spite of herself. "You certainly managed to attract the attention of scores of cads, rakes, scoundrels and bounders tonight. Is that why you came here, Fanny?"

She resisted the urge to cover her chest with her hands. "I've never been to the opera before. But since you come all the time," she said, imitating his offhand manner of replying, "I wanted to see what was so appealing. I believe I saw what attracts you, anyway."

"I'll tell you why I like the theater, Fanny," he replied. "It's because I know exactly who the actors are and what parts they're playing when I'm watching the stage. At other times, it takes more effort to figure out who's playing a role and what that role might be. For instance, are you really gentle little Fanny, or some brazen hussy determined to increase her horde of admirers?"

"I don't have a horde of admirers."

"Not yet, anyway. But you could, especially when you dress in such a provocative manner. Fop's Alley was all abuzz over you."

"I didn't come here to attract the attention of dandies and fops."

"No?" Brix's voice got a tone that was both dangerous and incredibly, undeniably exciting. "If you didn't dress to attract the notice of the dandies and their ilk, am I to assume, given our wager, that you dressed like that for *me*?"

Determined not to succumb to the temptation of his voice, resolved to remember that he was her enemy, and recalling his reaction to her behavior in the linendraper's, she ran her fingers along the neckline of her bodice. "You may think whatever you please. Plenty of other women in the theater were much more scantily attired than I, and not just the ones on the stage."

"They were prostitutes, Fanny."

She dropped her hand. "Are you saying I look like a cyprian?"

"I was merely pointing out that the women who were more scantily attired, as you put it, are harlots. Now I suggest you go back to Diana and Edmond before some stage door lothario mistakes you for one of the women who *are* harlots and offers you an indignity."

"I can take care of myself. As you just heard, I managed quite well against Lord Strunk and his friend."

"You might be able to triumph over drunkards and weaklings, Fanny, but if you persist in wandering about by yourself and dressing in this provocative manner, one day you might find yourself up against a more formidable, determined opponent."

"While you have complete freedom to do whatever you like!"

"I don't pretend that this is just, Fanny," he said softly. "But it is simply too dangerous for you to carry on this way. You could get hurt. Or worse."

For a moment, he sounded the way he used to—kindhearted and gently protective.

But she had to remember her vow to win the wagers and assuage her wounded pride. She couldn't go back to being mousy little Fanny Epping, not ever again.

He sidled closer, his proximity making her heartbeat race. "Why did you really come back here by yourself, Fanny?" he asked, his voice a low, seductive purr. "Will you tell me, or shall I guess?"

He didn't wait for her to answer, but supplied his own. "You thought you'd do as Diana did, with one difference. She studied Edmond because she didn't know much about men. You already know me as well, or better, than anyone, so it's Nellie you've ventured back here to study, isn't it? You want to understand the kind of woman I'm attracted to." He inched closer. "That I make love with."

She was so taken aback that he guessed correctly, she couldn't think of a word to say, not even when he took hold of her hands and drew her close, staring down at her with a look in his eyes that made her shiver.

"I have no qualms about telling you what I like in a woman, Fanny," he whispered as he ran his long, strong fingers up her arms, making her cloak spread open like a curtain being drawn back. "I prefer women who know what *they* like. Do you know what you like, Fanny? Do you even have any idea what there is *to* like?"

As he gently took hold of her shoulders, she felt as if she was one of Buggy's specimens, pinned to a board, powerless and immobile. "Shall we see?" he whispered.

She had no voice to refuse. Her reticule slid off

her wrist and fell to the floor. She made no effort to retrieve it.

He brushed his lips over hers in a way that made her senses reel. "Do you like to be kissed on the lips, Fanny? Or your cheeks?"

She closed her eyes. She shouldn't enjoy this. She mustn't enjoy this. But surely . . . if he was kissing her . . . she must be . . . making progress . . . of some kind. . . .

His mouth continued its tour. "Do you enjoy it when I kiss the lids of your eyes? What about the curve of your jaw?"

He untied her cloak and let it slip to the floor, too. She really ought to stop him. . . .

He pushed her gown off her shoulder and his lips moved lower still. "What about the slope of your shoulder?" His mouth was so warm and soft. "Or the lovely swell of your breasts?"

If he kissed her there, she'd swoon.

He didn't. Instead, he pulled her close and murmured, "Do you like kisses to be gentle and soft? Or hungry and passionate, like this?"

His mouth captured hers in a searing kiss. His arms encircled her and held her close, her body against his, as the heat of desire kindled within her.

She'd dreamed of this a thousand times, waking and sleeping. This was what she'd always yearned for. It was as wonderful and exciting as she'd imagined—and more.

His lips slid to the place where her jaw met her neck and his hand grazed her ribs, moving upward to cup her breast.

"Do you like it when I touch you there, Fanny?" he whispered while his fingers gently caressed her.

A low moan was her only answer as with persistent, yet gentle guidance, he steered her backward until she felt the solid wood of the armoire against her back, the firmness a welcome support.

She arched back. Her legs seemed as soft as butter in the sun, while a tension taut as a harp string grew elsewhere.

"I think perhaps you do," he murmured. "And here?"

He kissed her mouth again, rougher this time, while his hand cupped her between her hips.

She'd never known . . . never felt . . . anything like the sensations the firm pressure of his hand created. Gripping him tightly, she leaned into him more.

His tongue thrust between her lips as he slipped his hand into her bodice, so that his palm was against her bare skin. She gasped as her nipple pebbled beneath his fingertips. It felt so good . . .

His hand left her breast, to cup her again between her hips. He stroked her with a rhythm that matched the pulsing of her blood in her veins. Firm, yet also gentle. Constant, unceasing, and oh, so welcome.

Anticipation grew. Increased. Became stronger still. Almost unbearable.

His kisses were rougher. More insistent. Hungry.

The tension snapped, to become wave after wave of throbbing, blissful release as she clung to him, helpless and powerless and happily so. He held her for a moment, his breathing ragged in her ear, as she tried to calm her own.

What *was* that? She'd never felt anything like it. She never knew such a feeling existed. Like a kiss, only a thousand times more powerful. Like an embrace, but one that warmed her whole body.

He stepped back and regarded her steadily for a long moment, his face strangely expressionless, until a mocking smile slowly blossomed on his face. "I'd say you liked that very much, Fanny. All of it. But there's so much more you could learn. Shall I continue, or is that enough for this evening?"

The blood rushed to her face. She'd felt so much so intensely—hunger, desire, a passionate need that she couldn't deny—and this was just another joke to him? Another way to humiliate her?

Hadn't she learned anything?

Yes, she had. Despite that smile and the mockery on his face, she'd felt his need, his desire, as intense as her own.

She reached down for her discarded cloak and put it back on. Her fingers trembled a little as she tied the knot and brushed off the worst of the dust, but the visible sign of her distress strengthened her resolve and helped her overcome any shame she felt.

Vowing that he'd never make her feel ashamed

or embarrassed or humiliated again, she bent down and retrieved her reticule.

When she straightened, she met his gaze squarely. "I believe you quite enjoyed yourself, too, Mr. Smythe-Medway," she said, her voice firm and steady. "Only think how much better it would have been if I shared your enthusiasm and reciprocated."

His eyes flared with surprise.

But she wasn't finished yet. She grabbed his shoulders and brushed her lips over his. "Good night, Brix," she whispered, just as she'd imagined doing a thousand times, too.

Her voice hardened, like her resolve, as she let go and stepped back. "Perhaps we'll meet at Lady Jersey's fancy dress ball on the first of June—if you've been invited. Now that I know something of what *you* like, that could be rather interesting, don't you think?"

She didn't wait for an answer before marching from the room.

Chapter 7

London, the twentieth of May, 1819

Dear Aunt Euphenia,

First, the most exciting news. D'Arcy said his first word today! I'm sure he said "Da-da." Edmond tried to claim he didn't believe it, but you should have seen how delighted he was. And regardless of what Edmond thinks, I know that's what our dear boy said, because I've been doing all in my power to make it so, since Edmond is so foolishly, dearly besotted with his son. But this last should remain just between us, Aunt.

I know you'll also be anxious to hear more news of Fanny and Brix and this rather odd, baffling situation, which gets more odd and confusing every single day. It seems our dear friend Sir Douglas Drury has, shall we say, conceived a passion for Fanny that nobody expected. To make matters worse, Brix's brother, Humphrey, has arrived in Town. Given their rancorous relationship, that's sure to complicate things.

Lady Diana Westover Terrington

"**O**h, you can't really mean that, Mr. Smythe-Medway! The duke of Wellington never said any such thing!" Lady Annabelle Dalyrimple cried. She burst into high-pitched giggles as she fluttered her eyelashes at Brix, who was riding beside her carriage in St. James's Park.

"Ah, but he might have, mightn't he?" Brix replied, keeping his gaze on the young woman of nineteen ensconced in her carriage like Cleopatra on her barge. "I mean, the man can't have spent so much time in a tent and not worried about a leak now and then."

Lady Annabelle's duenna, Mrs. Wartworth, a sour-faced, gaunt woman of sixty seemingly without a drop of warm blood in her body, or the faintest glimmer of a sense of humor, regarded Brix as if he were infested with lice. Fortunately, these days he was getting a lot of experience ignoring women, even ones in pale pink silk who kissed him passionately and aroused him and made him forget where he was and inspired him to . . .

His gelding refooted, bringing him a bit closer to the barouche and reminding him that he was supposed to be attending to Lady Annabelle, not thinking about that night in the theater with Fanny. He shouldn't think about Fanny at all.

Lady Annabelle Dalyrimple was the belle of the season this year, and several young men were already said to be vying for her hand. One of them was most welcome to her—Brix couldn't imagine spending the rest of his life with that giggle—but in the meantime, he could think of worse ways to spend his time than riding in St. James's Park on a fine spring morning, entertaining the beautiful daughter of the sixth earl of Belden. It was certainly more enjoyable than being alone, or being chastised by an impertinent young woman.

But he wasn't going to think about Fanny.

"What a lovely hat, Lady Annabelle. From Paris, is it?" Brix asked, sure that Lady Annabelle knew she looked quite fetching in a light wool pelisse of blue, with black frogs to close it. Her chapeau, a feathery concoction, framed her face nearly as well as her blond hair.

Mrs. Wartworth frowned even more, while Annabelle put a slender hand up to touch her bonnet and smiled, revealing teeth that were not as fine as Fanny's. "Yes, it is."

"Tell me, will you be going to Lady Jersey's party on the first of June, by any chance, my lady?"

Annabelle blushed and simpered, "As a matter of fact, I am."

Gad, spare him women who simpered. In spite of that defect, however, Brix gave her one of his most charming smiles. "Then I shall hope to have the pleasure of a dance with you."

Mrs. Wartworth cleared her throat. Loudly.

"Oh, my," he cried, addressing the older woman with every indication of concern. "I hope you're not coming down with catarrh, Mrs. Wartworth. If you are, I suggest a poultice and plenty of rest." He leaned even closer to Annabelle and loudly whispered, "I'd suggest she refrain from speaking at all lest she strain her voice, except that she never says a word. She's not mute, is she?"

Annabelle giggled and shook her head.

Brix looked stricken. "Oh, dear. You mean she just doesn't like me?"

"That will be quite enough from you, Mr. Smythe-Medway," Mrs. Wartworth growled, her voice as deep and rough as a serjeant major's. "Home, Jasper!" She shoved the end of her parasol into the driver's back.

"Farewell, Annabelle! Until Lady Jersey's party," Brix cried as the carriage rumbled off.

Annabelle looked back and waved, while Mrs. Wartworth's annoyed words floated back to him. "Impudent rascal . . . those shocking wagers . . . I'll tell your father . . ."

Perhaps Annabelle would not be going to Lady Jersey's party, after all.

Ah well, Brix thought as he nudged his horse into a walk and continued along Rotten Row, there would be plenty of other young ladies there to take his mind off—

"Why, Mr. Smythe-Medway, what an unexpected pleasure!"

A quiver ran down Brix's spine at the sound of Fanny's voice, and he wheeled his horse to see Fanny, mounted on a very fine mare, trotting toward him.

She wore a riding habit of royal blue velvet. He

immediately recognized the fabric from the linen-draper's, which had been made into a trim little jacket and full skirt. The toes of shiny black boots peeked out from beneath the voluminous velvet. Her riding hat, of royal blue satin and taffeta, with a long, floating veil of matching blue silk, was the prettiest such creation he'd ever seen. As if in defiance of gravity, it was perched on Fanny's thick, wavy hair done up in braids and ringlets.

Fanny made Lady Annabelle look like an over-dressed doll.

Then he took a look at who was riding with her and nearly fell off his horse. It wasn't the happily married Edmond. It was Sir Douglas Drury, looking as if he'd been born in the saddle.

That bastard. What the devil was he doing riding with Fanny in the middle of the morning? Didn't he have to be in court? Or preparing a case? Or *something*?

Fanny was looking pretty damn pleased with herself, too, no doubt because she was riding in the park with the most famous lawyer in London. Who might soon be discovering what it was like to kiss Fanny.

Among other things.

But betray any feelings other than good humor, he would not.

"Why, good morning, you two!" he cried with every appearance of happiness when they caught up to him. "What a delightful surprise. I'm especially surprised to see you here, Drury. I thought fencing was your preferred form of exercise, when that nose of yours wasn't to the proverbial grindstone."

"I like a little change sometimes," Drury replied with his usual sangfroid.

"So today you're riding in Rotten Row with Fanny. How charming."

"Isn't it?" Fanny said with a smile. "Sir Douglas has just been telling me about some of his cases. They're fascinating." She tilted her head. Amazingly, that pert little chapeau didn't fall off. "You seemed to be having a most enjoyable conversation with Lady Annabelle Dalyrimple."

So, she'd seen that, and that her efforts to ruin his reputation with the ladies were not succeeding.

Brix gave her a smug smile. "We weren't talking about the law, of course. Lady Annabelle and I were having a very *entertaining* discussion."

Fanny laughed. It wasn't a throaty, earthy chortle like Nellie Teasdale's, or the irritating, high-pitched giggle of Annabelle. It was a lovely, mirthful musical sound he had long considered the perfect feminine laugh.

"I don't doubt you were very entertaining," she said. "You're an amusing fellow. Everybody says so. Of course, they're also saying certain other things about you that make me wonder what the good Mrs. Wartworth was about, letting you talk to Lady Annabelle at all."

She made it sound as if he were the most decadent cad in England.

Determined to retaliate, Brix made a great show

of scanning the horizon. "Since you bring up the subject of reputations, Fanny, where's your chaperon? Surely Edmond and Diana haven't let you go riding out without one, even if you're with such a fine, upstanding fellow as our Drury."

"They're right over there," Fanny replied, not a whit disturbed as she nodded to his left, where Brix spotted Diana and Edmond in an open barouche.

Naturally he was relieved to think they hadn't let Fanny do anything so shocking as ride out alone in public with a man who wasn't a relative. Nevertheless, they weren't doing a very good job of watching over their charge. Diana was holding little D'Arcy Douglas in her arms, and she and Edmond were smiling and talking with merry intimacy, the way happily married people did. To be sure, Fanny was within their sight, and he didn't really expect Drury to do anything impertinent, but who could say what might happen if Fanny started to flirt with the barrister the way she had with him in the shop and at the theater? Drury was no angel, after all, and his liaisons with women were the stuff of legend at their club.

A little wrinkle appeared between Fanny's brown brows, just as it had when she was confused by something when she was a child. "I must say I was surprised to see you with Lady Annabelle. She never seemed to have the time of day for you before our wager."

Brix refused to take the bait. "I don't doubt I owe her sudden and extreme interest to you,

Lady Francesca. I've often noticed that many women find notorious men fascinating. Isn't that right, Drury?"

The barrister didn't bat an eye at the reference to his celebrity. "For a short time, perhaps."

"Oh, come, come! You're being far too modest." Brix addressed Fanny as if he was happy to boast of his friend's prowess with the fairer sex. "Has he told you women slip notes under his door? And come to court just to watch him? That once, when he was delivering his closing statement, one of his female admirers swooned and had to be taken from the courtroom?"

"It was very hot that day," Drury said.

Fanny gave Drury another admiring smile, of the sort she used to give *him*. "I don't doubt your brilliance overwhelmed her."

"It was the heat, and certain gruesome details of the crime," Drury demurred.

What was going on? Drury wasn't one to shy away from acknowledging his skill.

"Very well, Sir Douglas, have it your own way," Fanny said, giving him another merry, charming laugh.

"Brixton!" a man's voice called from some distance away.

Good God! It couldn't be!

Brix looked back over his shoulder to see his older brother, Humphrey, heir to the earl of Parthington, torment of Brix's childhood, arrogant lord of Medway Manor, favored son of their father, trotting toward them on a magnificent black horse that had probably cost a thousand pounds.

"I didn't know Humphrey was in London," Fanny remarked.

"Neither did I," Brix muttered under his breath, wishing his brother far, far away. Borneo would be good. Or Australia.

"Who is it?" Drury inquired.

"Oh, haven't you met Mr. Smythe-Medway's elder brother, Lord Eastlake?" Fanny asked, as if she was greatly taken aback by Brix's apparent lapse of manners.

"You know Humphrey doesn't like London," Brix explained. "He doesn't come here very often, so I haven't been able to introduce him to my friends."

"No, Lord Eastlake doesn't like London," Fanny confirmed, addressing Drury. "It's harder for him to be important here, you see, so he generally stays at home, where he's the biggest rooster in the barnyard.

"Isn't that right, Mr. Smythe-Medway—unlike you, who fairly lives for London and its entertainments?" Fanny continued without waiting for Brix to confirm what he couldn't dispute, since he himself had used those exact words about his brother a few years ago, when he had been complaining about Humphrey's high-handed nature.

"There's not much of a family resemblance in looks either, as you can see. Lord Eastlake favors their father, the earl, who's a broad-chested, muscular man, while Mr. Smythe-Medway is slight and slender, like his mother."

As if he were a scrawny chicken! But he wouldn't play into her hands by responding to that.

"Oh, yes, it'll take more than age to slow Father down," Brix declared, even as he wondered if Fanny was planning to sweetly insult him, and his masculinity, some more.

She was. "You'll notice Lord Eastlake somehow manages to get his hair to lie flat."

"Bear grease," Brix lied. "He has it sent from Canada."

Fanny ignored him. "Lord Eastlake sports a beard because a woman once told him he looked like a Viking. He thinks it heightens the effect."

"He says shaving's a nuisance," Brix said, drawn to his brother's defense.

"Well, it's not as if he'd be shaving himself anyway. His valet would. Or has he lost another one?"

Before Brix could reply, Humphrey brought his black horse to a halt in front of them. "Hello, Brixton," he said, albeit without taking his eyes off Fanny.

Honestly, one would think Humphrey had never seen a woman before, and he'd known Fanny since she was born. "You remember Fanny, don't you, Humphrey?"

Humphrey's eyes widened and he gaped like an

awestruck child. "Fanny!" he cried. "Good God, I had no idea! What have you done to yourself?"

Brix barely refrained from scowling when Fanny smiled at Humphrey as if she was sincerely glad to see a man who'd tormented her for years. "I bought some new clothes. Do you like my riding habit?"

If she started batting her long lashes at Humphrey . . .

"Why yes, I do. Very smart."

"Have you met Sir Douglas Drury?" she asked, reminding Brix that he should be the one making introductions.

But if she wanted to play the queen, he'd let her.

"Oh, you're that lawyer friend of Brix's."

Brix mentally cringed, although he supposed he should be relieved Humphrey had remembered even that much about his friend. Yet to call the most famous barrister in London 'that lawyer friend' of his!

Brix became slightly less annoyed when he caught the look in Drury's eyes as he inclined his head about two degrees. "Lord Eastlake."

No doubt Drury was used to being deferred to at least as much as Humphrey, and for once, Brix didn't mind his brother's arrogance.

"I didn't know you were in London," Brix said to Humphrey.

"If you bothered to read your mail more than once a week, you'd have known I was coming," Humphrey gruffly replied.

"I do. If you sent me a letter, I didn't receive it."

"Simings must have forgotten to frank it."

Brix didn't believe that. Humphrey always blamed his steward when things weren't done, although the steward was rarely at fault. It was far more likely Humphrey hadn't bothered to write. He probably hadn't intended to visit his brother, either. They had their own town houses, and belonged to different clubs, and preferred different recreation, so Humphrey could have every expectation of successfully avoiding his brother's company when he came to London.

And vice versa.

"If you'll all excuse me, I really ought to be getting to my chambers," Drury announced.

Brix had never been so happy to have Drury take his leave.

"I've enjoyed talking with you, my lady," the barrister said to Fanny, with more deference than Brix had ever heard in his voice before. "Your insights into the law are very interesting."

Fanny had insights into the law that impressed the most renowned barrister in the city?

Drury fixed his gaze on Brix, catching him off guard. "Good day, Brix. Thank you again for an enjoyable evening at the opera."

Brix smiled at Fanny. If Drury was going to mention that night, he wasn't going to ignore the opportunity. "You're very welcome. It was extremely . . . entertaining . . . for me, too."

He felt a fiendish little glow of triumph as her cheeks turned pink. She could say what she would, but he knew what she'd felt in that property room, and that she'd enjoyed it, too. As he had. He'd never been with a woman whose kisses seemed so perfect, whose body excited him so, whose slightest touch aroused him so passionately. If he hadn't realized the danger not just to her honor, but to his peace of mind, and stopped when he did . . .

Fanny bade farewell to the barrister as if she was sincerely sorry to see him go, and Drury finally rode off, looking as dashing as if he were leading a cavalry charge.

Leaving her alone with him, and Humphrey.

He didn't dare ride off as long as Humphrey was with her. He shuddered to think what she might say to Humphrey about recent events if he weren't here to defend himself.

"What brings you to the city, my lord?" Fanny asked Humphrey as she nudged her horse to a walk. "Not problems with the bank, I hope?"

Gad, his family was hardly on the edge of ruin, Brix thought sourly, riding on one side of her horse while Humphrey rode on the other. Say what one would about Humphrey—and he and Fanny could both say plenty that wasn't flattering, or so he'd thought—his brother had a knack for making money.

"Not a bit," Humphrey declared, puffing out his barrel chest. "I hear Haliburton's thinking of selling his bottomland in the next little while. I want to purchase it, so I came to see my bankers."

This was the first Brix had heard of this.

"Shouldn't that be Father's decision? He isn't dead yet, you know."

"No, but he's more than happy to leave the running of the estate to me," Humphrey boasted. "He says I'll be running it soon enough anyway. In the meantime, he goes hunting."

Fanny laughed again. "That does sound like your father."

And Humphrey was going to turn out just like him. Couldn't she see that?

"So while I was here," Humphrey continued, "I thought I'd come to the park. I'm very glad I did." He leered at Fanny. "In fact, I wish I'd come to town sooner."

Humphrey had disgusted Brix plenty of times in the past, but never so much as at that moment.

"Well, it's been a pleasure, as always, Lady Francesca," he announced as he moved his horse to block their progress. "Now if you'll excuse us, my brother and I should be on our way."

Humphrey stared at him. "What?"

"I think we should be leaving, Humphrey."

Humphrey's stare became a glare. "I don't. My business can wait. Perhaps there's a horse race or game of cards that requires your attendance, though."

"Not at all."

"No doubt you're required at the theater, then," his brother retorted.

"Not at present." Brix slid a glance at Fanny. "As a matter of fact, I've invested in a factory in Yorkshire, and I've a meeting with the board of directors. They want to lower the wages and increase the hours of work."

Humphrey looked impressed, for about five seconds. "Well, off you go, then," his brother said, dismissing him. "Good luck getting those workers in hand."

"I think you misunderstand, Humphrey," Brix said. "I want the wages increased, not lowered, and the hours cut. I also want to ensure that the conditions are improved in the factory and that there's decent water available for the laborers' houses."

Humphrey's lip literally curled. "I might have known you'd turn out to be one of these reformers. You and men like you are going to bring about the economic ruin of England!"

"I prefer to think of myself as a humane employer."

"You've never had a head for numbers. With you on the board of directors, that company'll be bankrupt in a year."

"Perhaps I can't calculate income and expenditure with quite your cold-blooded speed," Brix replied, "but even you should be able to understand that a well-paid, well-fed labor force is a more productive labor force."

"Listen to him, Fanny!" Humphrey cried. "No doubt he'd like to tuck 'em all in their beds at night, too."

"I am listening," she said evenly, neither her tone nor her expression betraying what she felt or thought about either position.

Yet she must agree with him, not Humphrey, Brix told himself. They'd talked about this very subject when he was nearing the age he would come into his inheritance. He'd never forgotten what she said about the suffering of the people who made it possible for them to live in luxury, and how it was his Christian duty to see that they shared in the profits they provided.

Perhaps she didn't want to risk offending Humphrey, which was a distressing thought he promptly tried to dismiss.

"What about you, Humphrey? Shouldn't you see the banker without further delay?" he asked. "Then you can return to Medway Manor that much sooner. You're always saying the tenants don't have the first notion of how to do things unless you tell them. And you keep complaining that you have to keep an eye on the steward, even if Simings has been scrupulously honest for years."

Humphrey looked at Brix with an expression that was positively murderous. "Run along, Brix," he ordered. "Go play with your friends."

"Please, gentlemen!" Fanny cried, looking more annoyed than distressed. "Surely there's no need to quarrel."

Gad, he'd let Humphrey upset him! That was nearly as bad as letting Fanny think she could affect him. "We're not quarreling," he said as he smiled at her. "We're having a discussion. I'm so sorry if we've upset you. Isn't that right, Humphrey? Aren't you sorry for upsetting Fanny?"

"Yes," he growled. "Sorry, Fanny."

She gave Humphrey a bright smile. "Lord East-lake, Lady Jersey's giving a fancy dress party on the first of June. If she knows you're in town, I'm sure you'll be welcome. I suggest you leave a card at her house, and if I see her in the meantime, I'll be sure to mention you're here."

It was only because Brix was clenching his teeth so tightly that his jaw didn't drop. She wanted Humphrey to be at a party she was attending? Maybe he'd been right, and she was going mad.

Or maybe she really was becoming an outrageous flirt, and it didn't matter to whom she was talking, as long as he wore long pants.

And what did she mean by her references to Lady Jersey? That she could influence the woman who influenced all of London society? Was Fanny trying to tell him that she could destroy his social prospects with a word or two in Lady Jersey's ear, provided one could get a word in edgewise with a woman called Silence because of her loquaciousness?

As for Humphrey—he was grinning like an idiot and probably already planning his Viking costume.

"Yes, indeed, do come," he said to Humphrey, determined to hide his annoyance. "Most of the *ton* will be there, including Fanny's many admirers. Let's see, there's Drury, of course. Lord Bromwell, although he didn't seem very attentive at dinner the other evening. The earl of Clydes-brook. The marquis of Maryberry. Oh, and I mustn't forget Lord Silas Strunk and Sir Dickie Clutterbuck."

She flushed, and her smile became more like a baring of teeth before she addressed Humphrey. "Since you're only lately come to town, my lord, perhaps you haven't yet heard about the wagers your brother has made?"

Brix froze.

Humphrey's eyes widened as he looked from one to the other. "Wagers? What wagers?"

"Your brother bet his friends that he won't marry until he's fifty and he'll never marry me. Somebody even wrote it in the book at White's. Albert was incensed when he heard about it."

Humphrey's brow lowered, and for once, he really looked like a Viking—a savage Norseman ready to wipe out half a village. "Did Albert challenge you to a duel?" he demanded of Brix.

"Of course not. It was just a bit of sport, Humphrey," Brix replied.

"By God, he should have!" Humphrey roared, his loud voice making his horse prance nervously. "I would have, if it were my sister being wagered about."

"You'd have gladly shot me, too, no doubt." Brix regarded his brother steadily. "Care to challenge me anyway?"

"There's no need to get angry, Humphrey," Fanny said placatingly, and as if she hadn't been the one to raise the subject in the first place. "It was another of Brix's jokes, although one with serious consequences for me. I've had to leave Albert's and go to my friends, who were kind enough to take me in."

She made him sound like a ghastly villain from the sort of book Diana wrote.

Nevertheless, Brix still tried to act as if there was nothing at all wrong. "I told Fanny she should simply let it pass, but she wouldn't listen."

"No, I wouldn't," she replied evenly, "because he'd humiliated me and held me up to ridicule. I suppose I don't have to tell you that if he doesn't take things seriously, other people do."

Brix's knees gripped his horse's side so tightly, the animal whinnied in protest. "Yes, she was so distraught, she made a counter wager," he said, no longer hiding his annoyance and frustration. "She wagered she could break my heart in six weeks."

Humphrey couldn't have looked any more stunned if somebody told him his fine new horse was really a camel.

"Yes, it sounds incredible, I know," Fanny admitted with a smile—and without contrition. "As if your brother has a heart to break. I should have known better."

"It is theoretically possible that a woman could break my heart, Fanny," Brix retorted. "It just won't be *you*."

Fanny flushed at that, then looked past him. "Oh, Diana and Edmond are waving for me."

Brix followed her gaze. He'd suspected that

was a convenient falsehood, but it was, indeed, the truth.

"If you'll excuse me, I should go." She gave Humphrey another pleasant smile. "With you here, Humphrey, it's almost like old times at Medway Manor. I do hope to see you at Lady Jersey's, or perhaps Almack's before then. Good-bye!"

She rode off without a single word to Brix.

"You've done it now, you fool!" Humphrey snarled at Brix as soon as she was out of earshot. "What the devil were you thinking, wagering you wouldn't marry Fanny? Were you even thinking at all? Good God, she had every right to be angry." He looked after her. "She's being a bloody good sport about it, if you ask me."

"I didn't ask you."

"I don't know what Mother and Father are going to say—"

"I don't give a damn," Brix declared as he tried to control his prancing mount. "And I don't want to discuss this anymore."

"No, you never want to discuss important matters, do you?"

"Discuss?" Brix exclaimed. His horse took a step back. "Is that what you call being constantly harangued about what I ought to do and whom I ought to marry?"

"If you'd gotten Fanny to marry you, you'd have done something worthwhile for once. She's a duke's sister, for God's sake."

Brix glared at his brother. "Listen to me, Humphrey, because I'm not going to say this again. I'll live my life the way I want to. I'll run my factories as I see fit. And I'll marry when and where *I* decide."

"Don't you go all high-and-mighty on me, Brixton!" Humphrey snapped. "As the eldest I haven't got the luxury of waiting until I'm fifty to marry, or to pick any girl I fancy. I've got the estate to think about."

"How foolish of me to forget that you're the eldest son and will inherit the estate and our father's titles."

"You're jealous! You've always been jealous!"

Brix shook his head, and when he spoke, his voice was low, and firm. "Not of that, Humphrey, never of that. I don't envy you a single thing. You're welcome to Medway Manor and all that goes with it, but you shouldn't begrudge me what I have or what I do with it—and that I can please myself when it comes to marriage.

"Now if you'll excuse me, I really do have a meeting to attend where I intend to discuss my *ludicrous* ideas about the proper way to treat factory workers and their families—as human beings, instead of beasts of burden. But I don't expect you to understand that any more than you understand *me*."

With that, Brix punched his heels into his horse's sides and galloped down Rotten Row.

Chapter 8

London, the twenty-sixth of May, 1819

Dear Aunt Euphenia,

I suppose by now somebody has already written to you about the shocking incident at Almack's the other night. I would have written sooner myself, except that little D'Arcy caught a mild cold—have no fear, he's quite recovered.

What can I say? I had no idea Brix would ever do anything so shocking and scandalous.

Lady Diana Westover Terrington

S eated in Diana's charming and comfortable morning room, Fanny reached for her cup of tea. Diana was busy with little D'Arcy in the nursery, and Edmond had gone to his club. Outside, a steady drizzle fell, leaving Fanny little choice but to sit inside and try to read instead of dwelling on the twists and turns of fate, and some men's inability to see that just because they didn't consider something a serious matter, it could be to other people.

She glanced down at the book she was holding. She'd already enjoyed *The Castle of Count Korlovsky* more than once and usually found it occupied her mind completely, with its mysterious villain, ruined castle and brave Evangeline trying to escape to return to the man she loved.

But not today.

Fanny set the book aside and put the teacup back down on the table beside her. She rose and went to look out the muslin-draped window at the rain-slicked garden.

What was Brixton Smythe-Medway's opinion of her now? Was she having any effect on him at all?

Here, today, she doubted it, except for one thing. She was quite sure Brix didn't think of her as a girl anymore. He must think of her as a woman, or he wouldn't have kissed and caressed her as he had. He wouldn't have—

But that didn't mean he was falling in love with her. A man could lust after a woman and feel no pain at the end of the affair. Brix didn't seem particularly troubled by the termination of his relationship with Nellie Teasdale.

And outside of their intimate encounters, Brix acted as he always had.

Even when she'd been pleasant to the arrogant, selfish Humphrey, whom she loathed, Brix had reacted as he usually did when he was around his brother. When he'd argued with Humphrey, it had even been the same old quarrel; she might as well not have been there at all.

As for Humphrey's compliments and manner

toward her . . . She shuddered. Was he really so vain that he could believe she didn't hate him for the way he'd treated her and Brix all those years?

She wasn't any more pleased by Drury's attention. He'd appeared as if by magic, and she could hardly tell him to go away, even if he did make her uncomfortable, with his intense dark eyes and grave manner.

She scowled as she recalled the names of the other men Brix had mentioned to Humphrey and the things he'd said of them. Buggy Bromwell hadn't ignored her at the dinner party. He'd been polite, when he wasn't trying to get Lord Cheswick to contribute to the funding for his expedition. The earl and the marquis leered at every young woman they saw, even married ones; Brix knew that as well as she did.

Then there were Clutterbuck and Strunk.

Hoping she never saw either of those two men again, or heard their names, she turned back into the room and returned to the sofa.

To think she finally knew how it felt to be the object of men's curiosity and speculation and pursuit—and to discover that she hated it. All those years of believing it would be glorious and exciting, and instead she found it embarrassing, humiliating and even frightening.

Now, when she was alone, she even had to admit to some sympathy for the way Brix must have felt about her attention to him. Yet there were important differences, too. She'd kept her distance and hadn't been insolent or made unwelcome advances, and if he'd only told her how much it bothered him, she would have stopped. Or tried to.

"My lady?"

Fanny looked up to see Ruttles standing in the door. As always, the butler's face betrayed almost no emotion whatsoever. "Yes?"

"You have a visitor, my lady."

She couldn't help it. She thought of Brix, and blushed, then silently cursed herself.

"Who is it?" she asked firmly—so firmly, her words came out like pistol shots.

"Your brother wishes to speak with you. Are you at home?"

When she hesitated, Ruttles cleared his throat and said, "I should, perhaps, remind you, my lady, that I would have no hesitation in asking anyone to leave, should you desire it. If that person then refuses, there are several footmen I can call upon for assistance."

Fanny smiled. "Thank you, Ruttles. Show him in, if you please."

"Very well, my lady," Ruttles intoned.

When he was gone, Fanny arranged her skirts and sat up straight, preparing to face Albert's anger once again, yet still determined to stay where she was and try to win the wager.

Instead of marching into the room like an irate general, Albert came bounding into the room like an overgrown puppy. "Fanny!" he cried as if he was absolutely delighted to see her.

She couldn't have been more shocked if he'd arrived in sackcloth and ashes.

"Good afternoon, Albert," she said, trying to recover her calm. "What brings you here today?"

He perched his bulky body on the edge of the seat as if he couldn't even relax to sit down. "Why, to see you, of course, my dear sister," he declared as he looked her up and down. "You *are* looking pretty these days, Fanny."

Albert had never, ever paid her a compliment before. More baffled than ever, she gave him the ghost of a smile. "Thank you. How are Elizabeth and the children?"

"Fine, fine." Albert rubbed his hands on the arms of the chair as he always did when he was nervous or excited.

Fanny waited patiently for Albert to give some sort of explanation for his arrival, and his state.

"Fanny," he said when he finally realized he would have to speak first, "I've come to apologize for being such an ogre to you before. I was a selfish, pigheaded fool. Elizabeth is very sorry about how she treated you, too. She's been weeping bitter tears of remorse ever since you left."

Fanny didn't even try to hide her skepticism. "It's not like you to apologize, Albert, and I thought Elizabeth would be relieved to be rid of me."

"Never!" Albert declared. He reached out and took Fanny's hands in a strong grip, paying no heed to her book, which slipped to the carpeted floor with a dull thud. "Fanny, we were wrong to be so upset over that trifling wagering nonsense. Nobody blames you at all. Everybody's been most concerned and taken your side, putting the blame squarely where it belongs, on that fool Smythe-Medway. We should have, too. I see now that we were wrong to think society would be critical of my sister. And if you want to set up your own household someday in Bath or another out-of-the-way place, of course we'll do everything we can to help you."

He smiled as if sharing a great confidence with her. "But I don't think *that's* likely, do you?"

She gently pulled her hands free and retrieved the book, setting it on the sofa beside her. "I don't know what you're talking about, Albert."

He grinned, but with his wide lips, that looked more demonic than pleasant. "Playing coy, are you? Well, you're a woman, so I suppose that's to be expected." He winked as if sharing a great joke. "But I've heard things, Fanny, and it seems you've made *quite* a conquest. Quite a *famous* conquest."

"I really don't know what you're talking about, Albert," she replied, making no secret of her confusion. He couldn't mean Brix. For one thing, he wouldn't be pleased about that. They hated each other and always had. Nor had she conquered Brix. Yet.

Apparently deaf to her incredulous tone, Albert beamed. "Elizabeth tells me you're the talk of the *ton* because of the way Sir Douglas Drury was watching you in the theater. And I hear he's been riding in St. James's Park with you, too. I understand he's never been so blatant in his admiration of a woman before. Now *there's* a brother-in-law a man could be proud of! Or if he doesn't work out, I gather you've been turning quite a few *other* heads."

Fanny stared at him incredulously. She hadn't foreseen *this*.

Albert heaved a great sigh and leaned back. The wood frame of the sofa creaked. "God, Fanny, Sir Douglas Drury! What a coup!" He smiled at her as if she'd been made queen. "Who'd have thought it, eh?"

"Yes, who'd have thought it?" she echoed, wondering how many other people thought it, too. Surely Albert couldn't be the only one; he'd never had an original thought in his life. Elizabeth had probably put that into this head, and she'd likely gotten it from one of her gossiping friends. Who had, perhaps, passed that observation along to more of *her* friends. The whole *ton* might be infected with the belief that Sir Douglas Drury was courting her. Perhaps, like Albert, they also thought she ought to be pleased and flattered and do everything in her power to marry him.

"And I see, too, that Elizabeth and I shouldn't have tried to keep you all to ourselves," Albert continued, blissfully oblivious to her dismay. "We should have let you go out more, to plays and parties and things."

This was getting ridiculous. She hadn't gone to such events not because he hadn't allowed her to, but because she'd never been much for large gatherings, unless Brix was there.

The whole idea of her being courted by a man like Sir Douglas Drury was ridiculous, too, come to think of it. Or the height of vanity.

On the other hand, it was interesting watching her brother preen as if he was personally responsible for Drury's apparent interest in her, as well as the *ton's* sympathy for her plight.

Albert hadn't said anything about her staying with Diana and Edmond, or returning home with him, she noted.

She wondered just how far his magnanimous absolution extended. "So since all is forgiven, I'll pack up my things and return with you, shall I?"

She wasn't overly surprised to discover he hadn't been expecting that. "W-well now, Fanny," he began, stammering. "Let's not be hasty. After all, we don't want to . . . that is . . . things are going so well . . ."

His eyes lit up. "It would be better if you stayed here, Fanny," he declared with sudden certainty. "Sir Douglas is a good friend of the viscount's and staying here could only . . . you know . . ."

"Ensure that we're together more often, so that it's easier for Sir Douglas Drury to court me?"

"Precisely!" Albert cried. He leapt to his feet. "I must be off. Business and all that."

He wagged his finger at her as he backed toward the door, grinning. "Try for Sir Douglas, Fanny. Or if not him, somebody just as good.

Thank God you've come to your senses about that idiot Smythe-Medway at last."

Then he was gone, leaving Fanny alone with her book. And her thoughts.

A few days later, Fanny surveyed the famous, and noisy, assembly room of Almack's. Music from the gallery added to the din of conversation arising not just from the crowd of people in the main assembly room, but from those in the vestibule and refreshment rooms beside the ballroom, as well.

A bee must feel like this when reentering the hive after a long and peaceful sojourn gathering nectar, she thought, although this was a very exclusive, and expensively decorated, hive.

Two-tiered crystal chandeliers illuminated the gathering. Pairs of Corinthian pilasters and ornate swagged draperies added to the luxurious feeling of splendor, while rococo mirrors reflected the richly dressed people gathered there and made it seem as if they numbered in the thousands.

"Well, Fanny, what do you think?" Diana asked beside her.

Her friend was dressed in a very pretty evening gown of crimson crepe, with a white ostrich feather in her hair and a lovely pearl necklace that had been a gift from her husband when D'Arcy had been born. Although Diana didn't much care about her appearance, she looked very nice, and it was obvious her husband thought her beautiful.

Edmond loved Diana so much, he'd likely think she was beautiful if she wore burlap.

Although her very pretty lavender gown was as fashionable as Diana's, and she, too, had a feather in her hair, compared to the creme of the *ton* represented here, Fanny felt no more adequately attired than if she'd worn a dress of cambric muslin. At least at the theater, there had been plenty of other people more plainly dressed.

Her pale pink gown might have made her feel equal to the other women here, but she hadn't been able to bring herself to put it on again. At least, not yet.

"It's not quite what I imagined," Fanny admitted.

Diana smiled with sympathetic understanding. "It's rather disappointing, isn't it? I always imagined it as a very genteel, if crowded, place. Instead it's . . . well, it's not. It's just crowded. That's why I so rarely come."

"She hates large assemblies," her husband added, his eyes sparkling with secret understanding. "She prefers small gatherings, or wandering about labyrinths by herself, don't you, my darling?"

His wife laughed at their shared and secret joke. They didn't mean to, of course, but their intimate laughter and exchanged looks always made Fanny feel awkward.

Did bees ever wander into the wrong hive by mistake?

Perhaps she ought to ask Buggy, she thought as

she turned away to look at the crowd, although she doubted Lord Bromwell would be here. Almack's wasn't his sort of social milieu, either.

She hoped Drury wasn't. She also wanted to avoid Clutterbuck and Strunk at all costs, and Humphrey, too.

Brix was probably here somewhere. After all, this was his natural habitat, which was why she'd asked Diana and Edmond if they could come tonight. Even if she wasn't about to wear that pink gown anywhere Brix might be, she wasn't ready to give up yet.

She caught sight of one of her alleged suitors heading their way.

She quickly turned toward Diana and Edmond before she met his gaze. She'd rather interrupt their intimate reminiscences than endure Sir Douglas Drury's dark-eyed scrutiny.

Edmond's eyes lit up when he saw who was approaching. "Drury! What the devil are you doing here?"

"I heard a rumor you and Diana would be attending, and since you so rarely darken Almack's door these days, I thought I'd venture forth to see for myself if it was true." He bowed to Fanny. "Lady Francesca."

She smiled thinly and dipped a curtsy, and was very glad he didn't kiss her hand.

She kept smiling when she saw Brix at the top of the grand staircase, Lady Annabelle on his arm.

If only her heart wouldn't flutter! If only she could really be as calm as she pretended to be. Yet

she wouldn't look away from him, as if she
dreaded having to speak to him.

She wondered if he'd ignore her tonight, as he
had in Lady Cheswick's drawing room after the
dinner.

She had her answer sooner than she expected,
for Brix immediately sauntered toward them.
Once Lady Annabelle realized where he was leading her, her smile became more of a grimace, as if
her stays were too tight.

Other people in the immediate vicinity began
to watch. Fanny suddenly felt she was in some
sort of odd play, without a stage or script.

Brix obviously felt as at home under these circumstances as he did at the theater, for he addressed them with his usual pleasant geniality,
although with one important difference that
quickly became apparent. "Good evening, all. Diana, it's a pleasure to see you, as always. How
kind of you to take time from your maternal du-
ties to squire Fanny about. And Edmond, too, of
course. She's becoming very popular, thanks to
the two of you. But you know what you're doing,
I suppose. And Drury! There must be a dearth of
criminal cases these days. What a relief. Fanny,
my dear, you look delightful. Alas, you're not
wearing that pink gown I like so much. I hope
nothing's happened to it."

She'd never heard him use that cavalier tone to
say such biting things to his friends. It was as if
they were all his enemies now.

She wouldn't let that realization trouble her. If

Brix had lost his friends, it was his own fault.

And she wouldn't let his reference to their intimacy at the theater disturb her. "I save that gown only for particular occasions," she replied with just as jovial a smile.

"Really?" He ran a measuring gaze over her. "The mind boggles at what sort of occasions you're referring to."

She mustn't blush. She must not!

"Still, that's a nice dress, too. I'm sure Drury approves, don't you, Drury?"

"I agree that Lady Francesca is lovely," Drury said, his dark brows lowering ominously.

"Oh, and here comes Humphrey," Brix exclaimed, ignoring Drury's expression as he nodded behind them before giving her an insolent wink. "Another conquest in the making, no doubt. Good luck with him, my dear, although I thought you had better taste."

She would *not* let Brix upset her. And she wouldn't look away from him if it killed her, not even to see if he was telling the truth about Humphrey. "Perhaps I've realized my taste was suspect," she returned. "After all, I once thought you were wonderful."

Rage flared in Brix's green eyes, and his mask of jollity slipped. "A word of warning, Fanny. You mustn't get Drury jealous, not after the things he did in the war." The mask returned. "Humphrey's an arrogant bore, but he is my brother, so I'd hate to see him killed or maimed. You're quite welcome to break his heart, though. Now if you'll excuse us,

I've promised Lady Annabelle the first dance."

"With pleasure," Edmond declared as Brix walked away, Annabelle trotting beside him like an obedient puppy. "And if you can't be civil, Brix—"

Brix halted in midstep, then turned on his heel. He cocked a brow. "Don't trouble myself to speak to you or your wife or your *ward* again? If that's the way you want it, Edmond, that's the way it will be."

With that, he turned and continued to walk away. A baffled, but silent, Annabelle looked over her shoulder at them, then held tighter to Brix's arm.

Brix had brought this breach on himself, Fanny told herself again, and if he preferred Annabelle . . .

"Would you like to leave, Fanny?" Diana asked quietly.

And let Brix think he could intimidate her into running away? Never! "No, not at all. We only just arrived."

She smiled at her friends, and incidentally those people eavesdropping behind them. "After enduring the process of having my hair done this way, I'm not about to go so soon."

In spite of her smile and her tone, Edmond didn't look convinced. "Are you sure?"

"Absolutely."

"Hello there!" Humphrey bellowed behind her.

Fanny jumped as if his voice had been a pistol shot, then inwardly cringed. Brix hadn't been lying. She wished he had been. The last person she wanted to talk to now was Humphrey.

Unfortunately, considering that they were still the object of observation by several notables of the *ton*, she didn't dare ignore him completely, no matter how tempting that was.

"Good evening, my lord," she said, turning toward him. "You know Sir Douglas Drury. Have you met Lord Adderley and his wife?"

"Haven't had the pleasure," Humphrey declared, reaching out to shake hands with Edmond. He kissed Diana's hand, leaving a damp spot on her kid gloves.

"You're the ones who write," he noted, as if generously deciding to overlook a serious character flaw.

How could Brix even *suggest* she would consider Humphrey as a suitor? "Lady Diana's book sold thousands of copies," Fanny informed him.

Humphrey's bushy brows rose. "Thousands, eh? Brix didn't tell me that."

Brix didn't tell Humphrey much of anything, with good cause, because Humphrey made fun of nearly everything Brix said or did, and always had.

"Must have made a pretty penny, eh?"

Oh, God, why didn't he go away? Couldn't he see that he was annoying everyone?

The fact that neither Diana nor Edmond seemed disposed to answer his question didn't deter Humphrey. "So, where do you get your ideas?"

That was obviously the last straw for Diana. With the slightest hint of desperation, she turned toward her husband. "They're starting the dancing."

"If you'll excuse us, my lord," Edmond promptly announced, "my wife and I haven't danced together since our son was born."

He glanced at Fanny. "And Lady Francesca's already promised the first two dances to Drury," he lied. "Until later, my lord," he finished as he led Diana away.

Drury obediently took Fanny's arm. "Excuse us, my lord," he said in his deep, stern voice.

She didn't want to dance with Drury, but she would have danced with the devil himself if it got her away from Humphrey, so she gratefully took his arm and turned away.

To see Brix sweeping around the dance floor with Lady Annabelle Dalyrimple in his arms, and entertaining her marvelously, judging by the giggles.

Panting slightly and wishing her corset weren't quite so tight, Fanny gave Drury a woeful look after their first dance. "Would you mind if we sat out the next one? I'm rather winded," she admitted.

She was really thinking that one more turn around the dance floor, and she might swoon, or have a permanent crick in her neck from trying to keep an eye on Brix to see if he even noticed she was dancing.

If he had, he gave no sign as he expertly squired Annabelle around the floor.

"Of course, my lady," Drury replied, taking her arm. "Perhaps you'd like some punch?"

In spite of Drury's solicitous attention, she still

didn't feel any more comfortable in his presence. Once or twice as they'd danced, she'd caught him regarding her in a way that made her even more tense. Nevertheless, she managed a smile. "That would be very welcome."

Drury escorted Fanny to one of the refreshment rooms, and she was relieved it wasn't a crowded one. "If you'd like to wait here, I'll fetch you some negus."

"Thank you," she gratefully replied.

As he went in search of a drink, Fanny sidled toward a solitary corner at the very farthest end of the room. A window was open there, and a cool breeze, welcome even if it was redolent of coal and mist, wafted over her.

She looked outside, surveying the dim street illuminated by a glowing streetlamp. Carriages continued to come and go, discharging their occupants, or taking others from Almack's to private parties, or gambling hells, or clubs. A flower girl stood near the curb, her posies that must have been quite gay and pretty in the morning now wilted and sad, like the girl who continued to call for customers, her voice weary, her clothing a patchwork of ill-fitting castoffs.

She made quite a contrast to the people inside, except that so many of them were weary and sad and pathetic, in their own ways. The young women seeking wealthy, titled husbands, and caring only about how much wealth, and what titles. The cads trying to find innocents to seduce. The older men and women attempting to find partners for something that passed for love that their spouses—married for wealth and title—couldn't provide.

Where did Brix fit into this mixture? What was he looking for at Almack's? Amusement, certainly. Love?

Not from her.

"Well, if it isn't the little fugitive," a slyly familiar voice cooed in Fanny's ear. "But she's not got a bag to beat us with tonight, I see."

She turned to find Sir Richard Clutterbuck leering at her, with Lord Strunk by his side. Standing together, they were like a wall, effectively blocking her from the rest of the room. Strunk was only slightly taller than she was, but Clutterbuck towered over her.

"Did you enjoy playing me for a fool at Lady Cheswick's?" Strunk demanded, his beady black eyes gleaming with anger.

Fanny forced herself to remain calm. Even if she couldn't be seen, she wasn't alone in an alley. She was in a public room in a public place. "I did nothing more than refer to what you'd done. If that was cause for embarrassment at Lady Cheswick's, it should have been cause for shame before."

"We thought you were a maid," Clutterbuck said, his voice a nasal whine, his nose still red and swollen.

"Maid or lady, I don't think that will matter to Lord Adderley, or Sir Douglas Drury," she replied. "I'm sure they'll also agree that you shouldn't be accosting me here."

She craned her neck, trying to see past them. "Sir Douglas has just gone to get me some negus. Shall I call for him?"

The two men moved closer, backing her farther into the corner. The smell of their bodies made her feel even more trapped.

"I don't think you should make any noise at all," Strunk said, his voice low and menacing. "We won't hurt you. But you owe us a kiss at the very least."

"I don't *owe* you anything. I warn you, if you don't move away, I'll scream."

Strunk lunged forward and before she could cry out, he caught her in a tight embrace with one arm, while his other hand covered her mouth. Clutterbuck instantly shifted behind him, so that nobody could see what Strunk was doing. The moves were so well choreographed, they'd obviously done it before.

Desperate, she squirmed and tried to get free.

"Who do you think you are?" Strunk said as she struggled, his breath hot and smelling of wine and tobacco. "Traipsing about like some sort of queen as if we're not good enough to lick your boots."

Suddenly, and to his obvious astonishment, Clutterbuck was yanked backward, like a puppet on a string. In the next instant, Brix appeared behind Strunk. He clamped his hand on the short man's shoulder so tightly, he winced.

"I've never taken you for a criminal, Strunk, just a bounder," Brix growled, anger in his eyes. "Apparently, I'll have to reevaluate."

Strunk immediately let go of Fanny. "It was just a bit of fun. No harm done."

"No harm done?" Fanny exclaimed. "They tried—"

"I know exactly what they were trying to do," Brix interrupted, speaking with more malevolence than she'd ever heard in a man's voice before. "I know precisely the sort of men they are, too."

"You're no hero yourself," Clutterbuck retorted, straightening. "We weren't going to hurt her."

"I'm well aware of my own failings," Brix replied. "And of *yours*. Now take yourselves off, the pair of you. And don't trouble this young lady—or any other young lady—again. *Ever*."

Strunk stepped forward, sneering. "Or what? You'll challenge us to a duel?"

Fanny's gaze darted from the men to Brix. He never dueled. He'd never even held a gun since the time Humphrey had smeared his face with rabbit's blood after a hunt when he was ten years old.

"Yes, what'll you do about it?" Clutterbuck echoed, his hands on his hips. "You don't duel."

"An exception could be made."

Fanny had never, ever heard Brix sound like that—so stern, so fierce, so absolutely determined. She could believe he'd not only gladly duel with either one of them, but he'd shoot them without hesitation.

They obviously believed it, too. Clutterbuck

blanched, while Strunk's red face reddened even more.

"Now apologize to Lady Francesca and be on your way, or I'll have you thrown out of here," Brix ordered. Then the corners of his lips turned up into a wicked grin. "On second thought, perhaps I should do that anyway."

He glanced at Fanny. "What do you say, Lady Francesca? Should I give them the chance to apologize, or should I have them ejected, never to darken Almack's door again?"

Clutterbuck and Strunk didn't wait for Fanny to answer. They hurried from the room as if being chased by a brace of hounds.

Fanny leaned back against the windowsill and slowly let out her breath. She looked up at Brix and knew she had to say something to express her gratitude. "Thank you."

Brix smiled with what seemed like genuine warmth. "Think nothing of it. I couldn't resist the opportunity to come to the aid of a damsel in distress. Very storybook. Seems to have caused a bit of a stir, though."

He glanced over his shoulder, and she realized several people were watching them—several people who had done nothing to help her.

So much for the honorable folk of the *ton*!

"Smile, Fanny, unless you want to give them more to gossip about," Brix said under his breath.

"They're going to gossip about this anyway," she answered in a grim whisper.

"But we can affect that gossip. And you should smile to show them that you're not about to swoon or burst into hysterics, that you're not like every other hen-witted young lady in London this season."

Since he put it that way, she obediently put a smile on her face.

"That's better," he continued in that same low whisper. "Now, there are three things we can do here, Fanny. I can turn around and walk away and let you wait for Drury, who I last saw deep in conversation with another barrister, so it could be some time before he remembers you. Or you can leave me here and go find Drury, which might make people say you were ungrateful to your charming knight-errant. *Or . . .*"

His lips curved up in a mischievous grin, as if he was an impish boy again. "You can stand here and have a genial conversation with me and confound them all utterly."

She had to smile at that. And there was really only one answer to make. "Let's confound them utterly."

He laughed softly. "Good for you, Fanny. There's a time to retreat and a time to be bold, and I've discovered it's often better to be bold at Almack's." He turned toward the window. "Now, you look out the window, too, as if we're discussing astronomy or astrology or something."

Fanny did as he suggested, and then slid him a sidelong glance as they stood side by side. "Lady Annabelle might start to wonder where you are."

He cut her a look. "Jealous, Fanny?"

"Oh, yes, terribly," she said as if she wasn't and was lying for a joke. "What about you? Are you jealous of Drury?"

"Oh, yes, terribly."

She didn't think he was sincere, and his next casually spoken words told her what he really thought. "If you want to marry him, go right ahead. Might get a bit dull over the years, though. Still, he's very good at what he does, and justly famous."

Brix slid her another glance. "It must be pleasant for you to be the pursued instead of doing the pursuing."

She didn't find that amusing. "It must be very pleasant for you to be free of my unwanted attention."

"Not all the time."

Her heart skipped a beat.

"There are times I miss my little acolyte. She's quite gone, though. Grown up into a woman."

Fanny felt as if she were balanced on a high wire over a raging river. "A woman you rejected, Brix."

He nodded. "Yes, and a woman who's set out to make my life miserable in return."

"No, I didn't. I simply refused to surrender. I fought back the only way I could."

"Very effectively, too. My friends are annoyed with me, my reputation's almost in tatters . . . it must be very satisfying for you."

"I didn't set out to ruin you," she quietly

protested. "If you're having difficulties now, you should look to yourself and your idea of an amusing wager."

"All my fault, eh, Fanny?"

"Yes."

"You're not doing a single thing to contribute to my social downfall?"

She fought to keep her voice low. "No!"

"And I suppose you're not dressing to attract the notice of other men and that you hate their attention, too?"

"Yes!" she hissed, then sucked in her breath and silently cursed herself for letting that truth slip out.

"Can that really be so?" he murmured, gazing out the window as if fascinated by the lamplight. "You certainly seem to be enjoying their attentions, except for the odious Clutterbuck and Strunk, of course."

She wasn't going to surrender now, even if he'd come to her defense before. "I'm merely doing what I consider necessary to win our wager."

"It's all about the wager, is it, and nothing more?"

"Yes."

"I don't believe that, either, Fanny," he said, turning toward her.

"Well, it's true."

He leaned closer, his lips inches from hers, the look in his eyes more penetrating and intense than Sir Douglas Drury's stare. "I think you're lying."

When she opened her mouth to protest, he suddenly took her by the shoulders and kissed her with fierce, fiery passion.

For one moment, it crossed her mind to protest. To push him away. To make him stop.

For one instant, before his passion ignited hers and burned away all thought of stopping.

Yes, this was what she wanted. And who.

Not Drury, not any other man. This was the man who reached into her heart and set it beating anew every time she saw him.

On the edge of her senses, she heard a whisper. Then the murmur of low, condemning voices.

It was like being doused with cold water.

She twisted out of Brix's arms, horrified by the realization that they had an audience of blatantly staring people, more than one of them openmouthed with shock.

There was only one thing to do. She raised her gloved hand and slapped Brix across the face.

"How dare you?" she demanded as a red mark appeared on his startled face, her own burning as if she'd been struck, too. "You loathsome, lascivious cad!"

It was the only way to salvage her reputation—and she had to salvage it, or risk the virtual death of being an outcast from society and the stain of being considered immoral. She had to pretend Brix's scandalous kiss had been completely unwelcome. She had to feign indignation and disgust.

Head high, shoulders back, hiding her remorse, she marched out of the room.

* * *

His cheek stinging more from humiliation than her blow, Brix watched Fanny stalk out of the room, righteously indignant.

She had every right to feel that way, and he'd deserved that slap. He was deserving of the appalled stares of everyone in the room, too. He never, ever should have given in to his impetuous urge to kiss Fanny, especially in Almack's, that hothouse of gossip and rumor and scandal.

No matter what had passed between them, he had to undo the damage he'd done tonight. He had to prevent any further harm to Fanny's reputation because of his inexcusable loss of self-control.

He bowed to the spectators he'd completely forgotten. "I beg your pardon for my shocking breach of manners, ladies and gentlemen," he said, managing his usual genial tone. "However, I believe most of you are aware of the wager between Lady Francesca and myself. I understand some people are under the impression she has a chance of winning. Therefore, I felt it necessary to demonstrate quite clearly the impossibility of that outcome. Despite some undeniably interesting tactics on her part, you can all bear witness to the fact that I'm utterly unmoved by her kiss, or her anger. Obviously, she will never break my heart, and we are most certainly *not* destined for the altar."

He looked in the direction Fanny had gone. "Poor woman had no idea I was going to do that, of course. I judged a surprise attack would best prove my point."

A swift glance at people's faces told him he was succeeding in reducing an inexcusable public indecency to the mildly scandalous act of a prankster.

He grinned, ever the jester. "Now if you'll excuse me, I think I'd better retire from the field before Lady Francesca comes after me with a saber. I'd hate to get blood on my new shirt."

A few people laughed, and most of them smiled. Satisfied that he'd diverted any blame from Fanny, he strolled out of the room as calmly and casually as always.

And immediately went home.

Chapter 9

London, the twenty-sixth of May, 1819 (continued)

Edmond was furious when he heard what Brix had done, and went to see him first thing this morning. They had a terrible argument, and I'm afraid their friendship may be over.

Drury was also upset, although he hid it better. Nevertheless, if Brix hadn't already left Almack's, I honestly don't know what he might have done.

Oh, Aunt Euphenia, I hardly know what to do or say anymore! This isn't like writing a book where I can at least try to control things. Any advice you can give me to help me deal with this distressing situation would be greatly appreciated.

Lady Diana Westover Terrington

Brix was at breakfast the next morning when Edmond strode into the dining room and threw his hat on the table, narrowly avoiding the salt.

"Good God, Brix, you've finally gone too far. *Much* too far," he declared, his hands on his hips, his expression enraged.

This was no more than Brix had expected.

Gad, what a fool he'd been. He should have left Fanny the moment he got rid of Clutterbuck and Strunk. "Good morning, Edmond," he said, pretending he wasn't upset. "Care for some kippers? Spot of tea? Ham? Eggs?"

"I'm not hungry!"

"Then I suppose there's no point inviting you to sit down, either."

"How could you, Brix?" Edmond demanded. "How could you kiss Fanny like that?"

Brix wiped his lips with his napkin before responding. "It was quite easy, actually. I just leaned forward, and there you have it."

"You know what I mean! In Almack's, of all places!"

"Would you rather we'd kissed in a back alley?"

Edmond stared at him incredulously. "Haven't you caused enough trouble for her with those damn wagers? Why did you have to make it worse?"

"The case could be made that she's not entirely innocent, Edmond," he replied, fighting not to sound frustrated as he reached for a piece of toast. "It isn't as if she didn't want me to kiss her. She wasn't exactly struggling in my arms—or perhaps you didn't hear that part."

"It wouldn't matter if she threw herself at you. You were in Almack's, for God's sake, and you're supposed to be a gentleman."

"I'm well aware of that, Edmond, although I confess I forgot it at the time," Brix replied as he buttered the crisp bread. "So did she, I daresay, although she recovered quickly enough. Have you gone to her in such righteous indignation and demanded to know why she allowed me to kiss her?"

After a short, silent pause, he looked up at Edmond. "No, I thought not."

"You ought to have known better," Edmond repeated.

"And so should she!" Brix shoved back his chair and strode toward the sideboard bearing the silver warming dishes. "By God, she's *not* innocent. She's trying to win this game any way she can, by wearing those gowns and flirting with Drury and Humphrey and God knows who else to make me jealous."

He grabbed another plate. "I suspect Drury's got his own scheme. In that lawyerly mind of his he probably thinks he can win *his* wager by making me jealous. No doubt he believes that once he pretends to be interested, I'll immediately realize what a jewel I've been overlooking and fall madly in love with Fanny and want to marry her."

"Now you're ascribing devious motives to *Drury*?"

Brix spooned some coddled eggs onto his plate, the silver serving spoon hitting the blue Wedgwood china with a loud clink. "Why else would he suddenly find Fanny so fascinating?"

"Because he likes her. He's always liked her, but it was pretty clear to anybody who knew her that no man except you stood a chance with her."

Brix walked past Edmond to return to his seat. "As I told him, he's welcome to her. Really, I'll be delighted if he can win her heart."

"You *should* be after what happened to him during the war."

"He never talks about what he did in the war, or at least not to me."

"Perhaps because he's afraid you'll make jokes about it."

Brix fought off the anguished sting of that remark as he sat and pulled his chair closer to the table. "If he really wants her—although we both know he's not exactly the marrying kind—I give them my best wishes. Then she'll finally leave me alone, and I should definitely win our wager."

"Is that all you care about?" Edmond demanded.

"When it comes to Fanny, yes."

So it was. So it had to be.

"Then you're not the man I thought you were, Brix," Edmond said, turning on his heel and heading for the door. "You're not the man Fanny thought you were, either."

"No, I'm not," Brix murmured as his former best friend closed the door behind him.

Nobody really knew him. He'd made sure of that.

Confused and uncertain, Brix looked around the unfamiliar room. Music drifted toward him, soft and far away, as if played by a ghostly orchestra. No fire burned in the hearth, and glass-fronted bookcases lined the walls. White plaster busts of dead Greeks and Romans looked down on him from the top of the bookcases as if lined up to pass judgment on him.

He slowly came to recognize the room. He was in the little-used library of Lady Jersey's house at 38 Berkeley Square. What was he doing there?

The fancy dress ball.

He looked down at his clothes: pristine white shirt, white satin knee breeches, white stockings and buckled shoes. Not surprising, for he never wore costumes. Somehow, his jacket and cravat must have gone astray since his arrival, along with the mask he'd carried, a grinning jester's face.

This room was not intended to be used during a fancy dress ball. The ballroom, the drawing room, the long gallery—those would be crowded with well-dressed members of the *ton*.

Why wasn't he there, too? He didn't even remember coming into this room, or crossing the thick Aubusson carpet to stand near the tall windows draped with heavy indigo damask.

A shaft of light suddenly illuminated him. The sound of music increased. Someone had opened the door leading to the corridor.

He watched, oddly unable to move, as Fanny Epping came inside and closed the door. She wore clothes that were the mirror of his own: a dress shirt open at the neck, revealing her cleavage; satin knee breeches and stockings that emphasized her slender legs and hips; and buckled shoes.

She'd come as a travesty dancer. But unlike Nellie, she hadn't cut her hair. It was loose, and flowed over her shoulders in thick waves, the way it had when she was younger—when she came to him for comfort, and he'd been glad to give it.

Until that kiss in the rose garden that had changed everything.

He tensed, waiting for her to say something sharp and caustic. To hurt his feelings.

Instead, she smiled and strolled toward him. "Are you hiding from me, Brix?" she asked, her voice low and sultry.

He still couldn't seem to move his feet. "No," he said, trying not to sound defensive. He didn't know what he was doing there, but he was sure he wasn't hiding.

"I thought perhaps you saw me dancing with Drury."

Just like Almack's.

"I only danced with him because you were watching," she said, looking up into his face the way she used to when she was younger, as if he were the smartest, most important man in the world. "I wanted to make you jealous. I did, didn't I?"

God help him, he was jealous of every man who looked at her with desire, and especially Drury. Drury was smart, his life had a purpose; he didn't need Fanny, too. If anybody needed Fanny . . .

She ran her hand up his chest and he could hardly breathe. He willed his feet to move, to back away, to give him space and time to think. To run away, if he had to, but they simply wouldn't obey.

"What's the matter, Brix?" she purred. "You're not afraid of me, are you?"

"No, I'm not afraid of you."

That wasn't a lie. He wasn't afraid of her, not then and not ever. He was afraid of how she made him feel about himself.

Why couldn't he move? Why did she have to look at him like that, reminding him of what he'd lost with that damn stupid wager?

Why did she have to be so fetching in those clothes?

Fanny cupped his chin in her slender hand. "You don't want to run away from me, surely?" she whispered. "I won't hurt you."

"Yes, you will," he found himself confessing.

"I promise I'll be gentle."

He wanted to groan aloud. "Fanny, let me go."

"I'm not forcing you to stay, am I?" she asked as she released his chin. "I'm not *forcing* you to do anything."

Even as she spoke, she insinuated her hand into his open shirt, brushing her palm over the bare skin of his chest.

"What are you doing, Fanny?" he asked, his voice strained as she continued her slow, sensuous exploration.

"Don't you like this, Brix?" she murmured as she inched forward until they were hip to hip. "Don't you want me to touch you?"

He commanded himself to think of something else—a dunk in a freezing river. Falling into snow.

It didn't work. He hardened, and a burning, consuming desire to take her in his arms threatened to overpower him as it had before, in Almack's and the theater.

His teeth clenched. "Fanny, I—"

She put her finger on his lips. "Shhh, Brix. Don't talk. You spoil everything when you talk."

"Fanny, about the wagers—"

Her eyes gleamed as she pushed her body against his. "Never mind that. You were right in the theater, Brix. I liked what you did very much. Do you remember what I said, about how it would feel if I wanted you as much as you wanted me?"

"I recall that you said something like that," he replied, fighting for self-control, struggling against the desire raging through him. She wasn't like Nellie and the others, offering herself as part of a bargain, a simple business transaction between two people who understood exactly what was expected and required.

Fanny laughed, the delightfully merry sound unlike any other woman's laugh. Then she pulled his head down for a kiss.

Her mouth slid softly over his, teasing and grazing ever so gently. Her tongue pressed against his mouth until he couldn't resist the silent invitation. He parted his lips and allowed her entry.

Leaning against him, she deepened the kiss and began to stroke his chest. Then lower.

"I want you, very much," she said, drawing back a little, although her hands continued to meander over his body. "Make love with me, Brix. Please."

She was suggesting they make love here in Lady Jersey's library while not far away the cream of the *ton* danced and gossiped and ate and drank? "Fanny, think a moment!"

He searched her face, her bright blue eyes. She seemed perfectly serious, and absolutely sincere. "What if somebody were to find us?"

"Nobody will come in."

"But Fanny—"

She started to undo his shirt. "You want me, don't you?"

"God, yes!" He couldn't deny that any more than he could deny that he was breathing.

She tugged his shirt out of his breeches. "I want you, Brix. Now."

He was weakening. Giving in. Giving up the struggle. Because his desire was too powerful, his need for her too strong. "You're sure, Fanny?"

"Without a single doubt."

He lost the battle.

They kissed with fierce hunger. Not tenderly as before, but like two primitive beings determined to mate. His hands tugged at her shirt, ripping it from her and exposing a thin linen chemise. He tossed the shirt to the floor and, still kissing, worked feverishly to undo the buttons on her breeches. She, meanwhile, slid her hands under his open shirt, pushing it off his shoulders. He broke contact a moment to tear it off, while she wiggled out of her breeches.

He swept her up into his arms and carried her to Lady Jersey's expensive damask-covered sofa. He laid her down, then as she watched, her eyes gleaming, he shed the rest of his clothes.

"You're magnificent," she whispered, holding out her arms.

"You're beautiful," he replied, kneeling between her legs, bracing himself on his elbows as he studied her pretty face, surrounded by the wild, untamed corona of her thick brown hair. "You've always been beautiful, and I've been too stupid and too blind to see it."

"Kiss me again, Brix. Then make me yours, forever."

He needed no more urging. With her eager assistance, he removed the rest of her clothes, until she was naked beneath him. Her lithe, slender body was just as he'd guessed it would be: round breasts that fit perfectly into the palm of his hand, with small pink nipples fairly aching to be pleasured. Trim waist and narrow hips.

As he looked at her, the primitive passion she'd aroused returned, even stronger. With impatient desire, he began to kiss her again, starting with her lips, then slowly making his way lower. He lingered on her breasts, sucking a nipple into his mouth and swirling his tongue about the taut tip.

She wiggled and moaned with pleasure, increasing his already potent ardor.

He inched lower, brushing his lips over her flat belly and navel. And lower still.

She put her hands on his shoulders, stopping him. Their gazes met, hers questioning.

"Let me kiss you there, too, Fanny," he whispered, his voice husky with longing. "Please. It'll help make you ready. Trust me."

She nodded and closed her eyes. "I trust you."

She was the most wonderful woman in the world, and he didn't deserve her. He would never deserve her. He was only the jester to better, more accomplished men.

Yet he would make this as good for her as he could.

Restraining the primitive impulses surging through him, he concentrated on her body and her responses. She would be his guide tonight.

Or so he'd thought, until she began to kiss and stroke his body, taking control in a way he'd never expected. She seemed to know without being told how and where to caress him to send him soaring to the height of arousal. She sensed what pleased him in a way no woman ever had before.

Until he could wait no longer. With a low growl of pure primal desire, he thrust inside her warm, tight, moist body.

She held him close, wrapping her legs around him, then undulating beneath him. Accepting him completely. Without any apparent pain or surprise or doubt or fear.

He lost all control. All restraint dropped away, until his passion was as naked as his body.

"I love you," he whispered, panting as he thrust. "Oh, God, I love you, Fanny!"

She started to laugh, a rollicking, mocking laugh as if he was a clown who'd just performed a funny trick. "I've won then, haven't I?" she asked. "God, Brix, you *are* a fool."

He stilled and stared down at her disbelieving, while her lips turned up into a nightmare version of the same grin as his fancy dress mask—the jester, with its gargoyle smile—and her laughter echoed around him.

With a horrified cry, Brix sat bolt upright in his bed. Panting, his body drenched with sweat and tangled in the sheets, he stared at his surroundings.

The cream-papered walls. The dark walnut furnishings. The sand-colored damask bed curtains. The tall windows with thick draperies, closed except for a crack that showed the faint light of dawn.

His house. His room. His bed.

His body tense, he twisted and looked at the space beside him, half-expecting to see Fanny there.

She wasn't, of course, because he'd been dreaming. It had all been a dream. A blissful dream that had turned into a hideous nightmare.

He threw back his covers and, naked, went to his washstand and splashed cold water over his face until his breathing, and everything else, returned to normal.

What day was it?

Friday, the twenty-eighth of May. Four days until Lady Jersey's fancy dress ball. Of course he'd been invited—two months ago, before the wagers had become common knowledge. .

Regardless, he was going to go, provided Lady Jersey didn't have him barred at the door for kissing Fanny in Almack's, where she held the power of a reigning monarch.

Lady Jersey would have already informed him if she didn't want him at her ball, and she hadn't. Probably she was just as curious as the rest of the *ton* to see what would happen when he met Fanny again. Maybe she even had a wager on the outcome of their contest herself.

It was seventeen days until the term of his wager with Fanny was over and a winner would be declared.

He spotted the mask he'd ordered that had arrived for him that afternoon on his dressing table—the jester's mask, with its gargoyle grin.

He marched across the room and tore it into pieces.

Chapter 10

London, the second of June, 1819

Dear Aunt Euphenia,

I thought things were as bad as they could get, but I was wrong. As you shall hear, I should have tried harder to convince Fanny to stay home from Lady Jersey's ball, but she felt strongly that she had to make an appearance. Nor did I ever imagine things would turn out as disastrously as they did.

Lady Diana Westover Terrington

Fanny studied her costume in the large gilt mirror over the mantel in Diana's drawing room. She was supposed to look like a noble Roman lady, but she should have insisted the dressmaker give her some kind of sleeves and use some thicker fabric than this thin, diaphanous silk. The bodice was more low-cut than she liked, too. The thick ribbon of gold wrapped around waist and hips and crisscrossing the bodice between her breasts made them seem too prominent. More gold ribbon was woven into her hair, and she wore thin golden sandals on her feet.

She might as well have dressed as a travesty dancer. She could hardly have felt more undressed . . . Well, that wasn't precisely true. Her legs were hidden by the gown.

"Men!" Diana exclaimed from the door, where she was watching the stairs as they waited for Edmond to join them.

Diana was wearing a lovely costume, a slender gown of Lincoln green satin trimmed with embroidered leaves and little red flowers. She had a sort of velvet forester's cap on her head, sporting a jaunty red feather. A child's bow was slung across her chest, and fawn-colored gauntlet gloves completed the ensemble. She was supposed to be Maid Marian from the stories of Robin Hood, who had done his deeds in her native Lincolnshire.

"Men claim women keep them waiting, but I've often found it's the other way around," she continued. "I don't know what's taking Edmond so long. He's not even wearing a costume tonight."

"He's not?" Fanny asked, surprised. Edmond hadn't protested going to the fancy dress ball—at least not in her hearing.

Diana sat on one of the chintz-covered sofas. "He claims they're silly," she said ruefully, "but if you ask me, it's simple male vanity. He knows he looks wonderful in evening dress, but isn't so sure how he'll look dressed as Robin Hood."

"At the moment, I see his point," Fanny admitted. "Not that I don't think he'd look marvelous and dashing as Robin Hood, but about costumes in general. I feel silly, or rather . . ." She looked down at her dress. "You don't think this is too . . . well, scanty, do you?"

"No, you look like you've just stepped off a vase."

"I'm afraid I may take a chill," Fanny said with another dubious glance at her reflection. "I think I should have gone as one of Robin Hood's band, too."

"I'm sure Lady Jersey's house will be as hot as an orangery," Diana replied. She tilted her head to one side and studied Fanny. "It's no more revealing than many an evening gown. I think you only feel that way because you're not used to wearing such silky fabrics."

Maybe Diana was right. She wasn't used to soft, supple, expensive fabric.

In a slightly less anxious frame of mind, she joined her friend on the sofa to wait for Edmond. "You always know what to say to make me feel better."

As soon as she said it, she remembered the last time she'd said something similar: to Brix, six years ago, after he'd told her that Humphrey was nothing more than a pompous fool who was surely going to wind up with gout.

Diana's expression grew serious. "Are you still certain you want to go to this party, Fanny?" she asked as she folded her hands in her lap. "You're not worried about your reception there after what happened at Almack's?"

"Lady Jersey hasn't written to tell us not to come," Fanny replied, hiding any qualms she had about attending the ball. "She would have if I was in disgrace. Since she hasn't, I see no reason not to."

In spite of her conviction that she had little choice but to go, she toyed with the end of the ribbon around her waist and couldn't quite meet her friend's steadfast gaze. "I have to, Diana. I have to face the *ton*. Otherwise, it would be like saying I agreed to that kiss, perhaps that I even welcomed it. Although the *ton's* been on my side from the start, I can't risk that."

"No, you can't," Diana agreed.

An awkward moment passed before Diana spoke again. "I hope you don't mind me asking, but do you care for Brix at all, or do you hate him now?"

If it were anyone else asking, Fanny wouldn't have answered, but Diana was a good friend who had generously offered her sanctuary.

Moreover, her husband had been Brix's friend since childhood, and the wager was putting a serious strain on that friendship. If anybody had a right to know what was going on between her and Brix, Fanny decided, it was Diana and Edmond, although even so, there were some things she simply couldn't share.

"I don't care about him as I used to," she admitted, which was the truth. Her feelings for Brix had been constantly shifting, changing and altering from the moment she'd overheard him talking about the wagers in Diana's drawing room.

"Do you care what harm you're doing to him?"

Fanny regarded her friend with confusion. "I'm not hurting him."

"What about the damage to his reputation?"

Fanny refused to believe anything she did could harm Brix's standing among the *ton*. "I'm sure Brix will be able to laugh his way out of any temporary difficulties."

Diana didn't look as if she agreed. "There's something else, Fanny. He and Edmond quarreled about what happened at Almack's. I'm afraid their friendship may have come to an end over this."

Fanny fidgeted and tried not to feel guilty, but she wasn't responsible for Brix's actions or the things he said. "I'm sorry to think that Edmond and Brix aren't going to be friends anymore.

"It's not that I hate Brix, Diana," she clarified. "I don't, but I can't have people looking at me as if I'm some pathetic creature. I have to fight back." She clasped her hands together. "I *have* to."

Diana's eyes filled with sympathy. "Fanny, I understand how hurt and upset and humiliated you felt when you heard about those wagers. I agree that you had to do *something*. But what if you succeed? What if you break Brix's heart?"

Fanny stared at her hands. "He didn't care about breaking mine."

"So although you don't hate him, there's no affection left in your heart for him, either?"

Fanny shook her head. What she felt in her heart for Brix couldn't be called affection.

"What about Drury then?" her friend asked softly. "Do you have any feelings for him?"

Fanny raised her eyes. "Not the kind you mean. I wish he'd leave me alone."

"Oh, dear," Diana murmured as Edmond finally came trotting down the steps, looking as handsome and elegant as always.

"What, you're both ready to leave?" he demanded as he halted at the bottom. "Good God, Diana, if you're supposed to be an outlaw of the greenwood, all I can say is, kidnap me, and take me to your lair and never let me leave."

After a worried glance at Fanny, Diana rose. "Doesn't Fanny look lovely, too?" she prompted as Edmond walked into the room.

"Yes, she does," he replied with a warm, encouraging smile. He glanced from one to the other, and his smile became a little strained. "Am I interrupting something?"

"Just a little talk between two good friends," Diana said, taking his arm.

Fanny got to her feet and reached for her gloves and stole. "Yes, just a little womanly chat. Shall we go?"

Diana froze, then smiled, but it didn't reach her tense eyes. "We can't leave just yet."

"Oh, yes. Right," Edmond said, his suddenly nervous gaze darting from Fanny to the door and back again. "We're expecting an escort for you, Fanny."

Dread seeped over her. "Who?"

"Drury asked if he could come with us, and I said yes," Edmond explained.

"Even after Brix kissed me in Almack's?" she asked. "I would understand if he wanted to distance himself from me after that."

"He asked precisely because of that kiss."

Fanny regarded Edmond warily. "He's got a reputation of his own," she reminded them. "How will it look if I appear in public with him now? Perhaps they'll think that I'm licentious if I appear with Sir Douglas Drury."

"Drury's not reputed to chase after maidenly young women," Edmond replied. "His relationships are always with women of a certain . . . experience. If he escorts you in public, a few of the more decadent members of the *ton* may think he's trying to seduce you, but most of them will think that the most famous barrister in London doesn't hold you to blame for Brixton Smythe-Medway's outrageous behavior. Some may even think he has quite another, honorable object in mind."

"I don't want that, either," Fanny protested.

Diana and Edmond exchanged looks that Fanny couldn't quite decipher.

"Be that as it may, Fanny, I think for tonight, you should accept Drury's company," Diana said gently. "You can tell him how you feel if the opportunity presents itself. The main thing is, if you're determined to appear in public after what happened at Almack's, Drury's presence at your side will be of benefit."

Fanny couldn't refute their explanation or their reasoning. "Will Sir Douglas be in costume, too?" she asked. "His legal attire, perhaps?"

"No, I shall not be in costume."

They all turned to find Drury on the threshold of the drawing room, and in evening dress, like Edmond.

"Good evening, ladies, Edmond," he said. Even though he addressed all three of them, he looked only at Fanny. "My lady, you take my breath away."

Whatever Diana and Edmond thought, this sounded as if he were seriously interested in her.

"Thank you," she murmured, sliding a glance at her friend and her husband. They looked as if they hadn't expected him to say something like that, either.

"I hope you'll allow me the honor of the first two dances," Drury said as he bent down to kiss her hand.

It was no wonder he was so successful with women, with that voice, yet Fanny felt only dismay and dread, and an incredible urge to tug her hand from his grasp. When Brix had kissed her hand, her whole body had warmed.

Short of an outright refusal and subsequent explanation, and staying home from the ball and letting Brix think she was giving up, there was no help for it.

"I'll be delighted to dance with you, Sir Douglas," she said, although she gently extricated her fingers as she spoke.

After that, they couldn't get to Lady Jersey's soon enough to suit Fanny. She would feel better being with Sir Douglas in a crowd.

The carriage ride, a mostly silent affair with Diana attempting to make conversation once or twice until she gave it up, seemed interminable. It was as if Lady Jersey lived in Oxford or Dover, not a few streets away.

Eventually, however, they reached their destination, and a short time after that, Fanny found herself in an enormous foyer lit by a huge chandelier with several tiers of candles.

Other guests were already present, removing their cloaks and wraps and handing them to the waiting army of footmen. There were knights in armor made of silver crepe and ladies in medieval gowns with long, trailing sleeves and huge headdresses that looked like they'd be difficult to keep from falling off. One man was dressed as an oriental potentate, in satin and silk. Other people were wearing what were obviously intended to be costumes, but Fanny had no idea exactly what they were supposed to be. A few of the men clearly shared Edmond and Drury's distaste for costumes of any sort and were likewise in evening dress. A handful of ladies, most older, apparently shared that distaste; they wore ball gowns, although one or two carried masks.

She quickly spotted Humphrey, who was wearing a Viking helmet with enormous horns and what looked like an old fur rug over his shoulders. He was conversing rather animatedly with two young women who were smiling as if he were Eric the Red reciting an exciting tale of exploration and daring.

She didn't see Brix, but perhaps he was already in the ballroom or having refreshments, a distinct and distracting possibility. Or maybe he'd decided not to attend. Or perhaps he'd been told not to. Maybe she was wrong to think he would suffer no lasting social stigma from his actions.

She noted that there weren't any other women with bare arms, or so gauzy a gown, or so low-cut a bodice.

How she wished she was wearing an evening gown instead of this costume, especially when she saw Lady Emeline St. James surveying her costume as if appalled, then frowning and whispering behind her fan to Lady Mary Bredbone, who looked equally scandalized. The two sisters weren't the only ones behaving that way. Wager or no wager, perhaps she was wrong to come tonight.

"We seem to be attracting a lot of attention," Fanny murmured.

"I generally do. I rarely attend social functions," Drury quietly replied, "and I rarely have so beautiful a young lady with me."

She definitely should not have come.

"Oh, look, Edmond," Diana said, grabbing her husband's arm. "There's poor Mr. Pennyfogger, trapped in the corner with Lady Constance. He's a writer friend of mine," she explained to Fanny and Drury. "Lady Jersey heard of his latest book and invited him, but I don't think he knows a soul other than me. Excuse us, will you?"

"Of course," Fanny said, and she watched as Diana and Edmond forged their way through the crowd.

Their brisk progress turned a few heads, and more turned when they noticed Fanny and Drury.

Then, to Fanny's dismay, Albert and Elizabeth appeared in the foyer. When they saw who she was with, they looked as thrilled as if the wedding announcement had already been placed in *The Times*.

Fanny could envision what would happen next. They'd want to be introduced to Sir Douglas Drury, and she hated to think what they would say to him and the sort of innuendoes they would make. Worse would be the things they would say to her, with sly looks and winks and nudges, about Drury or any of the other men who waved, smiled, or otherwise intruded themselves upon her notice.

She was anxious enough without enduring that. She slipped her arm through Drury's. "Shall we go to the ballroom?"

"As you wish."

They made their way through the inquisitive, whispering crowd, and soon reached the elaborately decorated ballroom, brightly lit with chandeliers, their light reflected by the gilt-edged mirrors on the walls.

"Why, Lady Francesca, I didn't expect to see you here!" Lady Annabelle Dalyrimple cried as she intercepted them near the door. She smiled at Fanny as if she were happy to see her, but her eyes strayed toward Drury.

"Why not?" Fanny asked.

Annabelle obviously hadn't been expecting that direct a response. "I thought perhaps . . . in view of . . . well, what people are saying . . ."

"What *are* people saying?" Fanny inquired.

"That you . . . that is . . ." Annabelle was the very picture of feminine helplessness as she looked at Drury.

"Oh, I'm sorry," Fanny said. "Lady Annabelle Dalyrimple, allow me to present Sir Douglas Drury. Sir Douglas, Lady Annabelle Dalyrimple."

He inclined his head as he ran a haughty gaze over Annabelle's dress of heavy gold brocade. She had a thin white ruff around her neck and pearls in her hair. "Charmed."

"I'm very pleased to meet you, Sir Douglas," Annabelle simpered. "I've read all about your cases in *The Times*."

"Oh?" He raised a brow. "What did you think of the last one? Was I right to stop questioning the main witness when I did, or should I have allowed him to incriminate himself more?"

Annabelle blushed. "I'm sure I have no idea." She quickly turned her attention to Fanny. "That's a pretty dress, Fanny. What are you supposed to be?"

"Venus," Drury announced, his voice cold

and forbidding. "What exactly are you supposed to be?"

Annabelle looked nonplused and started to
stammer. "W-why, I'm . . . I'm . . ."

Fanny took pity on her and made a guess. "Are
you an Elizabethan lady?"

"Queen Elizabeth, actually," Annabelle said
with relief. She ignored Drury and addressed
Fanny. "Mr. Smythe-Medway was just saying I
look the way she must have in her prime, when
men were writing poems to her."

Fanny kept any reaction from her face when
she heard Brix was there, although she was
pleased to think he hadn't been told not to attend.
That would have broken his sociable heart . . .

She shouldn't be worrying about Brix's social
standing.

"You don't look at all like Queen Elizabeth to
me," Drury said. "She had red hair, and the style
of gown is all wrong, and the ruff is far too
small."

Annabelle's eyes went wide, and her face
flushed. She looked like she was about to burst
into tears before she hurried away without another word.

"Did you have to be so rude?" Fanny demanded, too upset by Drury's behavior to be anything but blunt.

"I wanted her to go away."

"And you succeeded," she said. "By upsetting
her."

He didn't look bothered a bit. "Lady Annabelle

will recover quickly. Her sort always do, as soon as she finds a man's shoulder to cry on."

Like Brix's?

Fanny pushed that thought away, even as she vowed that if she got the chance tonight, she'd tell Sir Douglas Drury how she felt about his attentions, and with as little regard for his feelings as he'd shown for Annabelle's.

"Fanny—Lady Francesca!"

Buggy Bromwell came charging through the crowd, waving. People immediately made way for him, and it had nothing to do with his title or his accomplishments. He had the most hideous, huge, ugly spider on his shoulder.

It was all Fanny could not to run away when he came to a halt in front of her.

"You look delightful, Fanny, really delightful," he said with more enthusiasm than she'd ever seen him exhibit before. "Like something off one of the pots in the museum. Your hair looks exactly like that of one of the caryatid figures of the Erechtheum on the Acropolis."

Ignoring Drury and everybody else, he took her hand and held it out, the better to survey her dress, while she did her best to keep as much distance as she could from the spider. "That's an excellent attempt at a Grecian gown. It would have been better with a peplum, but the simple lines are classic, like a Doric column. Your dressmaker did an excellent job."

"I'll let her know the famous Lord Justinian Bromwell approved. I'm sure she'll be pleased,"

Fanny replied, trying to smile, but keeping a wary eye on the spider.

Buggy ran a quick glance over Drury, who was also, Fanny noticed, keeping a careful watch on the spider. "You didn't wear a costume?"

"Obviously not," Drury said. He nodded at the spider. "I trust that's not poisonous."

Fanny hadn't even considered that possibility. She stepped back a pace.

"Of course not!" Buggy cried, reaching up to pat it affectionately. "It's not real. I made it myself, out of bits of cloth and wire and buttons. I wouldn't risk having somebody squash one of my live specimens of a Peruvian bird spider in a fit of manly protectiveness."

"But it moves," Drury said, still not convinced. "I saw it."

"Thread," Buggy replied. He held out his hand. A black thread ran out of his jacket sleeve and was tied around his index finger. "All I have to do is bend my finger, and he moves. You see?" he said, demonstrating.

Fanny slowly let out her breath. "That's very clever," she said, duly impressed.

"Oh, Buggy's tremendously talented, aren't you, Buggy?"

Fanny stiffened as Brix strolled around her and joined them. "He can cook, too. What was it you ate on that island? Some kind of lizard? I daresay Lady Francesca would love to hear all about *that*."

Before the astonished Buggy could answer, Brix

ran a measuring gaze over her. "Nice dress, Fanny. Mind, it doesn't leave much to the imagination."

"Perhaps not to a certain sort of imagination," she acknowledged, trying not to let his words upset her. "However, Lord Bromwell and I have attempted to use our imaginations in a different fashion. I see that thinking of a costume was too much of an effort for you."

"I have better things to do with my time," Brix said dismissively. He turned to Drury. "I didn't think fancy dress balls were your cup of tea, yet here you are with Fanny." He scrutinized her again. "I can see certainly the appeal. You're looking very pretty, Fanny."

Drury's eyes narrowed ever so slightly. "Developing some taste in your old age, are you, Brix?"

"No more than you. So are you really ready to tie yourself to a wife, my friend?"

Fanny realized several people around them were blatantly eavesdropping. She had to say something before speculation ran rampant. "Sir Douglas and I are not engaged."

Brix raised his brows. "Indeed?"

"I would be flattered to think Lady Francesca would consider me," Drury replied, an undercurrent of iron in his voice that took her aback. "So would any man of sense and discernment."

"Well, there you go, then! No wonder I didn't, since I have neither."

"Unless we're speaking of women on the stage, anyway," Drury shot back.

"Oh, but I'm not discerning then, either. A pair of nice legs, and I'm a lost man."

"This conversation isn't appropriate when we are in the company of ladies," Drury said, his deep voice firm.

Brix put his hand on his heart and drew back as if shocked. "Oh, but Fanny is desperate to learn what appeals to me, aren't you, Fanny? Isn't that why you were wandering around the theater the other night, all by yourself?"

Fanny could have shot him. Buggy stared as if she'd started to strip naked, while Drury stiffened. As for the people who were listening . . .

"I got separated from my friends," she said in her own defense as anger replaced dismay. "Unlike *some* people, I'm not familiar with theaters, or the people who work in them."

"But that's changing, isn't it, dear Lady Francesca? I'd say you're learning a great deal about acting . . . and other things."

Refusing to be cowed by any reference he might make, she bestowed a bright smile upon him. "Oh, yes, I'm certainly broadening my horizons. And to think, Mr. Smythe-Medway, that it's all because of you. Perhaps to show my gratitude, I should concede defeat in the matter of our wager."

His eyes flared with surprise—then she lowered the boom. "Or perhaps not. Now if you'll excuse us, the dancing is about to start, and I've promised the first two to Sir Douglas."

She took hold of Drury's arm and started forward, then turned back as if she'd forgotten something. "I believe Lady Annabelle Dalyrimple's in need of a shoulder to cry on, Mr. Smythe-Medway, and the sort of amusing, meaningless banter at which you excel."

Chapter 11

Letter of the second of June, 1819 (continued)

Oh, Aunt Euphenia, why must men duel? Why must they try to assuage their wounded pride in that potentially fatal way? I never, ever thought Brix would accept a challenge, just as I never, ever thought Fanny would be responsible for putting Brix's life at stake.

I can only hope good sense will prevail, but given who's challenged Brix, and why, I fear my hope is a vain one.

Lady Diana Westover Terrington

Making her way as quickly and unobtrusively as she could, Fanny slipped into the corridor and away from the ballroom. Diana and Edmond were dancing, Lord Bromwell was chatting with another potential sponsor for his expedition, and she'd left Drury deep in discussion with a judge. She didn't think anyone would notice she was gone for several minutes, at least.

She desperately wanted some peace and quiet. She needed time alone and time to think, away from the dancing and Sir Douglas Drury and everybody else with their curious, sly looks and speculative whispers.

She soon found herself in the more private area of Lady Jersey's house that was not frequented by guests. The few maids and footmen who saw her immediately halted and turned their backs as she passed, dutifully pretending to make themselves invisible to her. Under the circumstances, they would probably assume she was on her way to a rendezvous with her lover. She didn't think they'd alert anybody, and even if they did, it wasn't as if she was really going to meet anyone.

She cautiously opened the first door on her left and peered into the room dimly lit by the moon. She could make out bookcases along the walls, the glass catching the moonlight. This must be the library.

She went inside and closed the heavy door, leaning against it with a grateful sigh.

After a moment she pushed herself off and wandered farther into the large chamber full of mysterious shadows and the scent of wood polish. Like every other chamber in Lady Jersey's town house, the room was large and tastefully decorated. It was spotlessly clean, and the thick carpet cushioned her footfalls as she examined the books on the shelves. It was difficult to make out the titles, but she could tell some of the multitude of volumes bound with leather were very old, and all were probably expensive.

Diana would love this room. Edmond, too.

Fanny enjoyed reading, but not to the same extent they did. She preferred pleasant conversation. Jokes and stories that made her smile. Sharing a companionable silence.

She sat in one of the upholstered chairs near the empty hearth and thought again how lucky Diana and Edmond were to have found each other. They were deeply in love and so happy, it was almost painful to watch.

Here, alone in the dark, she admitted that it *was* painful. Seeing them so blissfully content made her realize how lonely she was; how lonely she'd always been. Only being with Brix had assuaged that deep, abiding ache.

Things had gone so terribly wrong between her and Brix in such a short time, and she doubted they'd even be friends again.

Brix's friendship with his closest friends was in jeopardy, too. She hadn't foreseen that when she'd impulsively made her wager.

She hadn't foreseen a lot of things.

"My lady?" a deep voice said from the doorway.

Fanny jumped to her feet as a man stepped into the room. "Sir Douglas?"

"I hope you're not unwell, my lady?"

Her heartbeat quickened, and not with the sort of excitement being alone with Brix engendered. She wordlessly began to back away as Drury approached. "No, I simply wanted to be away from the crowd and the noise for a bit."

His steps slowed as he continued toward her. What was it some people called him? The Court

Cat? That seemed very apt at the moment. "I could understand if you were upset," he said. "Brix's behavior has been unforgivable."

"In some ways, my own has hardly been laudable," she admitted, wondering if Drury would concur, or if his feelings had blinded him to her own less-than-sterling conduct.

"You've been more sinned against than sinning," he replied, still slowly approaching her. "Brix is far more the guilty party than you."

Although she didn't feel as physically threatened as she did by Clutterbuck and Strunk, she didn't feel safe, either, as she inched backward. She hit the bookshelves, the glass door cool against her back.

Drury halted a few feet away from her. "I'm glad I found you alone, my lady. There's something I have to confess."

"I don't think I'm the one to give anybody absolution," she said, mentally measuring the distance to the door even as she tried to make light of his statement.

Drury spread his hands. "I never meant for things to get so out of hand. I deeply, sincerely regret having caused you any trouble."

That wasn't at all what she'd expected. "What do you mean?"

"*I* wrote the wagers in the book at White's."

Shocked, incredulous, she gasped and stared at him. "You? Why?"

He shrugged. "I had my reasons."

He'd made her the subject of gossip and speculation at least as much as Brix had, and this was all he would say? "What reasons would those be, Sir Douglas?" she demanded.

"After a few glasses of wine one night, my envy of Brix got the better of me. I remembered the wagers, and decided to embarrass him by making them public, since I was certain he'd lose."

"You expect me to believe that one night, in a fit of envy, you got drunk and decided to write those wagers in the book," she repeated, making no secret of her skepticism. "You thought that, despite all his denials and denunciations, Brix would really marry me."

"I thought he would see the wisdom of it, yes."

He made it sound as if she were some sort of medication. A little dose of Fanny, and all would be well. "And before he was fifty?" she charged.

"Most definitely."

"Hadn't he made his feelings for me—or lack of them—perfectly clear to you and the others, if not to me?"

"I believed that no matter what he said, he did love you, in his own way, and that he would realize that eventually," Drury replied.

"*In his own way?*" she repeated as her hands clenched. "What is *that* supposed to mean? And *eventually*? Was I just supposed to sit and wait? I've done that, Sir Douglas. For years, and for what? To be publicly humiliated, by both you and Brix. You weren't thinking of my feelings when you wrote those wagers at White's any more than he was thinking of my feelings when he made them."

"No, I was not," Drury replied, making no excuses.

"You'll understand me, I hope, if I'm not disposed to forgive you. Or accept your explanation, either, for that matter. What is there about Brix that a man like you could possibly envy?"

He gave her an enigmatic little smile. "I can think of a few things, my lady."

No longer intimidated by Drury's manner, his voice or his dark eyes, she raised an inquisitive brow. "Such as?"

"He has the ability to make people comfortable around him, for one. I do not."

"That's certainly true," she retorted.

His gaze intensified. "For another, he has your devotion. I have never had any woman devoted to me. Ever."

"Your reputation would seem to belie that, Sir Douglas."

"A lover's fleeting passion is not devotion."

She was in no humor to debate. She went to go past him. "If you'll excuse me, Sir Douglas, I don't particularly care to hear your views on passion, devotion or love."

Drury put his hand on her arm to stop her, his grasp warm and unwelcome, as he looked intently into her eyes. "I'm very sorry for all that's happened, Fanny."

She yanked her arm away from him. "I daresay that sort of statement made in your most persuasive voice and with that particular look in your eyes is very effective with most women, Sir Douglas. However, I doubt they have as much cause to be angry with you as I do."

"Do you hate Brix now?" Drury asked, studying her face as if he expected to see a confirmation written on her forehead

"Does it matter?"

He answered quietly. Gently. "To me, it does. Very much. Or perhaps a better question would be, do you still love him?"

Perhaps if she just answered, she could get back to the ballroom and pretend this meeting never happened. "No. Even my devotion, as you call it, couldn't withstand the way he's treated me lately."

"He hurt and humiliated you, and you want to pay him back. Believe me, I understand the urge for vengeance, yet even so, I must warn you that it achieves nothing. I speak from bitter experience, Fanny. You'll wind up hurting yourself more if you try to win this wager. Forget Brix and start anew, with somebody who does appreciate you."

She stiffened. "Who might that be—you?"

He nodded. "Yes. Forget about the wager. Call off your bet with Brix."

There was the answer to her unspoken question: why would a man like Sir Douglas Drury have any interest in her?

He didn't. This was all part of a scheme, a plot to make her end the wager with Brix so that he would win by default. Surely if Sir Douglas Drury wanted her—or seemed to—she'd be willing to forget Brix and what he'd done.

Drury put his arms around her and pulled her close.

"What are you doing, Sir Douglas?"

The denizens of the British courts would never have guessed the barrister famous for his cool composure could look so taken aback. "I want to kiss you."

"Why?" The word came out like the accusation it was.

"Do I have to explain?"

Fanny glared at him with an expression of utmost contempt. "No, I understand perfectly. You and Brix think I really am a fool."

"I don't think you're a fool. Far from it."

Drury's expression of confusion might have tricked her earlier, but not now. "Oh, really?" she replied. "Tell me, Sir Douglas, how far were you to go? Were you to make me fall hopelessly in love with you? Were you to seduce me? Surely if you did that—and how could *you* fail—I wouldn't care about the wagers. Or was it going to be enough, did you think, to make me believe you were merely interested in poor little mousy me?"

As Drury stared at her, she jabbed his chest, which was as hard as a granite wall. "Tell Brix it won't work. Tell him I'm not stupid enough to think that Sir Douglas Drury, who can supposedly have any woman in London, is seriously attracted to me. It's too incredible." She crossed her arms over her chest. "I suspect you didn't even write the wager in the betting book."

Drury seemed to grow larger, looming over her

in the silvery light coming in through the tall windows. "I am not in league with Brix."

"Then you didn't write the wager in the book at White's?"

"Yes!" he hissed.

"So you *are* his confederate, helping to humiliate me!"

"I told you why I did that, Fanny."

"And for the past several days, I've apparently forgotten that you're one of Brix's oldest friends." She tilted her head as she regarded him. "What exactly did you do in the war, Sir Douglas? Some sort of espionage, wasn't it? No doubt you're very good at acting and pretending to feel what you don't. Brix asked you to put your skills at his service, because you're such old friends, didn't he?" Her voice dripped with scorn. "What is my shame and humiliation when weighed against such a request?"

Drury reached out and grabbed her shoulders, hauling her close so that she could see the moonlight glinting in his eyes. "What I did in the war is my business. As for Brix asking me to help him, you couldn't be more wrong. Damn it, Fanny, you're an incredibly attractive woman, and I'm not the only man who's noticed. Brix certainly has, no matter what he says or does. If anything, I've risked his abiding hatred for riding with you in the park and dancing with you and wanting you in my arms. If you don't understand that, you don't understand Brix, or me, at all."

"And you don't understand *me*!" she charged,

struggling to get free of his unwelcome hold. "I know I'm no beauty, and a few new gowns can't make that much of a difference. You never even noticed me before, but suddenly I'm supposed to believe you find me so appealing, you'd be willing to sacrifice your friendship with Brix for me."

"I did notice you before. I've noticed you for years, but I believed I stood no chance as long as you were in love with Brix." He searched her face. "You're still in love with him, even now. Aren't you?"

She wrenched herself free. "I'm not in court, Sir Douglas. I don't have to tell you anything."

"Then I'll find out for myself another way."

Before she could protest, he grabbed her and tugged her into his strong embrace.

She instantly discovered the difference between being kissed by a man she *thought* she didn't want, and being kissed by a man she truly didn't want. She most certainly did not want Sir Douglas Drury.

Just as she put her hands on his chest to shove him away with all her might, they were caught in a shaft of light from the open library door.

"Sorry to interrupt this intimate little *tête-à-tête*, but don't you think you should be more careful?" Brix said as he sauntered into the room and closed the door behind him, his tone no more distressed than if he was announcing it looked likely to rain.

Fanny pushed Drury back. "We're not having an intimate *tête-à-tête*."

"Really? I didn't just see the two of you kissing?" Brix asked as he flopped onto the nearest sofa, spread his arms over the back of it and crossed his long, lean legs. "Honestly, Fanny, there's nothing wrong with my eyes, you know. You both should be very glad it was me wandering by, and not any of the ladies of the *ton*. Imagine the gossip."

Hands on her hips, she glared at him. "Have you come to see if your plan's succeeding?" she demanded. "In spite of what you saw, it's not."

"Plan? What plan?" he inquired, quirking a brow at Drury. "Do you know what she's talking about?"

"Of course he does—but I've seen through your scheme, Brix."

"Are you drunk, Fanny?"

"No! Are you, to concoct such a plan?" She turned to glare at the stone-faced Drury. "Were *you* in your cups when you agreed to help him?"

"Fanny, I'm *not* conspiring with Brix," Drury said sternly.

She didn't believe him, because the evidence was against him. The only way his attention to her finally made sense was if he was in league with Brix.

She crossed her arms and tapped her toe, eyeing Brix scornfully. "Well, if you're not in a conspiracy with Sir Douglas, you may take yourself off, Mr. Smythe-Medway."

He uncrossed his legs. "A private party, is it?" He got to his feet. "Well, pardon me, I'm sure."

Drury blocked Brix's way as effectively as he'd

blocked hers. "Since when have you taken to spying on people?"

His harsh accusation began to make her wonder if she was wrong to believe that they were scheming together. That didn't sound as if they were even friends.

"Spying? That's your game, isn't it?" Brix replied as if the charge didn't particularly bother him. "Really, Drury, there's no need for such animosity. I just happened to be passing by and glanced in because I don't normally cover my eyes when walking down a corridor. That might lead to tripping and falling and other disasters. So I think I can hardly be held at fault for looking into the room and seeing you *in flagrante*. As a friend, I'm trying to warn you that other, less discreet people might see you."

"We were not *in flagrante*," Fanny exclaimed.

"Well, whatever you want to call it, my lady," Brix observed with a raised brow, "you should be glad it was me and not Lady Jersey or your sister-in-law who witnessed that shocking display of familiarity. You're already notorious enough, don't you think?"

"If I am, whose fault is that?"

"I'm not the one sneaking off in theaters, or during fancy dress parties and kissing anybody who finds me there."

"Drury kissed me. I didn't kiss him—just as I didn't kiss you in Almack's."

"Nothing's ever your fault, eh? Well, unless I'm an utter idiot—which I'm not—there could be no mistaking your enthusiasm once you got started, at least when *we* were kissing."

Fanny sniffed disdainfully. "With your *vast* experience, you'd know exactly how I feel, of course."

Brix's green eyes glittered with rage. "My *experience*, as you put it, is not nearly as vast as you think, although I'm well aware of the difference between bogus desire and true passion. You were *not* pretending, Fanny."

Drury strode toward the door. "It seems the pair of you are forgetting that you're not alone. Perhaps you should be."

Fanny started. She had indeed forgotten he was there.

For an instant, Brix looked just as surprised, until Drury slammed the door. Then he regarded her with his usual insouciance. "My word, Fanny, I do hope I haven't ruined anything."

Fanny scowled. "I assure you, Mr. Smythe-Medway, you have not."

"Really? It certainly looked like something. I had no idea you were quite so . . . how shall I say it? *Adventurous?*"

"I'm *not* adventurous," she retorted, hating his smug, self-satisfied tone. She straightened her shoulders. "I'm playing at love, Brix, just the way you men do. Sir Douglas's reputation as a lover is well-known, and since—unlike *some* people—he seems to find my company appealing, I decided to see if his kisses are as intoxicating as I'd heard."

Brix's brows lowered. "And are they?"

She shrugged. "I hardly know. I have so little experience, you see. You're the only other man who's ever kissed me, except for him. I need more experience." She put her finger to her chin. "Perhaps I'll try Buggy next, or maybe . . . Humphrey?"

"You'll ruin your reputation."

"It's already damaged because of you. And wouldn't it be better for you if I came to care for another man—Sir Douglas or Buggy Bromwell, perhaps? Then surely I'd be willing to forgo our little wager."

"Be quiet, Fanny!" Brix ordered, his whole body tense.

She walked up to him until they were nose to nose. "I won't be quiet because *you* tell me to. Once upon a time, Brix, I would have done nearly anything you asked of me. That was before, though. Now I'll do exactly what I want to, with whomever I want."

"No, you won't," Brix growled as he tugged her into his arms. "And you won't kiss anybody but me."

He took hold of her face and brought her mouth to his, crushing it in a kiss that robbed her of breath.

His primitive, unbridled passion reached into her soul and ignited her smoldering desire. She forgot all the reasons she shouldn't want him and returned his kiss with pure wanton abandon, his yearning hunger matching her own.

She wanted, needed, to be held and kissed and caressed and loved by Brixton Smythe-Medway.

In spite of all that had happened, she wanted him still, with every fiber of her being. In his arms, she was wonderfully, vibrantly, intensely alive.

He was the one person who'd always made her feel safe and cherished. He was the one who had first stirred her girlish thoughts of love.

He was the one she'd fantasized about during the long, lonely nights. She'd imagined him touching and kissing her with fierce longing, just as he was doing now.

He wanted her, too, no matter what he said. The proof was here, in his kisses and caresses, in his voice and body.

He *did* care for her, or he wouldn't have gotten angry. He would have sauntered out of the room with the same easy, unconcerned gait she'd witnessed a hundred times.

But he hadn't.

Sure she was right, convinced of his feelings for her, she kissed him deeply, fervently, her mouth gliding over his. There was no point trying to deny what was between them, as they'd foolishly been trying to do. It was too strong, too powerful, too perfect.

When his hand found her breast and kneaded it, she moaned soft encouragement. As his palm lightly brushed the taut tip of her nipple, she wanted to cry out with wanton abandon.

And run her fingers over his naked skin.

She shoved her hands under his jacket, lifting it up and away from his body. He broke away long enough to shuck it off, letting it fall unheeded to the floor. Her hands tore feverishly at his cravat as he steered her toward the sofa and sat her down.

She managed to rip off his cravat as he joined her and lifted her into his lap. Through the thin fabric of her gown and petticoat she could feel him hard beneath her. Grabbing his face, she captured his mouth and plunged her tongue inside.

What she had done that first day was but a prelude, like dipping a toe into a pond. Now she wanted to submerse herself completely.

She shifted, the sensation of his arousal between her thighs nearly overpowering, while his hands and fingers still worked their sensual magic, dancing over her skin.

She moved backward and grabbed his shirt and pulled him to her so she was beneath him, his legs between her limbs, before taking his mouth in another ardent kiss.

He levered himself up on one elbow. He pleasured her breasts and stroked her hot skin with his free hand, while his kisses continued, making her gasp for breath. His hand slid slowly down her ribs, her belly, her hip. He began to bunch the fabric of her gown, exposing her bare leg to the whisper of cooler air.

She got his shirt unbuttoned and finally put her hands on his naked chest. Her fingers brushed across the hairs spreading between his nipples, and from his navel to his trousers, exploring his body that was familiar, yet not.

She arched back, letting Brix kiss her chin and

neck and collarbone, then raised herself to press her lips to his magnificent, well-muscled chest. Holding tight to his shoulders, she slowly grazed his smooth skin with her mouth. He moaned softly, the sound almost a plea, as the muscles in his neck tightened.

She could feel tightening elsewhere, too, while deep in her body, she throbbed with answering need. She desperately, urgently, wanted him to make love with her. To take her here and now. To join in that most intimate of unions.

To forget even the strictest rules of the hypocritical *ton*.

Lying back, she looked up into his wonderful, beloved face, and smiled.

Such a look he gave her in return! Horror mingled with revulsion, as if he'd kissed a woman only to have her turn into a monster.

He shot back and got to his feet, hurriedly buttoning up his shirt. "More games, Fanny?" he muttered as she slowly sat up, staring at him in dismay and disbelief. "If you think you're going to win the wager this way, you're wrong."

He thought she was with him like this because of *the wager*?

She scrambled off the sofa. "I'm not one of your mistresses, Brix."

He looked at her with absolute scorn. "No, you're not. They're more honest."

"Honest?" she cried as rage and shocked disbelief replaced passion, and all her dreams that had come back to life died again.

Her hair disheveled, her gown wrinkled, she marched to stand in front of the man who'd killed them. Once again, he made her feel like a fool for having them, and an even greater fool for loving him.

"I'll tell you what would have been *honest*," she cried. "It would have been *honest* to explain that my affection wasn't wanted instead of allowing me to go on, until I was forced to discover it in that terrible way. It would have been *honest* to admit you liked having me follow you about like a lovelorn schoolgirl—don't think I don't know the truth! Tonight it would have been *honest* to tell me that, in spite of everything, you want me."

Brix's whole body tensed, as if every nerve and muscle was locked into rigid stiffness. "Would a declaration that I want you satisfy you, Fanny?" he demanded. "Would it make you stop tormenting me? By God, you know I do!" He jabbed a finger at the sofa. "I want you so much, it's taking all my strength not to throw you down there and make love with you until we're both too sated to move." He slowly crossed his arms. "But when I've done that, Fanny, when I've made love with you, you'll have me right where you want me. Vengeance will be yours at last. You'll be able to break my heart."

"What about *my* heart, Brix? Do you care at all that you shattered it?"

He picked up his cravat and began to retie it. His hands shook, but his voice was steady as he answered. "I didn't mean to do that, Fanny."

"How could you not realize that you would? It was obvious to all the world that I loved you. You had to know that making fun of that love, telling everyone I only annoyed you, would hurt me."

How he looked at her then! "Yes, that's right, Fanny," he retorted. "It's only *your* feelings, *your* hurt, *your* pain, that need be considered."

He marched toward her and glared down at her, righteously angry as she'd never seen him before. "Did you ever stop to wonder, Fanny, how *I* feel? That perhaps I was as upset as you when I discovered that what I thought was nothing more than a little wager among friends had been written up at White's? How do you think I felt when you threw my apology back at my face, as if it—and me—were beneath your contempt?

"Do you think I *enjoy* having to pretend that I don't care what people say about me? That I'm happy they're talking about me as if I'm the worst sort of cad, like Strunk? Pretending I'm impervious to sly looks and cutting remarks? Acting as if I'm just amused by it all, when it stings like the devil?

"All my life nobody's cared about how I feel about anything—not even you," he declared, silencing her before she could protest. "Even when you were my adoring little shadow, did you give a moment's thought to how *I* might feel about it? No. You *assumed* I must be pleased and flattered, because you didn't see beyond your own needs and desires. I wasn't a person to you, Fanny, but a romantic ideal.

"Well, surprise!" he cried, spreading his hands. "I don't want to be anybody's romantic ideal. I want somebody to love me the way I *am*. Because when *I* love, Fanny, it won't be to worship from afar, or with an acolyte's distant devotion. When I love a woman, Fanny, I'll love her completely, flaws and all, and with all my heart and soul and body."

Fanny stared at him, shocked, speechless. And ashamed.

She'd never thought . . . never guessed . . . never even *suspected*. . . .

The door to the library flew open and a man stood silhouetted on the threshold, his hands on his hips.

"What the devil is going on here?"

Fanny stared, stunned, as Albert stormed into the room. "You'll have to marry her now, Sir Douglas," he declared, and never had he sounded so arrogant or pompous.

Brix slowly turned around.

"Good God . . . *Smythe-Medway*?" Albert cried with horrified disbelief that quickly turned to red-faced rage. "What the devil were you doing with my sister?"

His demand energized Fanny. She ran to her brother and took hold of his arm to steer him out of the room. "There's nothing to get upset about, Albert."

"The devil there isn't!" Albert cried as he twisted out of her grasp and glared at Brix.

"Must you call on Beelzebub with such frequency?" Brix inquired coolly. "The repetition is getting rather aggravating."

"You shut that damned mouth of yours," Albert retorted before running an equally scornful glance over Fanny. "I know what's been going on here, you bounder."

"Really? What?" Brix inquired with annoying sangfroid, even as he put on his coat.

"Brix, you're only making things worse. Albert, calm yourself. There's no need to be so upset. Mr. Smythe-Medway and I were not engaged in the sort of activity you assume," she said, lying without remorse because she was willing to do anything to get Albert to be quiet before he made even more of a scene, inadvertently summoning the servants, or other guests curious to see what the commotion was.

"Do you think I'm blind, or stupid?" Albert demanded of her. He raised his arm and pointed at Brix. "He was putting on his damn cravat. Your hair's a mess, your gown wrinkled as if you've been . . . I don't have to say it, do I?

"How dare you take liberties with my sister!" he bellowed at Brix. "Those wagers were bad enough, but now this, you disgusting libertine. You've besmirched the honor of Fanny—and my family."

"Oh, Albert, be *quiet*," Fanny ordered, trying to keep her own voice low. "Are you trying to alert the entire household?"

Ignoring her, Albert walked up to Brix and

struck him hard across the face. "I demand satisfaction. Meet me in Hampstead Heath with your second in two days, pistols at dawn."

"That's ridiculous, Albert!" Fanny cried. "Brix hasn't even held a gun in years."

Brix's gaze darted to her, but he focused on Albert when he spoke, his voice betraying nothing of the anger she'd seen in his glimmering green eyes. "Really, my dear fellow, apart from the very real possibility that you'll kill me and be charged with murder, isn't dueling a bit old-fashioned?"

"If you don't meet me, the whole world will know you for a coward."

Brix calmly brushed the sleeve of his coat and remarked, "I've never claimed to be a model of bravery, but I don't particularly want to die an ignominious death over a trifle."

Fanny stared at him, incredulous. He was dismissing what had happened between them in this room as a *trifle*?

"What was it you proposed when you thought I was Sir Douglas?" Brix mused aloud as he tapped his chin with his finger and leaned his weight on one leg. "Ah, yes, honor would be satisfied if your sister and I were to marry."

Fanny's jaw dropped.

He ran an insolent, measuring gaze over her, then addressed her brother. "How unfortunate that I have a wager to win that prevents that. No matter what little schemes your sister concocts to tempt me, I will not marry until I'm fifty, and never Fanny. Mind you, she can be *very* tempting, so don't worry, Albert. Just because *I* don't want her doesn't mean other men won't. I wouldn't give up hope she'll snag Drury yet. Pity he's not the sort who marries, but he is famous, so maybe your family will be willing to overlook that small detail."

Any remorse, any guilt, any tender feelings that lingered within her were instantly destroyed by his horrible implication.

"You dog, how dare you speak of my sister and . . . and *us* . . . in that . . . that impudent manner!" Albert raged, spittle flying out of his mouth as his whole body quaked—and for once, she sided with her brother. "How dare you accuse *us* of having such base motives. You ought to be ashamed of yourself. You can't deny you weren't trying to take advantage of her." He shook his fist at Brix. "We all know the kind of man you are!"

"If there's anybody here who was trying to take advantage of somebody and who ought to be ashamed of themselves," Brix replied, sliding her a disdainful look, "it's your sister, wearing that astonishingly seductive gown, tempting every man in the place and snaring me in here. If I went beyond the bounds of decency, I did no more than I was encouraged to do." His eyes were full of bitterness as he looked at her. "And all to win a wager."

"I didn't try to seduce you to win the wager," she protested. "I didn't try to seduce you at all. Besides, you're a fine one to talk. What were you doing in the theater, except trying to seduce *me*?"

Albert gasped, but it was too late to take back what she'd said.

"This is what comes of letting you be friends with Adderley and that writing wife of his," Albert snarled. "You never went to the theater when you were living with *us*. I knew no good could come of that friendship. I was too kind, too generous—but no more. I'm taking you home, Fanny, where you belong and where you'll stay and where there'll be no more talk of wagers or parties and theaters. You've disgraced us for the last time."

Fanny planted her feet. "I'll be going back to the viscount's, and there I'll stay under I can find a house of my own."

"The devil you will! You're my sister and you'll bloody well do as I say!"

"I will not."

His face twisting with fury, Albert raised his hand.

Brix instantly grabbed it and slowly, inexorably forced it lower. "If you ever hit her, I'll break your bloody arm," he growled, his voice stern and commanding in a way that made her tremble.

"You have no right to interfere!" Albert blustered.

Brix's expression and manner didn't change. "You gave me that right when you accused me of trying to seduce her and challenged me to a duel. And rather than run the risk of having you denounce me for a coward as well as a cad— although both charges are equally unfounded—I'll meet you in Hampstead Heath at dawn in two days, with a second." He gave her brother the ghost of his usual grin. "I do note, Albert, that you didn't allow me the choice of weapons. Even if I'm not much better with a sword, that hardly seems sporting."

Albert's face turned purple as Brix strode from the room, slamming the door behind him.

Fanny glared at her brother, then left him without a word.

"Brix?"

At the sound of his name, Brix raised his heavy head from his folded arms. With bleary, unfocused eyes, he looked around, vaguely realizing he was still in a dark corner of a tavern in Drury Lane that reeked of smoke, sawdust and ale. Then he focused on the person addressing him. He blinked twice before he recognized him.

"Buggy!" he cried with sodden bonhomie when he did. "Good ol' Buggy." He banged his fist on the scarred tabletop. "Sit down and join me, Buggy old friend. Molly, more wine!"

Buggy remained standing. "How much have you had to drink since you left Lady Jersey's?"

"Not enough if I can still talk," Brix said with a drunken chortle as he brought the nearly empty glass to his lips and downed what wine remained.

Buggy reached out and took the glass away. "I think you've had plenty."

"Well, you're no fun," Brix mumbled, rubbing his eyes. "You're never any fun. Always too busy with your spiders and your books. And Fanny. You were pretty busy with Fanny at the party. I saw you dancing with her." He raised his index finger and waggled it shakily. "You weren't the only one, you know. Drury was with her—and doing more than dancing, too. I caught them kissing. She tried to tell me she didn't want to, but I know better. He's Drury, after all." He saw Buggy's shocked expression and brandished his empty glass in a triumphant salute. "Ah ha, didn't know *that*, did you? Well, they were—right in the library." He began to lower his head, to rest it on his arms again. "The little minx. The damned tempting little minx."

"I think it's time you went home."

"No!" Brix raised his head again and frowned. "I like it here." He waved his arm to encompass the dour patrons, most of whom were even more in their cups. "*They* like me. Molly likes me." He squinted at a female shape across the room. "Don't you like me, Molly?" he called out.

He didn't see her reaction, because Buggy came around the table, blocking his view as he unceremoniously hauled Brix to his feet. "Come on. I'll take you home."

Despite Buggy's iron grip, Brix tried to sit down. He wasn't ready to leave yet. He could still envision Fanny in that incredible gown, with her hair disheveled and her lips swollen from their passionate kisses.

"You're not my mother, you know," he muttered petulantly.

"I know," Buggy said through clenched teeth as he tugged him upright.

"You're not my father, or Humphrey. You can't tell me what to do. If I wanna stay here—"

"I'm not a relative, but I *am* your friend, so I'm not going to leave you in this stinking tavern another moment." With a mighty effort, Buggy hauled Brix to his feet. "Now move!"

"You surprise me, Buggy, you really do. I had no idea you could be so commanding," Brix declared as Buggy half helped, half dragged him toward the door. "You and Fanny—full of surprises. But I don't wanna kiss *you*."

"Thank heavens for small mercies," Buggy said under his breath as they made it outside, where he all but shoved Brix into a waiting carriage.

Brix flopped against the seat, then wiggled around until he was sitting properly, albeit as loose-limbed as a cloth doll.

"Since we're all alone, answer me this, Buggy ol' boy, do you want Fanny, too?"

"All I want to do is get you safely home," Buggy grimly replied.

Grinning, Brix put his unsteady finger to his lips and whispered, "All right. Don't admit it. Be like Drury. He wants Fanny, although I'm not sure if it's for marriage or just a good—"

"Brix, be quiet!" Buggy snapped. "Say another word, and you'll likely lose another friend, and right now, I'd say you need all the friends you can get."

Brix slumped back against the squabs.

"Are you forgetting what happened this very night? With Fanny's brother?"

"Oh, that."

"Yes, that. Albert lost no time telling everybody how he challenged you to a duel because you were trying to take advantage of Fanny."

Brix sniffed and didn't meet his friend's censorious gaze. "I wasn't. No more than she was taking advantage of me."

"It doesn't matter who was doing what to whom. Your reputation was already in serious jeopardy because of the wagers. After this, you'll be lucky if decent people receive you, even your own family. Humphrey was livid when he heard what Albert was saying. And aren't you the least bit worried about the duel? Albert's a good shot, and you're . . ."

"And I'm not. Damn it, Buggy, I know it. He didn't give me the chance to pick the weapons, the bastard."

"Listen to me, Brix. Whether it's swords or pistols, if you duel with Albert, you could be killed."

"Should have paid more attention to my sporting father and brother and gone hunting, eh?"

"Brix, be serious. For once in your life, be serious!"

Brix sullenly shrugged his shoulders. "Oh, all right. I'll be serious." He crossed his arms. "What's it matter if I'm killed? I'm not good for much anyway."

Buggy's expression altered. "Of course you are."

"You think so?" Brix asked with a bleary smirk. "Ask my brother. Ask my parents. Ask Fanny. Hell, ask Drury and Edmond, too. They'll tell you otherwise."

"Nobody wants to see you dead, Brix."

"Fanny does."

Buggy sighed and spread his scarred and slender hands. "Look, Brix, I don't know what's going on with Drury, and I'm not saying we haven't been annoyed and frustrated with you. As for Fanny, I can't blame her if she's very upset with you. But even so, I'm sure she doesn't want you to risk your life in a duel with Albert."

"Well, I've got to," Brix said. "My honor's at stake."

Buggy didn't answer, and Brix took this for agreement, or acquiescence, at least. "I ought to have a second, you know, when I meet that pompous, arrogant bore. How 'bout you?"

Buggy frowned. "If you insist on going through with it."

Relieved, Brix reached out and clapped his friend on the shoulder. "I should have known I could count on you. You like spiders, not Fanny. And maybe you could give me a few shooting lessons, too? It's been years, you know."

"Yes, I know," Buggy said with a sigh.

Chapter 12

London, the third of June, 1819

Poor Fanny! She may not like Albert, but he is her brother, and she couldn't have wanted such an outcome, under any circumstances.

Lady Diana Westover Terrington

In the wee hours of the morning of the duel, Fanny crept down the back stairs of Diana and Edmond's town house. Her last remaining hope, that it would rain so hard the duel couldn't possibly take place, had been destroyed when she'd awakened from a fitful sleep and seen the stars shining. There wasn't even a hint of mist or fog.

Now dressed in a footman's trousers, shirt, jacket and cap she'd surreptitiously taken from one of their rooms, she cautiously unlocked the back door and slipped into the garden. It was a short distance from there to the mews, where Edmond's horses were stabled.

The most difficult part of her plan was going to be getting a horse saddled and out of the stable without waking a groom or stableboy sleeping in the loft above.

She wrapped the jacket more tightly about herself and pulled down the hat covering her hair. Diana had told her about the time she'd dressed in disguise when she was in Bath, and Fanny had decided doing the same would make it easier for her to be out on the London streets alone at such an hour. If any of the watchmen queried her, she would say she was returning the master's horse after he'd gotten too foxed to ride home.

She made it to the stable, then cautiously opened the door and slipped inside. The horses shifted, but made no other sound.

She surveyed the stalls. Edmond kept four carriage horses and a gelding for riding. Diana hired a mare if she wanted to ride while in London, as she had done, or went out with Edmond in the barouche.

The gelding it would have to be. Fanny bit her lip as she slowly approached the stall holding the beast. She was used to a more placid mare, not this great black creature.

She began to whisper soothing words to the horse as she set about finding a blanket, saddle and bridle. Once she had those things, she cautiously opened the stall door and went inside. Inching her way forward, she reached out a trembling hand to stroke the gelding's muzzle.

So far, so good, she thought as he stood still.

He stayed still as she struggled to saddle him. She'd always had a groom or stableboy to prepare her mare for riding, so she had no idea how complicated a process it was, or how heavy a saddle could be. The effort of raising the saddle high enough to put it on the gelding's back made her shoulders ache and her muscles quiver, but she wasn't about to give up. This was a matter of life, or death.

She finally succeeded, although by the time she was finished, the shirt and her chemise were soaked through with perspiration. She thought she'd allowed ample time, yet a quick glance through the east-facing window high in the wall made her fear she was going to be too late to stop the duel. She was determined to do just that, even if that meant standing between Albert and Brix as they took their aim.

She led the horse out of the stable and shivered in the cooler air before mounting. She could barely get her foot in the stirrup, and wouldn't have managed it at all if the gelding hadn't stood perfectly motionless.

She nudged the gelding with her heels. It broke into a desultory trot. She felt like a bag of potatoes bouncing along on the gelding's broad back, but as long as no one stopped her, she'd survive.

It was too early for even the street sellers to be about their business. In fact, she'd never seen the streets of London so empty. It was as if the whole city were under quarantine, a thought that made a different sort of shiver run down her spine.

She should mention this to Diana as something she might be able to use in a book someday.

The sound of a lone horse's trotting hooves in

the distance added to her dread. That diminished when she turned a corner and saw a hack stopping in front of a house where a light burned in the upper windows. A man clad in black, carrying a doctor's bag, ran up the steps.

A sick child, perhaps. Fanny sent up a quick prayer for whoever was in need of a physician at this hour, in addition to her nearly constant silent prayers that Brix would come to his senses and not try to duel with Albert. Or that Albert would hurt himself so that he wouldn't go. Not a serious injury—just enough to keep him at home.

When she arrived at Brix's street, she slid off the huge animal and led the gelding inside the entrance of the mews behind the row of houses. She was fairly certain Brix wouldn't be walking to the duel. He'd take either a horse or his carriage. Either way, she'd see some activity in the stables, and given the early hour, she could assume it would be in Brix's service. Then she'd follow him.

After waiting for what seemed an eternity, she saw a man leading a horse from the stables and recognized Brix's mount from their meeting in St. James's Park.

A familiar figure came out of Brix's house—albeit walking without his usual jaunty stride—and mounted his horse. As his groom went back inside the stable, Brix turned the animal.

He was going to ride right past her. She couldn't scramble into the saddle without raising suspicions.

She had to make him believe she was a stableboy.

Effecting what she considered a burly sort of rolling masculine stride, she led her horse down the mews as if returning it to a stable farther down the row.

Brix didn't even look at her.

She kept on walking, right to the other end of the mews and out into the street. Mounting quickly, she joined the main street shortly after Brix had ridden past the intersection of the two roadways. She waited until he was several yards in front of her, then followed, keeping her eyes on his broad shoulders.

Brix nudged his horse to a trot. Fearing she would lose him if she didn't match his pace, she brushed her heels against the horse's sides to try to get it to trot again.

But this time, the horse leapt into a gallop, tearing down the street. She frantically clutched the reins, too terrified to scream. Her hat flew off, and her hair streamed out behind her like a banner.

Somebody shouted; she had no idea who it was or what they said. She desperately tried to pull the horse to a halt or turn him down a side street, but the headstrong gelding wouldn't obey. It was as if she were no more to him than a pesky fly, and he would gallop until he felt like stopping.

Or hit the milk cart a man pushed into the road. Fanny cried out a warning and yanked back on the reins with all her might.

The gelding finally, finally, stopped. Her heart

pounding like a piston, Fanny struggled to catch her breath.

"Are you all right?"

She half turned, to see Brix on his prancing horse beside her as if he, too, had just gotten his galloping beast to halt.

Brix started, then stared. "What the devil? Fanny, is that *you*?"

He quickly dismounted and walked toward her. "What are you doing here, dressed like that and—" His eyes widened as he ran his gaze over her mount. "On Edmond's horse?"

She didn't answer, because all she wanted to do was get down from the hellish horse's back. She shakily began to dismount.

Brix rushed to help. His strong hands encircled her waist, and he held her steady as she slipped to the ground. She let her head rest against him briefly, just as she had so many times in the past when he'd comforted her. Hearing his heartbeat, feeling the warmth of his body, she again felt that sense of safe security she'd experienced so often when she was with him.

His breathing quickened. So did hers.

He put his hands on her shoulders and held her slightly away from him, regarding her with a puzzled, worried expression. "Are you hurt?"

She shook her head.

"You're wearing men's clothing," he noted, his gaze holding her as effectively as his arms.

"I wanted to—"

" 'Ere now, 'ere now, wot's all this then!" a voice cried out.

Brix didn't let go of her as they turned to see a watchman trundling toward them as fast as his bow legs would carry him. Glaring at them, he reached up to grab her horse's dangling rein. Brix immediately released her.

Fanny stepped forward. The charley could detain Brix, if she told him Brix's intentions. "Sir, you have to stop him. He's going to—"

Brix pulled her back into his arms. "Oh, my darling, what a scare you gave me!"

Holding her firmly against him, he muttered into her ear, "I can guess why you're here and dressed like that, and it won't work. Now either follow my lead, or I'll tell him you're my mistress who's in league with a gang of horse thieves."

"You wouldn't dare," she whispered hoarsely.

"I would."

He spoke so fiercely, she believed him, and since she wouldn't be able to prevent the duel if she were in prison, she reluctantly nodded.

Brix smiled remorsefully at the watchman. "We had a lover's spat, you see, and she's out so early in these outlandish clothes because she's been following me. Poor girl thinks I've got a mistress." He looked at Fanny beseechingly as he took hold of her hands. "I don't, my darling, truly I don't."

Fanny tried to pull her hands free, but Brix had them in a grip of iron.

"There's no need to be jealous, my dear," he

continued insistently. "Even if it's flattering, there's absolutely no reason for it. It's you I love, and only you!"

Then he swooped down and captured her mouth with a fervent kiss.

For once, Fanny wasn't immediately overwhelmed with desire when Brix did that.

"Stop it," she said under her breath when she managed to break the kiss.

Brix turned back to the charley and became once more the sophisticated, amicable aristocrat. "Obviously, my beloved's skills as a horsewoman leave a great deal to be desired. However, no harm's been done, so there's no need for you to stay. Isn't that right, my darling?"

He nudged Fanny with his elbow.

She made herself smile. "Yes, that's right."

The charley didn't look convinced, until Brix reached into his jacket and tossed the man a gold sovereign.

The watchman snatched it in midair, grinned and doffed his hat. "As you say, sir, no harm done."

"No harm at all," Brix seconded as he pulled Fanny into his arms and kissed her with surprising, almost numbing thoroughness, far more than playing a part demanded.

Far more than he would if he was still angry with her.

"Rich folk today," the charley mumbled as he ambled away and joined the milkman, where they began to rather loudly and disdainfully discuss the decline of the upper classes.

Meanwhile, Brix grabbed hold of Fanny's arm and the horses' reins. "Come with me," he muttered.

Since he had hold of Edmond's horse, she had no choice but to follow him into the nearest alley. He paid no heed to the rubbish or the stench, and neither did she. She wasn't going to leave him until she'd convinced him not to risk his life dueling with Albert.

Brix looped the horses' reins over a broken door leaning against the brick wall, then faced her, his expression stern and unyielding. "Go home, Fanny, and stop trying to interfere with my business."

She squared her shoulders. "I will not. I'm trying to save your life."

"You have no control over me, Fanny," he replied, his voice grim as he crossed his arms. "If I choose to duel, there's nothing you can do about it."

"If I saw a man standing in front of a runaway horse," she said, gesturing at his gelding, "I'd do everything in my power to make him see that he's in danger. This is just the same. Albert's an expert marksman. You aren't."

He ran his gaze over her clothes. "And riding about London dressed as a man isn't putting *you* in danger?"

"I wore these clothes to be as safe as I could be. I do know what might happen to a lone woman, thanks to Lord Strunk and his friend. But I had to stop you."

"To assuage your guilt for enticing me in Lady Jersey's library?"

Fanny's hands balled into fists. "I didn't entice you!"

Brix moved closer. "Or perhaps this has little to do with me at all. Albert could be charged with murder if he killed me."

"I can't deny that, but—"

"That would cause another, even more serious scandal, and play havoc with your new role as beauty of the season, too. How distressing."

Her temper flared. "I don't care about that."

"Really? Then you are a most unique woman." He ran his gaze over her again, but this time he made her feel naked. "Perhaps your plan wasn't so very far-fetched. Seeing you dressed like that might have rendered Albert and me too dumbfounded to aim our weapons."

He glanced to the east, where the sky was tinged with the orange glow of the rising sun. "Unfortunately, your little scheme has failed. Go back to Diana and Edmond's, Fanny, and stay there."

"Don't treat me like a child!"

"Believe me, Lady Francesca, I haven't thought of you as anything but a woman for several weeks." Brix sidled a little closer, and his expression turned as hard as a granite tombstone. "It's no wonder you're distraught, though. If I'm dead, you can't win the wager."

She couldn't believe what she was hearing. "You think I'm worried about our wager? I'm worried that you're going to be *killed*. That's why

I've stolen these clothes and Edmond's horse and risked my neck to try to stop you. Brix, please don't go!"

Her emotions were so raw and near the surface, she didn't trust herself to say more.

He didn't seem to care how upset she was. "Obviously the thought of my possible demise is more serious than I considered. There must be something I'm missing—"

She grabbed hold of his lapels. "Don't be a fool, Brix! Whatever Albert said, it's not worth dying over."

He shook himself free. "You still don't understand, do you, Fanny? I *am* a fool—that's the role I play, that I've always played. It's the role I was born for."

"You're *not* a fool," she protested. "I've never believed it, and I still don't—and neither would other people if you'd come out from behind that merry mask you wear all the time. You have plans and ambitions—good, noble ones that your family doesn't appreciate, but *I* do. You want to help people, Brix. You *do* help people. You're a good man. A wonderful, generous, kindhearted man.

"You were right to tell me I'd been selfish before. I wasn't thinking of your feelings, but only what I felt for you."

Exasperation, distress, fear all combined in Fanny, and restraint gave way to desperation. "Don't you see, Brix?" she cried. "I love you! I'll always love you!"

She grabbed his jacket and hauled him close and kissed him. Fervently. Passionately. With determination and resolve, to show him that she really did care for him, and his death would kill her, too.

But instead of responding to her passion, Brix abruptly pulled away and stumbled backward, staring at her as if she'd done something too horrible to contemplate.

He grabbed his horse's reins and swung into the saddle. "No matter what you do, I won't give Albert the satisfaction of claiming that I was afraid to duel," he said, his eyes blazing. "I won't have him telling everybody I was a coward. I won't have him spreading the lie that I was trying to seduce you. Now go home, Fanny, and *leave me alone*."

He wheeled his horse around in the narrow confines of the alley, then spurred it to a gallop.

Once out of the city, Brix encountered only a few farmers on their way to London with their produce. As he'd passed some cottages, a watchful dog barked a warning; otherwise, all was quiet and still, except for birds heralding a new day. Occasionally he looked back over his shoulder to make sure he wasn't being followed by anyone.

He commanded himself not to dwell on his unexpected and disturbing encounter with Fanny. He needed to concentrate on the task at hand, and he couldn't let her sudden appearance, like some sort of guardian angel in male attire, or her heartfelt declaration of love, impede his focus. As she'd said, he was not an expert marksman, and Albert was.

And no matter what she said, or how she looked when she said it, or the way she kissed him, he was adamant. He wasn't going to let Albert destroy what was left of his reputation. Even the Honorable Brixton Smythe-Medway couldn't laugh off an accusation of cowardice, or the charge that he'd been attempting to seduce a virtuous young lady.

Nor was he about to let Fanny witness his possible demise at her brother's hands.

He reached the secluded place Albert had chosen for the duel, a small clearing in the midst of a stand of alders, well shielded from the road and any curious eyes. Dew was heavy on the grass, glistening in the early-morning light.

When he entered the clearing, he discovered Buggy waiting by his horse. His friend, who had become more used to tropical temperatures in recent years, wore a heavy blue greatcoat. His hands shoved in the pockets, his hat pulled down over his ears, his shoulders hunched, shifting his weight from foot to foot, Buggy looked as if he was freezing.

Or very worried.

Albert and his second, the marquis of Maryberry, were standing beside Albert's barouche. They, too, wore greatcoats and hats, but Albert's was unbuttoned, and the marquis was yawning. The middle-aged driver of the carriage was seated on the box, and by his disgruntled expression, he wished he was anywhere else. Given the clandestine nature of the meeting, there were no other liveried servants in attendance.

"And here I was thinking you weren't going to come," Albert jeered as Brix dismounted.

"You were never noted for your intelligence," Brix replied, leading his gelding toward Buggy and tossing the reins over a convenient bush. "As it happens, I had an unforeseen delay on the way."

Buggy was looking very pale, and another explanation for his manner came to Brix. "You're not ill, are you?" he quietly asked.

"No, I'm not," Buggy said. "I'm afraid I'm about to see one of my best friends killed before my very eyes. I was hoping you were going to show some sense and stay home."

Buggy's genuine concern wasn't exactly conducive to calming Brix's nerves.

He tried to diminish the gravity of the situation by affecting a cavalier manner. "Judging by what I read in your book, you've seen worse things," he noted as he started toward his opponent.

The grass was very slippery, and he made a mental note to be careful. He didn't want to slip and fall like some kind of clown.

"I don't need to be reminded of some of the things I've seen," Buggy said, dutifully following. "Are you sure you won't reconsider?"

"Yes, are you sure?" Albert mocked. "All you have to do is take back what you said about my sister."

Brix came to a halt in front of Albert and handed Buggy his beaver hat. "If it were simply a matter of apologizing for my impertinent observations about your sister, I might consider it," he said as he began to remove his coat. "However, you're an arrogant, conceited bully, and it's time somebody called you to account."

Albert shrugged off his greatcoat. "You're a lazy, lascivious, decadent cad," he sneered as he gave it to the marquis. "I can't wait to shoot you."

Brix gave his coat to Buggy, so that now he was wearing just his shirt and cravat, waistcoat, breeches and riding boots. "The feeling is quite mutual."

"We'll use my pistols?" Albert haughtily inquired as the marquis put Albert's coat and hat in the carriage.

The marquis then pulled out a narrow, polished ebony box with brass fittings, which he opened to reveal two very fine dueling pistols.

"Since I don't own any, I have no choice," Brix said with a smile, although his eyes betrayed exactly what he thought of Albert. "Lord Bromwell's explained the procedure to me thoroughly, so what do you say we get it over with? I haven't had my breakfast yet."

Albert grinned malevolently. "As you wish."

"Whatever you think, Brix, I should check the pistols first," Buggy announced.

"No," Brix replied, shaking his head. "Albert may be a bully and a braggart, but I believe he wouldn't tamper with the pistols. I'm sure he's quite certain he can beat me without resorting to cheating."

Albert bowed. "You may have your choice of pistol," he declared with great magnanimity.

"Damned decent of you, old boy," Brix said, "although of course, that's no more than my right." He grabbed the closest. "Where would you like me to go?"

"To hell," Albert muttered, leading him instead to a level patch of grass in the center of the clearing.

"My, you do have an affinity for all things satanic," Brix remarked as he followed him. "One can only wonder why."

"Now we stand back-to-back," Albert ordered, scowling.

"As I said, Lord Bromwell's told me the basic rules of dueling," Brix replied as he went to stand uncomfortably back-to-back with his opponent.

"I'm really going to enjoy silencing you," Albert sneered.

"If you can," Brix countered. "I daresay it'll take more than a bullet."

"Then I'll do whatever's necessary."

"Temper, Albert, temper. Better not get all hotheaded under the circumstances, don't you think? Only my humble opinion, of course. You're the expert."

"Shut your damn mouth!"

"If you say so."

"Start the count, Maryberry!" Albert called out.

His second obediently followed his command. "Ready, gentlemen?"

"Yes!" Albert snarled.

"Whenever you are," Brix replied.

Trying not to betray any dread whatsoever, or slip on the grass, Brix slowly walked forward as the marquis numbered the paces.

He tried to remember everything he'd ever learned about shooting—but all that came to his mind was Fanny's eyes. Her beautiful, sweet eyes that used to look at him with such innocent admiration and devotion.

Her eyes full of womanly desire before they kissed in the library.

Her eyes that morning, begging him not to risk his life.

She'd thought he was about to make the biggest mistake of his life.

She was wrong. He'd already made the biggest mistake of his life when he made fun of her affection and held her up to scorn and ridicule.

"Nine . . ."

"Ten!" Albert shouted.

Brix wheeled around. Albert was already aiming. He fired, the report reverberating in the early-morning stillness and sending a flight of startled sparrows up into the sky.

The pistol ball whistled past Brix's ear as the scent of sulfur and gun powder filled his nostrils.

I'm not dead. I'm not dead!

A quick survey proved he hadn't even been hit. Brix's knees went momentarily weak with relief as he sent up a fervent prayer of thanks. Albert, the expert marksman, had miraculously missed.

It dawned on Brix that Buggy was shouting. His friend was furiously angry, marching toward Albert as if he wanted to shoot him himself.

"You cheated!" Buggy cried. "You didn't wait for the count to finish!"

Albert had *cheated*?

The marquis looked sick, and the color drained from Albert's face as he dropped his smoking pistol.

"You can shoot him at your leisure, Brix," Buggy declared. "It's your right."

Triumph and pride surged through Brix as he looked at the trembling duke of Hetley. Albert had cheated and handed him a victory.

"Y-you can't shoot me," Albert stammered, looking as if he was about to burst into tears. "My family . . . my sister . . . they *need* me."

Brix thought of all the times Albert had bullied the sister he now claimed needed him. "You think Fanny needs you? For what? To make her life miserable? To point out her shortcomings?" he asked as he slowly raised his gun. "How many times have you made Fanny cry, Albert?"

"Please, don't," Albert pleaded, falling to his knees. "I take back everything I've ever said about you."

"Do you think I care what a sniveling cheat thinks of me? I want your word you'll never bully Fanny again."

Albert nodded with rapid desperation. "Yes!"

"You'll allow her the freedom to live where she

wants, as she wants. You'll respect her decisions and her right to make them."

"Yes! Anything!"

"You'll get that wife of yours to stop criticizing her all the time, to anybody who'll listen."

"Yes! Please, don't kill me!"

"All right." Brix pointed his pistol to a spot about three feet from Albert's left shoulder and fired.

Albert let out a screech and fell to the ground, clutching his arm.

Cursing, Brix tore across the clearing as the marquis ran to Albert's side.

He couldn't have hit him. He'd aimed wide . . . but a red stain grew on the sleeve of Albert's shirt.

Oh, God. Fanny would think he'd tried to kill her brother.

"I should have missed him," he cried as he slid to a halt on the wet grass.

The marquis held Albert up in a sitting position and pressed a linen handkerchief to the wound.

"Stay away from me!" Albert screeched when Brix knelt in front of him.

"It's just a flesh wound," the marquis muttered.

"Thank God," Brix murmured as his shoulders slumped with relief.

"Flesh wound or not, you tried to kill me in cold blood," Albert shrieked.

"Shooting one's opponent is the general idea of a duel," Brix said as he slowly got to his feet.

A very pale Buggy joined them. He had a dueling pistol in his hand, and Brix discovered he didn't. He must have dropped his when he realized his bullet had struck Albert.

"Brix shouldn't have hit him at all," Buggy declared with disdain. "The barrel of this gun has been altered to shoot to the right. If Brix had been aiming for Albert's body, he would have missed. But since he *wasn't* aiming for Albert, he hit him." He regarded the duke with contempt. "It's your own fault you got shot."

Albert had cheated *twice*?

The duke turned even paler, and the marquis's ministrations suddenly became less gentle.

Whose reputation was at stake now?

"Well, well, well, Albert," Brix noted, cocking a brow, "so you cheated in more ways than one. I must say, I'm surprised you felt the need, considering you're the best shot in three counties. Just wanted to be sure, I suppose."

"There's nothing wrong with that pistol," Albert objected. "Bromwell's only trying to make sure you're not charged with attempted murder—but you will be. I'll see to it."

"I'd think about that, if I were you," Brix replied. "We have the gun as evidence, and Lord Justinian Bromwell for a witness. Whatever the *ton* may think of me, I doubt anyone would question anything he says."

"*Albert!*"

Brix stiffened, cringing, as Fanny rode into the clearing on Edmond's big black gelding. He should have known Fanny wouldn't do what he said and go home, and sure enough, she'd found them.

Fanny's heart didn't flutter when she saw Brix standing by her brother, obviously uninjured. It lurched. And then fear replaced her joy when she saw the blood on Albert's shirt.

She scrambled off the back of the horse, hit the ground, stumbled, righted herself and ran toward them.

"Oh, Albert!" she cried as she fell to her knees in front of her wounded brother and the marquis of Maryberry. In spite of all that Albert had done, he was still her brother, and she didn't want him dead, Elizabeth widowed, and her nieces and nephews left fatherless.

Albert ran his gaze over her. "Fanny, what the devil—?"

Brix shot him a look.

Albert gulped, then his lips curved upward tremulously as if he thought this would be his last opportunity to address her on this earth and he wanted to leave her with a smile on his face. "Dear sweet Fanny." He held out his hand, which she grasped. "I feared I'd never see you again."

Relief cascaded through Fanny. If Albert were really seriously hurt, he wouldn't be playing the martyr nearly so well.

"It's only a flesh wound," Brix offered.

"And he got shot because he *cheated*," Buggy declared disdainfully.

Fanny's astonished gaze flew from one man to

the other. She knew Albert hated to lose, but that was a far cry from what Buggy was suggesting.

"We don't need to discuss this now," Brix said as if that was of no importance. "We should all go home before the Bow Street Horse Patrol appears to arrest us."

Buggy didn't pay any attention. He held out the pistol, apparently expecting her to examine it then and there. "Brix wasn't even trying to hit him. He aimed wide after your brother shot before the count was finished—as Brix had every right to do—but the duke had tampered with the weapon. His own dishonorable conduct got him shot."

Fanny let go of Albert's hand and straightened. "Is that true, Albert?"

His eyelids fluttered closed and his cheeks, previously pale, flushed pink. "Can't . . . speak . . . the pain."

Albert's reluctance to deny the charges Buggy leveled at him were as good as a confession for Fanny, and any lingering animosity she'd felt toward Brix for wounding her brother dissipated.

More than that, if the shoe were on the other foot, Albert wouldn't be generously acting as if the cheating were of no consequence. Even if Brix had been seriously wounded, Albert would be taking him to Bow Street to be charged with attempted murder.

"The duke should see a doctor without further delay," Brix said briskly. "We wouldn't want that wound to turn septic."

"*Septic?*" Albert gasped. "Get me home!"

Both Brix and the marquis put their shoulders under Albert's and helped him toward the barouche. Buggy crossed his arms and watched the duke's progress with an expression of the utmost contempt.

Albert made a very good show of being nearly unconscious, but he couldn't fool Fanny. She'd seen him fake too many illnesses when they were children and he wanted to avoid something to be taken in by his obvious ruse.

Once Albert and the marquis were in the barouche, Brix leaned on the sill of the open window. "For your family's sake, Albert, I'm willing to keep the truth about your dishonorable behavior quiet. I think it will be enough punishment for you to know that everybody will know that *I* won the duel."

His voice and expression altered, to become hard as steel. "But if you're ever tempted to forget out little conversation this morning, I'll tell everyone how you cheated. Lord Bromwell will be able to back me up. And if you try to deny it, I'll have your pistol for proof. I'll also sue you for slander for implying that *I'm* lying. So good day, Your Grace. I do hope you're feeling better soon."

With that, Brix thumped the side of the barouche. The driver jerked the reins, and the carriage bounced over the grass toward the road.

Fanny reached out and touched Brix's arm to get his attention. "Brix, I—"

"Buggy can tell you what transpired here this morning," he said as he faced them, his expression inscrutable. "Take her back to Diana and Edmond's, will you, Buggy? That's Edmond's horse she's riding."

His gaze softened for the briefest of moments. "Farewell, Fanny."

He couldn't leave her here just like that, not after what she'd told him that morning. Not after he'd shot her brother. "Brix!"

He didn't even hesitate before heading toward his tethered horse on the other side of the clearing. As she started to go after him, he swung himself into the saddle and kicked his horse into a gallop.

Powerless to stop him, she watched him ride away.

Obviously, he didn't care that she still loved him.

She thought her heart had been broken before?

Her heart had merely been cracked when she'd heard of those wagers. *Now* it was shattered, into a million tiny, separate, lonely pieces, every one with a jagged, painful edge.

"Come on, Fanny," Buggy said quietly. "I'll take you home."

Anguish in her eyes, she looked at Brix's friend. "Yes, Buggy, I want to go home."

Chapter 13

London, the fourth of June, 1819

So, Aunt Euphenia, Brix has left London. We're not sure where he's gone. Fanny received a note from him addressed to us here, which naturally I took to her at once. I didn't presume to question her on its contents, especially when I saw her face as she read it.

Lady Diana Westover Terrington

After asking Buggy to take the horses to the mews, Fanny hurried up the steps to her brother's house. This was where she needed to be right now—where they would need her.

She banged the knocker to announce her arrival, then went in without waiting for the butler to open the door. The air was filled with a series of high-pitched, mournful wails coming from upstairs.

Elizabeth, of course.

Laughlin appeared, and he frowned with vast displeasure. "Young man, if you do not get out of this house, I shall—"

"It's me, Laughlin," Fanny said, taking off her hat. "Lady Francesca."

The butler put his hand on the wall to steady himself. "Lady Francesca?" he repeated dully.

"I haven't got time to explain my clothes. Is my brother in his bedroom?"

Laughlin nodded.

"Has a doctor been summoned?"

Buggy joined her, glancing uneasily upstairs. "Oh, dear."

"That's Elizabeth." She addressed Laughlin again. He was staring at Buggy as if he expected him to turn out to be a woman in disguise. "*Did you send for the doctor?*"

Laughlin started. "Yes, my lady. At once." He remembered to close the front door behind them. "He is with the duke at present."

Another howl of despair wafted down the stairs. "Where's the duchess?" Fanny asked.

"She's with them, my lady."

That was reassuring. Albert's condition couldn't be critical, or surely the doctor would have sent Elizabeth somewhere else while he attended to his patient. "Where are the children?"

"With their tutor and governess, my lady."

Fanny turned to Buggy, who was hovering near the door. "I'm going to suggest that Miss Mapples and Mr. Hepplewaite take the children to the park while I try to convince Elizabeth to rest, or at least be quiet. I'm sure they'd be more likely to go if you went with them. The boys especially loved your book."

Buggy gave her a sympathetic smile. "Anything I can do to help."

"Thank you. If you'll wait in the drawing room, I'll be as quick as I can." She turned to go, then paused and addressed the butler. "Laughlin, Lord Adderley's gelding is in the stable. I, um, borrowed it this morning. Please have one of the grooms return it, with my compliments."

Laughlin didn't look as shocked as she expected. "Very good, my lady."

As Fanny left them and hurried upstairs, she realized it would probably upset her sister-in-law even more if she appeared dressed in men's clothes.

She went into her old room, to see if there was a gown of hers to change into. She discovered nothing had been moved or altered, except that the mess she'd made packing had been tidied and the clothes she'd discarded and left behind had been put away. Her books still lay on the rosewood table beside the bed, the candle half–burned down in the pewter candlestick beside them. Her box for hair ribbons was still open on her dressing table. Her bed was made, with the same thick satin coverlet. It was as if Albert had hoped—or expected—she'd soon return.

As she went to the armoire, she glanced at the bed. How many hours had she lain awake there, daydreaming of Brix? How many times had she sat in that brocade chair near the muslin-draped window, thinking about him? How often had she gone to this armoire to select a dress for a party, wondering if Brix would be there?

How much of her life had she spent in love with Brixton Smythe-Medway?

What was she going to do now?

Another plaintive wail from Elizabeth prompted her to focus on what she had to do. Blinking back tears, she got out of the footman's clothes and folded them. She'd send them back with a footman, and a note of explanation to Diana as soon as she had things under control here.

She dressed quickly in a gown that required no assistance to lace. She splashed some water on her face and tied back her hair with a bit of ribbon she found on her dressing table. That done, she hurried to the schoolroom on the upper floor of the vast house.

It was a bright chamber under the eaves painted a pale yellow. There was a bookcase along the wall, and each child had his or her own table on which to work. Pictures of British birds and animals lined the walls, along with a print of the Prince Regent, and another of the king.

One look at the children gathered there, and Fanny knew that the injury to their father, and their mother's reaction, had terrified them. Young Albert was trying to be brave, but he looked as if he was on the verge of tears. Peter's eyes were red-rimmed, as if he'd been crying and only just stopped. Unabashedly sobbing, Clarissa and Geraldine were clinging to the tall, gaunt Miss Mapples, whose hair was as dark as theirs was fair.

Mr. Hepplewaite, a balding man of forty whose

facial creases indicated the toll taken by tutoring spoiled young noblemen, was frowning, and obviously worried. Miss Mapples stood so stiffly, it was as if she was expecting another disaster at any moment.

"The duke's going to be all right," Fanny hastened to assure them as she walked into the room.

Geraldine, the youngest, immediately ran to embrace her. "Aunt Fanny, Aunt Fanny!" she cried, while the other children hurried to gather around her.

Putting aside her own emotional distress, Fanny spoke gently and with complete confidence. "Your father isn't seriously hurt, and the doctor's with him now, taking excellent care of him, I'm sure. Your mother's crying because she gets upset when anything bad happens to anyone in the family."

"What *did* happen?" her eldest nephew demanded. "Nobody will tell us. Did Father fall from his horse?"

Fanny bit her lip, unsure what to say, until she decided upon the truth. Young Albert admired his father a good deal and sought to emulate him. She wouldn't have him emulate her brother's propensity for dueling, and the truth might prevent that. "He was shot in a duel."

The boys' eyes widened, and the girls stopped crying.

"What happened to the other man?" young Albert asked warily.

"Fortunately, he was unharmed—but I remind

you," she said to both boys, "dueling is extremely dangerous. Your father was lucky."

"He's a good shot," young Albert said stoutly.

"Good shot or not, he lost today. So bear that in mind if you're ever tempted to indulge in dueling when you're older."

She looked away from the older boy to address the younger children. "Lord Justinian Bromwell is downstairs in the drawing room, waiting to take you all on a little expedition to the park while the doctor tends to your father, and I help your mother."

Peter whooped with delight, and young Albert looked pleased. "Will he tell us about the time he was nearly eaten by cannibals?"

"Perhaps, if you ask politely," Fanny replied.

Geraldine looked up at her with more worry in her eyes. "He won't make us touch spiders, will he?"

"Not if you don't want to," Fanny answered, hoping she was telling the truth. But she doubted Buggy would terrorize a girl with a spider, as Albert had once done to her. "Now come along, and I'll take you to meet him."

Mr. Hepplewaite cleared his throat.

"I'm sure you'll both be welcome," Fanny replied in answer to his unspoken question.

Mr. Hepplewaite beamed, while Miss Mapples flushed and surreptitiously patted her sleek hair before ushering the children downstairs.

That accomplished, Fanny carried on to Albert's bedroom. She knocked softly, then entered the large bedroom decorated with very masculine furnishings: an enormous four-poster bed canopied in a rather lurid blue, heavy walnut armoire, dressing table and side tables. A brilliant Aubusson carpet covered the floor.

Albert looked like a child in the huge bed, and it was obvious, from the snoring, that he was in a deep sleep. She was pleased to note that his color was much better.

Elizabeth was half-reclining in a chair beside the head of the bed, dabbing her eyes and sobbing as if she'd just been told Albert had only moments left to live.

The white-haired physician, unperturbed by Elizabeth's lamentations, stood at a side table near the window packing things into his medical bag with careful deliberation. There was a dark brown bottle and an empty glass with white residue at his elbow.

A sleeping draft would explain Albert's ability to sleep despite the pain of his wound and his wife's wailing.

Elizabeth spotted her sister-in-law. "Oh, Fanny!" she cried, rising and tottering across the room to fall into Fanny's arms. "It's so terrible! That horrible Smythe-Medway tried to kiiiiiilll the duke!"

"Mr. Smythe-Medway didn't try to kill Albert," Fanny said firmly as she tried to ease Elizabeth away. Her sister-in-law wasn't exactly light.

Elizabeth choked and stared at her, but Fanny

was in no mood to explain right at that moment. "How is he, Doctor?"

"It's not a serious wound," he replied with a gentle smile. "All that's required is rest and quiet now that it's been cleaned and bandaged. I'm also happy to say that I don't think he'll suffer any permanent injury."

"Oh, but he could have!" Elizabeth cried.

"Yes," Fanny agreed, "and that's why he shouldn't duel ever again. This should be a lesson to him."

Demonstrating that she wasn't completely prostrate with grief, Elizabeth stepped back and glared at her. "A lesson to *him*? It's all that Smythe-Medway's fault!"

Fanny kept her voice calm and level so that her sister-in-law wouldn't get any more agitated. "It wasn't. Albert challenged him, remember?"

"He had to! Our family honor was at stake." Elizabeth frowned, as if suddenly realizing that Fanny could be held responsible for the duel, too.

Fanny wasn't going to accept any blame for Albert's decision to duel. "Elizabeth, Albert was shot because he *cheated*. He tampered with his pistols, so the one Brix used didn't aim properly." She regarded her sister-in-law with resolute intensity. "You know how much he hates to lose, Elizabeth, and how vain he is of his skill with a pistol. He obviously didn't want to take any chances."

"I-I don't believe it. I won't!"

"Lord Bromwell has the pistol for evidence, if you'd care to see it."

Elizabeth blanched and wobbled toward the chair, into which she collapsed. "Oh, no. Oh, dear. Cheating? What will people say?"

She cast a horrified glance at the doctor.

"I'm sure the doctor knows how to keep a confidence," Fanny said. "And nobody else has to hear about what happened this morning. Brixton Smythe-Medway has generously, graciously said he won't reveal the exact circumstances, and I believe him. But if Albert's ever tempted to challenge anybody to duel again, *I* will."

Elizabeth stared at her, openmouthed. "You'd do that to us, Fanny?" she whispered. "What about the children?"

"It's they—and you—I'm thinking of, as well as Albert." She softened a little. "Come, Elizabeth. You don't want your husband killed over something as silly as gossip, do you? Given the number of times Albert's dueled, he's been fortunate that he hasn't been wounded before, even if he is the best shot in three counties."

His bag in his hand, the doctor stepped forward. "Pardon me for intruding in this conversation, but I must agree with the young lady," he said. "The duke was fortunate—this time. Who can say what might happen the next? And a man of his age and station surely has no need to prove himself by such means."

Elizabeth nodded as she dabbed her eyes again. "Yes, yes, you're right."

Grateful for the physician's diplomatic assistance, Fanny smiled at the doctor, and she could have sworn there was an answering twinkle in the brown eyes beneath his snowy brows.

"Now, Your Grace," he said, addressing Elizabeth, "I've left some of the medicine I gave your husband in that bottle on the table. One spoonful the next time he awakens, then as he needs it to dull the pain and help him sleep. I'll come back tomorrow afternoon to check the bandage and ensure that the wound hasn't become infected."

"In-*fect*-ed!" Elizabeth cried, covering her mouth.

"Yes. At this point, I believe that's all we need fear. I've cleaned it quite thoroughly, however, and he hasn't lost nearly as much blood as he might have. So try to stay calm, Your Grace. I don't want to have two patients the next time I come to call. Now if you'll excuse me, one of my patients has had another attack of gout, and I'm already late."

"Oh, yes, yes. Thank you for coming," Elizabeth said, rising and going to him. She seized his free hand between hers and squeezed it. "You saved my dear husband's life!"

The doctor managed to pull his hand from Elizabeth's grip. "Are you going to be able to help tend to the duke so that the duchess can get some rest?" he asked Fanny.

"Yes, I'll be here."

"Oh, you'll stay?" Elizabeth exclaimed.

"Yes, I'll stay," Fanny replied.

Albert needed somebody sensible to look after him and run the household until his arm healed.

Later, when he was better, if he sought to restrict

her life again, she could leave as she had before. She would live on her own, in some quiet, out-of-the-way place. And have as little to do with men as possible.

For once, Elizabeth's smile was genuine and sincere. "Oh, thank you, Fanny!"

"Elizabeth, why don't you rest now?" she suggested. "The children have gone to the park with . . ."

Elizabeth hadn't asked her how she came to be there. It would no doubt be better if explanations came later. "With Miss Mapples and Mr. Hepplewaite."

"All right. I'll be in my room, Fanny. Call me at once if Albert awakes," Elizabeth said, sniffling as she left through the adjoining door to her bedroom.

"I don't believe the duchess is suited to nursing," the doctor noted, his careworn face wrinkling with a wry smile.

"No, she's not," Fanny agreed as she escorted him out of the room.

Fanny wasn't surprised by Diana's arrival later that day. She expected her friend to come to see her as soon as she could.

When she joined Diana in the golden drawing room, she wasn't surprised by the grim expression on Diana's face, either. After all, the duel and its aftermath had been serious, although just how serious, only she knew.

"How's your brother?" Diana asked as she sat on the Grecian couch.

"He's doing very well. I'm happy to say Elizabeth's been able to nap. As you might expect, she was very distraught."

"Yes, I'm sure she was." Diana's gaze didn't waver. "I daresay she required some attention herself."

"Some," Fanny acknowledged as she sat beside her friend. "I hope Edmond's not angry that I used his horse. I wanted to stop the duel and thought that if I could find them before it began, I could. I couldn't bear the thought of my brother charged with murder if he shot Brix. I didn't ask you for permission because, well . . ."

"Because you were afraid I'd try to stop you, or talk you out of your plan?" Diana suggested. "I might have."

Fanny nodded and looked at her hands in her lap. She couldn't bring herself to tell Diana about her encounter with Brix, just as she couldn't tell Diana that it was Brix she'd been worried about, far more than Albert. "I was too late. It was only by chance I was on the right road and heard the pistol shot."

Diana patted her hand. "You tried, Fanny. I admire you for that. And thankfully, no one was killed."

"Yes, no lasting harm's been done."

"Hasn't it?"

Fanny pretended she hadn't heard that. "I'll send a servant for my things tomorrow."

Diana suddenly took Fanny's hands in hers and

looked intently into Fanny's eyes. "How are *you*, Fanny?"

"I'm fine," she lied.

Diana was silent for a moment, then reached into her reticule. "This came for you. Obviously Brix didn't realize you'd come here this morning instead of returning to us."

Fanny took the letter. Her hands trembled as she broke the seal and read the terse message:

Lady Francesca:

Be advised that I do not return the sentiments you expressed so forcefully this morning.

It was signed *The Honorable Brixton Smythe-Medway.*

"Fanny? Dear? Would you like me to leave?" Diana asked softly, her face full of sympathy, and understanding. "Or if you'd like to talk about this . . ."

Fanny shook her head as she crumpled the letter in her hand.

"There's one thing more, Fanny," Diana said. "You might as well hear everything at once."

Just like when she'd told Albert about the wagers, Fanny thought. "Very well," she said, mentally bracing herself.

"Brix has left London. When we realized you were gone, we suspected you'd gone to Brix to try to stop the duel. We were sure of it when we discovered Edmond's horse was missing. Since we didn't know where the duel was to be, Edmond immediately went to Brix's house, but he was too late, too. Edmond decided to wait, and when Brix returned, he said almost nothing to Edmond, except to ask him to deliver this note, and that he was going to Medway Manor."

Brix hated going there. Why would he now?

The obvious answer came to Fanny, and it filled her with anguish.

He wanted to get away from her, once and for all.

This time, she'd let him. She'd spent too long trailing after him, hoping he'd notice her. Hoping he'd say one word, or just glance her way.

No more.

She got to her feet and reached for the bellpull. "Thank you, Diana, for bringing me this, and for all your hospitality. I'm very grateful. Now if you'll excuse me, I have to see the housekeeper about the meals. Elizabeth's too upset to think about food. Laughlin will show you out."

Diana rose. "If you need anything, Fanny, anything at all, at any time—"

Fanny made herself smile. "I'll be fine, Diana, really. Things are going to be very different now."

Diana's blue eyes regarded her with unflinching candor. "Yes, I can see that. I'm so very sorry, Fanny."

Fanny squared her shoulders. "There's no cause to be sorry, Diana. I've gotten over my girlish infatuation with Brixton Smythe-Medway at last."

* * *

After making the journey to Medway Manor in record time, Brix took a moment to gather his thoughts—and his explanations and excuses—before he sauntered into the familiar, shabby library. His hands in his trouser pockets, he strolled into the room as if he visited his father all the time, instead of once every couple of years.

It was as if nothing had changed since the last time he was there, except to gather more dust. The books were still where they'd always been, unopened, he was sure, since his school days and for years before that. The prints of horses and hounds were the same. Several huge hunting dogs lay about the room. One was slumbering on the hearth, one was sleeping at his father's feet, two more lay in the sunlight streaming in through the mullioned window, and another two were curled up on the only chairs not occupied with guns, or powder bags, or various bits of horse harness. The animals, harness, oil and polish contributed to the general odor that always hung about this room.

His father, dressed for hunting even though it was raining, and peering at the pieces of a gun scattered on the table in front of him, added his own unique scent of whiskey and wool. He might well have been sitting there since the last time Brix had been to the family estate.

"I told you, Michaels, that I didn't want to be disturbed until I figured out what was wrong with this gun," the earl of Parthington muttered without looking up.

"Michaels did tell me that, Father, but I thought perhaps you'd rescind that order to greet the prodigal son. I don't expect a fatted calf, but a hello would be nice."

The earl started and looked up as if a ghost had appeared and started to speak. "Brixton?"

He bowed. "In the very flesh."

His father's bushy gray brows narrowed with suspicion. "What the devil are you doing here? Not in trouble, are you? Or debt?"

It was no more than Brix had expected, and yet, as always, he'd hoped for something different. A little genuine affection, perhaps, or a sign that his father cared about him.

But then, as he'd told Fanny, he was a fool.

He shoved one of the dogs off the nearest chair and sat down. "I'm not in trouble the way you mean, although I did shoot the duke of Hetley."

His father fell back against his chair and stared at Brix as if he'd announced he'd assassinated the Prince Regent. "*What?*"

Brix forced himself to look pleased by what he'd done. "Albert challenged me to a duel and I accepted." Brix had no desire to even hint that Albert had cheated. His father would never believe it, anyway. *He* could barely believe it, and he hated Albert. "He missed, and I hit him in the shoulder."

His father's expression changed, to one of proud, if incredulous, wonder. "Albert *missed*?"

"Yes."

With the alacrity born of good health and much exercise, the earl jumped up from his chair and rushed forward to clap his son on the shoulder.

Brix winced as his father exclaimed, "Congratulations, my boy! You beat Albert. Well, well! I never thought you had it in you." His father headed for the brandy bottle. "Just as well you didn't kill him, though, and not just because it's Albert. Makes things a bit sticky with the law, don't you know."

He hesitated in midpour. "Is that why you've come home? Bit of legal trouble because of the duel? Couldn't that lawyer friend of yours help you there? Dudley or Drummond or whatever his name is?"

"No, I'm not in any legal trouble," Brix replied. "I just thought it might be a bit prudent to leave the city, that's all."

His father handed him the glass of brandy. "What possessed Albert to call you out? What'd you do, play some sort of prank on him?"

"Not exactly." Brix wondered how much his father was likely to hear about what had happened. All he talked about with his friends was hunting and horses, but his mother wrote frequently and she was always well informed, even if she was in Bath.

"It was about a woman," he prevaricated, deciding to let his father reveal how much he knew of what had been happening in London.

The earl settled his large frame in a worn chair beside the chimneypiece and deftly nudged one of the sleeping dogs out of the way with his foot. "Ah, a woman. I should have guessed. Still, it's a bit of surprise, considering Albert's married. Wonder what that wife of his will make of that, eh?"

Grinning, the earl raised his glass in an impromptu toast. "Here's to your being a man at last."

He downed his drink, then frowned when he realized Brix hadn't raised his. "What's the matter?"

"I'm not very thirsty," Brix said, setting down his glass.

His father relaxed in his chair. "So you're here till things die down a bit, eh?"

Brix nodded. "If I may stay."

"Of course! Good thing you've come, as a matter of fact, what with Humphrey in London."

"Yes, I saw him there."

"Well, the tenants are making some kind of fuss about something or other. You have a way with them—better than Humphrey, come to think of it. See if you can figure out what the devil it's about and how to make 'em stop."

"I don't want Humphrey to think I'm trying to step on his toes."

"He'll probably be glad to have it all sorted before he gets back."

"That isn't why he left, is it?"

"Gad, no," his father retorted. "He wants to purchase some land and had to see the bloody bankers. I had a letter from him yesterday." He waved his hand at the pile of papers on the age-darkened oak secretary desk in the far corner.

"He's met some gel. Tells me he'll surprise me with the particulars when he gets home. Poor fool sounds utterly smitten. I wouldn't be surprised if he comes back with a wife."

Brix didn't say a word.

His father hoisted himself to his feet. "Come on out to the stable, my boy. I want you to see my new horse. Quite the fine beast and worth every penny I paid, if I do say so myself."

"Have you had any news from Mother?" Brix inquired as he rose.

"Got a letter this morning. Haven't read it yet. All that gossip bores me. As long as I get a letter, I know she's well, and that's the main thing. Say, while we're there, you can see Matilda's latest litter. Maybe I'll even give you one of the pups, eh?"

"Perhaps another time," Brix murmured as he followed his father out the door.

Chapter 14

London, the eighth of June, 1819

I suppose I should be pleased that Fanny's returned to her brother's, especially since he seems to have reconsidered his treatment of her, but I miss her. I can't be sure how truly happy she is, either. When she's come by for tea lately, she seems very merry—until I get a good look in her eyes.

There's no word yet as to when Brix might return to London.

Lady Diana Westover Terrington

"I'm *so* looking forward to this party at Lady Dalyrimple's," Elizabeth said with a blissful sigh as she regarded Fanny in her dressing table mirror while her middle-aged maid fussed with her hair. "That's a very pretty dress, Fanny. That color suits you. I've always said pink would look good on you, and you can see I was right." She glanced at her maid. "Aren't I right, Ceddars?"

The maid nodded and kept on working, trying to get the string of pearls to loop just so. Her mistress's elaborate gown of green silk, with puff sleeves and embroidered trim, was quite a contrast to the maid's plain black woolen dress and white cap.

Fanny forced herself to smile. "I thought of your advice when I purchased the fabric."

Elizabeth beamed, and Fanny tried not to frown.

She'd been dressed and ready to leave for Lady Belden's party for the past half hour. Since she had nothing better to do, she'd joined Elizabeth in her boudoir, with the halfhearted hope her presence would provide an impetus to be on their way. Unfortunately, it seemed that nothing less than an emergency would compel Elizabeth to depart before she was sure every hair, pearl, feather and bit of trim was in its proper place.

"It's too bad Albert can't come," Elizabeth continued, "but the dear man's so fatigued, I didn't have the heart to insist. Well, he *says* he's fatigued. I think his wound must be very painful. Yet he was adamant we go. He's so sweet-tempered these days, Fanny, and I daresay it's because you're home. Even the children are so much quieter. Miss Mapples tried to tell me it was her management of them that made them so much softer spoken, but I said it was your influence, without doubt. You should have seen her face."

Fanny continued to bare her teeth in a strained smile, but if the girls were quieter these days, it was because both she and Miss Mapples had told them it would help their father get well if they didn't quarrel and make a lot of noise. The boys had been told the same thing, and they were doing quite well in that regard, too.

As for the dinner party at Lady Belden's, Fanny didn't believe it was fatigue or any lingering pain from his wound that kept Albert at home that evening, especially since he'd been well enough to go to his club the day before. It was more likely because he hated Lady Belden and thought her husband a bore.

Yet Elizabeth was right—he'd been very keen that they attend, even if he did not.

No doubt he still harbored hopes that Sir Douglas Drury would ask for her hand. One of these days, she'd have to disabuse him of that belief, but not right away. If it meant she could get out of the house for an evening so she wasn't alone with her thoughts, and Albert treated her like a capable adult and not an overgrown child, she'd let him continue to believe that there was a possibility Sir Douglas Drury wanted to marry her, until she had to reveal otherwise.

Fortunately, she hadn't encountered Drury again since that horrible night at Lady Jersey's.

"So then we decided on the Nile green. And a wise choice it was, don't you think?"

Fanny realized an answer was required. "Yes, it's very lovely, Elizabeth."

Her sister-in-law gave her a significant look. "Sir Douglas Drury once told me this color suited my complexion. You should have told me he'd be there this evening."

Fanny stiffened. "I didn't know he would be."

"You don't look very happy about it," Elizabeth remarked with a frown.

"You surprised me, that's all."

Elizabeth smiled. "Well, it's true. Lady Belden was all aflutter, to hear Marion Morrison tell it. Apparently she's invited him several times before, but he's never accepted." She slid Fanny a surreptitious glance in her mirror. "I understand Lord Bromwell's going to be there, too. Such a nice young man, and so intelligent!"

And famous, Fanny finished for her. No doubt Albert and Elizabeth would consider him an acceptable suitor, too. "Yes, he's very nice."

"I could never understand why they were so friendly with Brixton Smythe-Medway. They're such ambitious, clever fellows and he's—" Elizabeth gasped and put her hand to her lips. "Oh, dear, I've been doing so well not to say that man's name. Albert gets so upset when I do."

"Albert's not here, Elizabeth," Fanny pointed out, glad she could hear Brix's name and not be upset. Enough to show, anyway.

Elizabeth studied Fanny in the reflection of the large mirror before her. "Tell me, Fanny, now that we're alone, how *do* you feel about Sir Douglas?"

"I'd rather not discuss my private life in front of Ceddars," Fanny quietly replied.

The maid blushed, while Elizabeth regarded Fanny as if this were some sort of odd eccentricity. Then she cast a critical glance at her reflection and

waved her hand at Ceddars. "That's fine, Ceddars. You can go."

The maid obediently sidled from the room. After
she was gone, Elizabeth turned to face her sister-
in-law. "So, how do you feel about Sir Douglas?"

It was insolent of her to ask, but Fanny supposed Elizabeth's curiosity had reached a fever
pitch. Perhaps she would be wise to prepare them
for the inevitable disappointment. "I fear we
might not suit."

Elizabeth frowned. "Not suit? Why, he must
think you do. He's never singled out a young lady
as he has you. I'm not the only one who's noticed,
and now that Smythe-Medway's finally gone,
what's to stop him?"

"The fact that I don't love him?"

"Oh, but surely you feel something for the man!
How could you not? He's so handsome and mysterious and fascinating. And the stories I've
heard . . ." Elizabeth leaned closer and spoke in a
confidential whisper. "He's *quite* a lover, Fanny. I
have it on the very best authority."

Fanny's eyes narrowed as she regarded her
vain sister-in-law. Perhaps Elizabeth had her own
reasons for wanting Drury in their family.

"Oh, not personally!" Elizabeth cried and in
such a horrified way that Fanny, to her relief,
could believe her. "From other ladies of the *ton*
who can be counted on to know."

"The fact remains, I don't love him, Elizabeth,
and I don't want to marry him."

Her sister-in-law pursed her lips. "No?" she said after a moment.

"No," Fanny said firmly. "And I doubt I ever will."

"Ah ha!" Elizabeth cried as if she'd just discovered jewels lying on the carpet. "You do allow for some doubt." She waved her hand, silencing Fanny before she could reply. "I won't press you any further, Fanny. Let's just leave it at that, shall we? And perhaps it's best to let the gossip about those wagers die down a bit. After all, a man in his position wouldn't want to be involved in the *scandal du jour*."

"If Sir Douglas were seriously interested in me, I don't think he'd let a scandal stand in his way, do you, Elizabeth? But I haven't seen him since before the duel."

"Perhaps he's been busy with his latest case."

Exasperation began to get the better of Fanny. "Or perhaps he's also realized we really don't suit."

"Nonsense, Fanny. Of course he'd be willing, with some encouragement. He was very interested before."

Fanny sighed and gave up trying to convince her sister-in-law that she didn't care for Sir Douglas Drury and never would. She rose and shook out the skirt of her pale pink silk gown. "If you're ready to leave, Elizabeth, I'll ask Laughlin if the carriage is waiting."

Lady Belden was all solicitousness when Fanny and Elizabeth arrived in her crowded drawing room, which reflected the hostess's mania for whatever was deemed fashionable in decor by the *ton*. The furniture was an odd clash of Chinese-inspired decorative items and wallpaper, and Egyptian-inspired furniture in ebony and brass, along with the requisite pieces, like the large pianoforte. Two huge, intricately painted chinoiserie vases stood on pedestals on either side of the door like sentries; the top of Fanny's head barely reached the rim of them.

"Oh, dear me, what a time you've both had! I heard about that *horrible* business with the duel," Lady Belden cried, her garnet earbobs dancing, the several inches of pin-tucked trim of her dark red gown swinging, as she met them at the door and briskly led them farther into the room, which was stifling. It was a warm evening, and the candles added to the heat.

Several people turned to look at them, and more than one quickly turned back to exchange murmured comments with their companions. The tone of the subsequent whispers told Fanny she was still very much the subject of gossip and speculation and fervent curiosity.

She wasn't surprised. The duel was a recent event, and it was only three days until the fateful six weeks would be up. Still, it would be a relief to find a friend or two here, even if she was fairly certain Diana and Edmond wouldn't be among the guests. Lady Belden had once had the poor judgment to mention in Edmond's hearing that lady writers were not much better than ladies who got paid for other services.

To her chagrin, Humphrey was near the pianoforte, with Lady Belden's daughter, Annabelle. The young woman was looking up at him as if enraptured, and for once, she wasn't giggling.

Buggy Bromwell wasn't in the room, either standing near the musicians or hidden by one of the vases. Given that Elizabeth, and probably Albert, considered him another candidate for her hand, she was rather relieved he wasn't.

As she'd feared, though, Drury was, deep in conversation with an elderly gentleman near a pair of French doors leading to what must be the garden. If he noticed she had arrived, he gave no sign.

Perhaps she could manage to avoid him.

Elizabeth gracefully slid onto a sofa—taking up most of it—and looked as mournful as if Albert had died. "Oh, it's been terrible, Lady Belden! Awful! A *nightmare*. I can't begin to tell you the effect it's had on my nerves. I've hardly been able to eat a bite, or sleep a wink." She clasped Fanny tightly by the hand. "If it hadn't been for dear Fanny, I don't know what I would have done."

As grateful as Fanny was to have her help acknowledged, she felt like her hand was in a perfumed vise. She managed to extricate herself, and was inching away in the opposite direction of Drury, when Humphrey bustled toward her, Annabelle in tow.

"Fanny! I'm glad to see you," he cried, wringing her hand.

Annabelle clung to Humphrey's arm, not unlike a leech, and gave Fanny a victorious smile, as if she'd beaten her at something.

Because she was with Humphrey? Good God, Annabelle was more than welcome to him!

"I can't forgive my brother for what he's done," Humphrey declared. "I never thought he was a bright light, but I never thought he'd do anything so stupid. I'm only shocked he didn't shoot himself. Must have been pure chance he got Albert and devilishly unlucky for the duke."

Although Fanny kept her tone calm, she regarded him as she might a rather unusual kind of rodent. "Would you feel better if Brix had been shot?"

Humphrey blinked, then reddened. "Gad, no! But Brix should have known better. He's a terrible shot—always has been. Couldn't hit a house at ten feet."

Fanny raised a brow. "Obviously he's a better shot than you know."

"But to agree to duel with *Albert*—"

"Albert challenged him, Humphrey. Would you be any happier if he'd begged off? Then you would have told everyone he was a miserable coward. Whatever else you may think of your brother, he's not a coward. As for Albert being unlucky, ask Albert about that the next time you see him."

She stepped closer to Humphrey and, ignoring Annabelle's peeved expression, leaned in to whisper, "A word of warning, Humphrey. I'd stop treating Brix as if he's the village idiot. There's a reason he has the friends he does—and a reason he has so many more friends than you do."

Humphrey's jaw dropped, while Annabelle looked at him as if she feared he might have some sort of attack.

Sir Douglas Drury appeared at her side. "Good evening, my lord, Lady Annabelle." He turned toward Fanny, his dark eyes gleaming. "You look very lovely tonight, Lady Francesca. That color suits you."

Her eyes narrowed. What was he up to? Was this his standard gambit? And if so, why was he trying it after what had happened at Lady Jersey's? Surely he had to realize she did *not* appreciate his attentions. "Good evening, Sir Douglas," she said, her tone cool.

He took hold of her elbow. "Would you excuse us, please? I'd like to have a little chat with Lady Francesca."

Humphrey's eyes widened, and Annabelle looked as if she feared Drury would bite her if they refused.

Although she was taken aback by the request, Fanny didn't protest. There were a few things she'd better say to him, too.

Drury led her toward the French doors. Elizabeth watched their progress like a hawk eyeing a mouse, and she wasn't the only one.

"Are you taking me to the garden, Sir Douglas?" Fanny asked.

"I'd prefer a little privacy." He glanced down at her, reminding her of a wolf in a child's story. "We'll stay on the terrace, in full view of anyone near the doors."

She thought of suggesting they stay inside, except that she didn't want anyone to hear what she had to say, either. As long as they could be seen, it couldn't be too dangerous. "Very well."

Drury opened the door and they stepped outside, into the fresh, cool air. A full moon hung in the sky, shining upon a formal garden.

The barrister didn't offer any comments on the garden, or the evening. He made no preamble at all. Instead, standing beside her, he placed his hands on the stone balustrade and spoke without looking directly at her, as if he was seeing something only he could see. "As you know, I was engaged in espionage in France during the war. I was caught and imprisoned there for a good many months."

He shoved himself off from the balustrade and faced her. His eyes were deep in shadow, but she felt his intense gaze nonetheless. "My lady, being locked up in a very small room for a very long time gives a man plenty of opportunity to think, about what he's done and not done. Happy memories sustain you, and regrets gnaw at you.

"I had one regret that troubled me the most of all, and it was one I've been trying to spare Brix— the realization that you've lost the chance for love and happiness."

Fanny felt as if she was on the back of Edmond's runaway gelding again. She listened, astonished and speechless, as he continued.

"It's long been obvious to me that you two were made and meant for each other," he said, his deep voice soft, yet resolute, "whether Brix was willing to admit it or not. I thought I could make him see that if he persisted in pretending he felt nothing for you because he didn't like everybody telling him that he should, he'd lose you. I was trying to make Brix stop wasting precious time without coming right out and saying what I thought he should do.

"I daresay I should have been completely open and honest about my motives from the beginning, especially considering how terribly my plans have gone awry, but when secrecy has become a way of life, it's difficult to be less so." His deep voice lowered as he regarded her steadily. "Despite my actions, I haven't been trying to make you love me, in any way."

"You haven't?" How conceited that must sound, and yet she certainly felt justified in asking the question. "After that kiss at Lady Jersey's, I believe I could be forgiven for thinking you were."

"Other people were supposed to think I was falling in love with you. I was trying to make Brix jealous, with the hope that he'd finally admit his feelings, to both himself and to you." He looked out over the moonlit garden, his lean features in profile.

Fanny's eyes narrowed. "I thought you were

the jealous one—that's why you wrote the wagers in the book at White's, you said."

"I was being honest about my reasons for that. I just didn't disclose everything. Unfortunately, my clever scheme hasn't worked."

He didn't sound very contrite. He sounded only mildly disappointed, although his actions had made her troubles much worse.

Anger and indignation at his behavior boiled up and over within her. "So instead of telling us what you really thought, instead of suggesting I put a little distance between Brix and myself, or ask his family not to keep suggesting that he marry me, you decided to treat us as if you are a puppet master and we're your marionettes? You pretend to be seriously attracted to me, well enough that most of the *ton*—and my own family—believe it, and that's supposed to make Brix want me, too? You decide to write the wager in the book at White's, believing my humiliation will help me win Brix's affection? For an intelligent man, Sir Douglas, I must say your plan was terrible. It's achieved exactly the opposite of what you claim you intended—if that's really what you were trying to do." She tilted her head and crossed her arms. "Or is this claim of a 'clever scheme' supposed to make *you* feel better? I daresay not many women aren't attracted to you, and you're not used to failure. Perhaps once it became obvious that I was the exception, you decided to assuage your pride by pretending you had no intentions toward me in the first place."

The barrister's eyes flashed like steel glinting in the moonlight. "I told you, I was trying to help, and I'm sorry for the way things have turned out."

"And kissing me was nothing more than part of this ludicrous plan to spur Brix on to a declaration?"

His gaze becoming even more intense, Drury shook his head. "Not precisely. You've a very attractive young woman, Lady Francesca, and I'll gladly confess that if it weren't for Brix, I'd be pursuing you in a way that would leave you breathless."

She backed away a step.

"But Brix has always had your heart, and he has it yet."

At his words, her heart fluttered the way it always did when Brix walked into the room.

But she had to ignore that feeling, and Drury's observations. He'd been wrong about too much to give credence to his opinion now.

"You can see into people's hearts, can you?" she coldly inquired. "You can tell just by looking at me that I still love him?"

"A blind man could see it. And Brix would see it, too, except that he still stubbornly clings to the pride that refuses to comply with his family's notions of what he ought to do.

"But I don't blame him entirely," he continued, stepping forward. She moved back, until she hit the balustrade. "You meet many people in the legal profession, Lady Francesca, and you learn to recognize those who would hide their true natures. That's what you've been doing, and if Brix didn't appreciate your merits before you discovered the wagers, it's not been entirely his fault. You've also had a hand in it, for blindly trying to conform to society's dictates instead of showing the world what you're really like."

"Oh, really? And what am I really like?"

"You're a vivacious, clever, lively woman who wouldn't shirk from confronting the most famous barrister in London when you feel an injustice has been done. Or defending a man who's maligned you, as you did just now." His lips jerked up into a sardonic little smile. "You needn't look so surprised, my lady. I could hear you defend the man for whom you claim to feel nothing across the room. Deny it all you like to me, and even to yourself, but you love him still, with a devotion some men would die to experience for just one day in their lives." He took hold of her shoulders and stared into her face. "Are you willing to let him go, my lady? Is your pride that important to you? Will it hold you in its arms at night? Will it comfort you? Will pride give you joy, or make you laugh?"

She twisted from his grasp. "I have no other choice!" she cried. "He doesn't love me. He told me so himself."

"To your face? He said he didn't love you, and you saw the sincerity of that denial in his eyes, felt it in your own heart?"

She shook her head. "He sent a note."

Drury's laugh was without mirth, and yet it brought a buried hope pulsing back to life. "A note? Oh, my lady, did it not occur to you that he had to do that because he didn't trust himself to lie to you in person?"

She leaned back against the balustrade for support. "You think he loves me?"

"You've just given me all the evidence I need to believe it," he said with such conviction, she could believe it, too.

She gave up trying to deny it, and let her hope break free.

He loved her. She loved him. But she was in London, and he was not.

"Oh, God, what should I do?" she murmured, thinking aloud in her dismay.

Drury shrugged his broad shoulders. "That, my lady, I leave up to you. I'm giving up interfering in other people's love lives. The outcomes are too uncertain. Now I'd better get back to the party before people assume we're doing more than talking."

"Yes, yes, of course," she muttered, still too wrapped up in her thoughts and her burgeoning hope to pay attention to his words, or his departure, or worry about what the *ton* might think of her.

She turned and looked up at the moon and its ageless face.

Drury was right. Her pride wouldn't comfort her or make her laugh. Winning the wagers wouldn't make her happy.

It was time for one last, desperate gamble.

* * *

Waving a letter, the earl of Parthington strode into the library, where Brix had carved himself out a space to work on account books and tenant requests. For one brief instant, Brix allowed himself to wonder if the letter was for him. He didn't expect Edmond or Drury to write, but he'd had hopes that Buggy might, and tell him what was going on in London.

Unless he'd gotten all the funding he needed for his expedition, and was too busy preparing for it.

His father pushed one of the hounds off a chair and threw himself into it, then dashed Brix's half-hearted hope. "Well, Brixton, your brother's engaged at last."

Brix pretended to be intently studying the page of figures before him. But surely Fanny hadn't . . . she wouldn't . . . it had to be Drury who won her.

"Didn't you hear me? I said Humphrey's engaged."

Brix raised his head. "Who's the lucky girl?"

"Some chit named Annabelle Dalyrimple."

Brix almost went limp with relief, then commanded himself to get a grip. Of course Fanny wouldn't accept Humphrey, and that proved she'd been friendly with his brother only to upset him. "Lady Annabelle's the daughter of the sixth earl of Belden."

"Really?" his father exclaimed, examining the letter again. "He doesn't say that. Just that she's agreed to be his wife. Seems quite tickled about it, actually."

"Annabelle is a very lovely young lady."

His father frowned. "A beauty, eh? That could be trouble."

Brix shrugged. "That's Humphrey's lookout, not mine."

The earl glanced at the letter again. "And what's this about a wager you made?"

Damn Humphrey, Brix thought as he got to his feet.

"He says the time's nearly up," his father continued as he perused the letter, "and people are saying you ran away rather than risk losing." He glanced up at his rapidly approaching son. "I thought you said you left London because of the duel with Albèrt."

"May I see the letter?" Brix asked as he snatched it out of his father's hand without waiting for an answer. He scanned the contents quickly.

Mercifully Humphrey hadn't gone into any details, or mentioned Fanny's name . . . until the very end.

Albert's convinced Fanny Epping's going to marry that lawyer, Drury, he read. *He's thrilled.*

Brix started for the doors that led out to the garden.

"Where are you going?" his father demanded. "We should have a drink to celebrate your brother's engagement."

"Later, Father."

Once outside, Brix strode across the terrace and

down the formal garden path. He didn't know exactly where he was going, nor did he care. He just wanted to be away from his jubilant father.

At least Fanny wasn't marrying Humphrey. That would have been completely unbearable. Whereas Drury . . . He was rich, titled, successful. Fanny deserved a husband like that, not a jester good only for amusing people.

Oh, yes, he had his factories where he was trying to be a humane employer, and yes, his father's tenants came to him with their problems, but his accomplishments were minor compared to those of Drury and Buggy and Charlie and Edmond, whose wife wasn't the only successful writer in the family.

Brix halted by the yew hedge and stared at the wood beyond the sheep grazing on the lawn, imagining his future.

A future without Fanny.

She wouldn't be waiting anxiously for him in foyers and doorways anymore, making him feel as important as a king. She wouldn't be watching him with her shining eyes, smiling shyly. She wouldn't need him to comfort her sorrows, or to try to make her laugh, a sound that made *him* happier than she would ever know.

She'd never kiss him again or let him kiss her. She'd never rouse him to heights of passion and desire such as he'd never experienced before, and probably never would again.

He envisioned a life without Fanny making

him feel he was worth something, as if even a jester, good only to make people laugh, could be important, too.

A scent wafted to him on the breeze.

Roses, from his mother's rose garden, where he'd kissed Fanny that very first time. Where he'd first felt desire. Where he'd first fallen in love.

Crumpling the letter he still held in his hand, he turned on his heel and strode into the house.

Chapter 15

London, the fourteenth of June, 1819

Dear Aunt Euphenia,

To think it's been six weeks since my dear boy was baptized! Where does the time go? You were right to tell me to enjoy these precious hours, because I can see that all too soon, little D'Arcy won't be a baby anymore.

You'll also realize, I'm sure, that today marks the end of the term of Brix and Fanny's wager. Edmond and I were talking about it at breakfast before going to church, and you can imagine our surprise when the duke of Hetley appeared, quite frantic, looking for Fanny. She'd left the duke's home sometime before dawn. Again. When he realized she wasn't with us, the duke proposed that she'd gone to Sir Douglas Drury. I didn't think so, and had another optimistic hope, but decided it wouldn't be prudent to mention it.

The duke declared his intention to go to Drury's chambers, and it was obvious he hoped Edmond would go with him. I think he didn't want to confront Drury alone. I would have liked to go with them, but little D'Arcy required my attention, so I remained at home.

Edmond returned a short time later. Fanny wasn't there, and Drury was quite offended that anybody would think he would entertain a young lady in his chambers.

Given his reception, the duke didn't linger. He decided to go to the Bow Street Runners. Drury then confided to Edmond that he thought he might have some idea about where Fanny had gone—Medway Manor.

Oh, Aunt Euphenia, am I wrong to hope that Drury's right, despite what Brix has done? Or am I just incurably romantic and want to see Fanny win the man she's loved so devotedly for so long? And who, if anyone were to ask my opinion, loves her, too, in spite of all his denials?

I can almost see your skeptical expression, Aunt Euphenia, but you haven't watched him when he's with her. I have. And I must tell you, Edmond agrees with me. If anybody knows Brix well (besides Fanny), he does.

Lady Diana Westover Terrington

L ate in the afternoon, Brix galloped through the high-arched gate in the wall surrounding the courtyard of the Saracen's Head in Upper Dropples, the town at the halfway point between Medway Manor to the north and London to the south. Stables and storerooms lined three sides of the yard; the two-storied, half-timbered inn made up the fourth side. Chickens scratched in a patch of dirt near the well, and straw spilled out of one of the lofts. Smoke rose from the kitchen chimney at the back of the tavern.

Steering his mount around the cumbersome coach that was having its horses changed, Brix brought his sweat-slicked horse to a halt so abruptly, it sat back on his haunches. The animal's flanks, like Brix's boots and breeches, were splattered with mud from galloping along country roads.

One of the stableboys, recognizing Brix from his previous stops on journeys between London and his family's estate, immediately abandoned the large horses being harnessed to the coach and hurried to take hold of the gelding's bridle.

"Ah, Freddie!" Brix cried as he swung down from the saddle. "I need a fresh horse at once. And take good care of this one. My father paid a small fortune for him."

Brix reached into his blue coat and threw the lad a sovereign as shiny as his brass buttons. "Quick as can be, my boy. I've got to get to London without delay."

"It'll be dark soon, sir," Freddie noted as he pocketed the coin.

"Makes no different," Brix said with a dismissive wave as he strode toward the inn. "I've got business that can't wait."

He walked into the Saracen Head's familiar taproom, redolent of sawdust, ale, sweat and roast beef. The small mullioned windows didn't allow for much natural light, so there was, as always, a fire kindled in the enormous hearth that took up one whole wall. Trestle tables had been set up for meals, with benches for seating, and an ancient oak settle stood beside the fireplace, as it had ever since Brix could remember.

The coach passengers, judging by their hats and cloaks, and some local farmers, judging by their smocks, were seated around the scarred oaken tables, finishing a meal of meat pies slathered in thick gravy, bread and ale.

"Johnson, some wine and a loaf of bread, if you please!" Brix called out to the innkeeper as he continued toward a table. "I'm in a hurry."

One of the women, who was wearing a violet pelisse and a straw bonnet, and was seated by herself at a table near the hearth, suddenly raised her head. The action caught Brix's attention— then he came to a dead halt and stared as if seeing a heavenly vision. "*Fanny?*"

She half rose. "*Brix?*"

He took a tentative step forward. "What are you doing here?"

She finished standing and regarded Brix steadily, her hands clasped. "What are *you*?"

Brix took off his hat, ran his hand through his hair, disheveling it even more, and walked slowly toward her. "I'm on my way back to London. I was coming to see you."

Despite his words, Brix could read nothing in her face as he continued toward her, his footfalls muffled by the layer of sawdust. "It's been six weeks," he said.

She nodded, her cheeks blooming with the pink of a blush as she stepped away from the bench and table. "I know."

He reached her and looked into her beautiful, inscrutable face.

Then he went down on one knee and took her gloved hand in his. The time had come to confess and admit everything. With complete, heartfelt sincerity, and not a hint of humor.

"Fanny," he began, "I've been a selfish, stupid, stubborn fool. I've treated you terribly. I was as cruel and thoughtless and mean as Albert and Humphrey ever were, and I'm thoroughly ashamed of myself. I should never have ridiculed and denounced your affection. I've publicly humiliated you, and I can understand if you hate me. If you tell me to go and never speak to you again, I won't protest. But I can't let another day, or hour, or minute go by without telling you how I really feel about you. How I've felt for a long time, but didn't want to admit, not even to myself."

He pressed a kiss to the back of her hand, then gazed up into her limpid blue eyes. "I love you, Fanny Epping. I've loved you since I was twelve years old and kissed you in my mother's rose garden. I love you so much, it terrified me. What have I to offer you, after all, but a jester's devotion?

"But I've realized that I'm more terrified of finding out that in spite of everything, you love me still, and I let you go. I love you with all my foolish heart, Fanny Epping, and I'll never care for any woman as I do for you."

He took her other hand and held them both in his own, which had grown cold with fear as she silently listened. He might be wrong to think her being here meant she still cared for him. Perhaps she was on her way north for quite another reason.

Nevertheless, the time had come, and he would accept her answer, whatever it was. "Lady Francesca Cecilia Epping, is it possible . . . dare I hope . . . could you even consider the possibility that you might marry me?"

Her expression still told him nothing. "If I say no, will I break your heart?"

Oh, God. He'd been wrong.

Fool. Stupid fool, to have thrown away his chance for happiness with those damn wagers.

Whatever he felt, whatever he thought, she deserved to enjoy her victory, after all that he had done. "Yes, Fanny," he admitted. "You'll break my heart completely and win our wager without question."

"I have something to tell you, Brix," she solemnly said. Then a smile more brilliant, more joyful, more wonderful than any he had ever seen, blossomed on her face and she pulled him to his feet, "I'll gladly marry you!"

"You will?" he gasped, hardly daring to believe his ears.

Laughing, her eyes sparkling with happiness, she cupped his face between her gloved hands. "I love you, Brixton Smythe-Medway, and I want to

be your wife. I was on my way to Medway Manor
to tell you I still love you."

"Oh, Fanny," he whispered, intently studying
her lovely face. "Do you mean it? Do you really
mean it?"

"I mean it, with all my heart."

As joy, relief and gratitude overwhelmed him,
he pulled her into his arms and held her tightly,
aware of how very close he'd come to losing her
forever.

"I convinced myself that what you felt for me
was just a lingering affection from our childhood," he whispered. "That your love wasn't really love at all, but an infatuation that wasn't
going to last. I thought that one day, you'd wake
up and wonder what you ever saw in me. So I pretended your attention annoyed me. That you
were a nuisance. That you were just little Fanny
Epping playing a troublesome game. I was afraid
that if I let myself love you, if you got close to me
again, the way we were as children, you'd discover I wasn't worthy of that devotion."

He drew back and looked down into her eyes,
and gave voice to the doubts and fears that had
haunted him for so long. "I don't deserve you,
Fanny. You do know that, don't you? I'm not particularly clever, or accomplished, or famous—"

She covered his lips with the palm of her hand
and shook her head. "I won't hear a word against
the man I love, not even from the man I love. Oh,
Brix, I didn't fall in love with you because I thought
you were clever—although you are. And I don't

care a fig for fame. I fell in love with you because you're good and kind and generous. Because you comforted and listened to me when I was upset."

She smiled tenderly. "Do you think making people feel better and helping to ease their burdens isn't an accomplishment? I assure you, it is, and one I value far above fame and ambition and glory. A person may do one great deed and be lauded by society as a hero, but a person who does many smaller deeds, known only to those he helps, is just as great and deserving of respect and admiration to me.

"You have a rare and wonderful gift, Brix—one others recognize and appreciate. You make people happy. Everybody feels better when they're with you." She put her hands on his shoulders and tipped forward to brush her lips across his. "Who wouldn't want to be married to somebody like that?"

One hand around her waist, Brix swiped his hand across his eyes and smiled tremulously. "You'd better stop it, Fanny, or I'll be become so vain, I'll be insufferable."

"You'd better get used to being complimented and told how much you're appreciated, my love," she said, caressing his cheek. "You're owed much in that regard, and I'm going to do my best to make up for it, every day of my life."

"And I'll do my best to make certain you never regret marrying me, every day of my life."

Someone cleared his throat. Loudly.

Startled into remembering they weren't alone,

they both turned to see the landlord, a brawny fellow in homespun and a stained apron, standing near the door. "Coach is leavin'," he announced.

The other passengers began to head out the door, and more than one looked back over their shoulder as if reluctant to go. The farmers went back to their meal, although they exchanged wry glances and smiles.

"Ah, Johnson, my good man," Brix said, loosening his hold on Fanny, but keeping one arm about her slender waist. "Please have Lady Francesca's baggage brought back. She'll be returning to London with me."

"If you say so, sir," Johnson said, a hint of wariness in his hazel eyes. "Lady Francesca, is it?"

Brix laughed, then winked at Fanny. "I fear the good Mr. Johnson has his doubts about your identity, my lady. I believe I can guess where the confusion set in. Were you traveling alone?"

She flushed, looking so pretty, he had to tighten his embrace. "I didn't want anybody to know where I was going."

"Ah, there it is, then, just as I suspected," Brix said. "Mr. Johnson, surely you know Lady Francesca Cecilia Epping, the sister of the duke of Hetley, who's visited Medway Manor before. She's just agreed to be my wife."

As a look of recognition dawned, along with a blush, the brawny innkeeper mumbled an apology, then his congratulations and best wishes.

"In fact, to celebrate my joy, I believe a round for the house is in order," Brix declared.

That made the landlord smile, exposing several gaps where his missing teeth should be. "With pleasure, sir," he cried as the farmers called out their congratulatory remarks and touched their forelocks in appreciation.

Brix nodded at a table apart from the others, near one of the windows. "There's a table in the corner that's a little more private," he said to Fanny. "Shall we sit and apologize and declare our love some more?"

"Absolutely." Her eyes twinkled with happiness, and something else that made him remember being in the theater property room. Vividly.

"I believe you're owed several compliments, too," he said as he led her there. "A few years' worth, in fact. I think I'll start by saying how beautiful you looked in that pale pink gown."

"Then I should tell you how marvelous you always look in evening dress."

"Really?" he said, as pleased as a boy as he pulled her onto his lap.

"I also especially like your hair," she said as she wrapped her arms about his neck and kissed him on the cheek, "and I don't want Ramsbottom to ever try to get it to lie flat."

"I like *your* hair," he murmured, trailing his lips along her cheek. "I can hardly wait to see it spread upon the pillow, like a halo."

Her breathing quickened as she turned her head to capture his mouth.

"I can hardly wait to get you in my bed," he

whispered as they kissed and nipped and tasted and touched. "I've been dreaming about it for weeks."

"I've been dreaming about it for years."

Mr. Johnson, busily handing out mugs of ale, glanced in their direction and cleared his throat again. A frown creased his broad brow before his customers called for his attention.

Brix frowned with mock dismay. "We'd better not kiss anymore, at least not here, or poor Mr. Johnson will be utterly scandalized."

"We couldn't have that," Fanny solemnly agreed. "Still, it seems a pity we have to behave ourselves when we're so far from London." She brushed a lock of his hair from his forehead. "The coach doesn't come until the morning."

Brix's eyes widened and, as his body responded to the notion of spending the night upstairs with Fanny, his incredulity at what she said wasn't feigned. "My dear young woman, what are you suggesting?"

She looked down as if suddenly bashful, her dark lashes fanning across her cheeks, while she toyed with the end of his cravat. "What did you think I was suggesting?"

"Given your behavior recently, the mind boggles." He shifted and told himself to control his desire, until they were married.

Glorious, wondrous thought!

"I'm determined to behave in a gentlemanly manner," he continued with mock severity, "no matter how difficult that may be under the circumstances and in view of your outrageous, brazen innuendoes. I don't want Albert challenging me to a duel again."

"I don't think you need worry about *that*." She sighed with resignation. "But if you insist." Then she smiled gloriously. "I didn't expect anything else. You're too honorable."

"Fanny Epping, was that some sort of test?"

"No," she gravely replied. "I'm very tempted to spend the night with you. But you're right. We shouldn't. We should wait for our wedding night. If we can."

She smiled so seductively, he nearly picked her up and carried her upstairs right then and there, and regardless of what Mr. Johnson might say. "I sincerely hope you don't want a long engagement," he muttered.

"After waiting for you to ask me to marry you since I was twelve years old?" she exclaimed, her eyes dancing. "Certainly not!"

"I don't need your brother's permission or anything?"

She caressed his cheek. "No. I'm of legal age, and there's nothing else to stop me from marrying whom I wish. Indeed, Brix, I think my mother would approve, if she were alive. She always liked you. And I can't wait to tell Diana and Edmond."

She frowned, and he wanted to press his lips to the little wrinkle of worry that appeared between her brows to ease it away. "What's wrong?"

"I hope you can be friends with Edmond again."

"I hope so, too, and I'll apologize and make amends or do whatever else is called for. He was right about the wagers and the trouble they'd bring us. I should have listened to him from the start, and I'm certainly willing to say so." He pressed another kiss to her fingertips. "It's been awful thinking everybody I cared most for in the world hated me."

"I don't think they hate you. But you were acting so . . . so . . ."

"Foolishly? Stupidly? Like a dunderheaded idiot?"

"Different."

"So were you."

"I was really being myself, Brix. I stopped pretending to be what the *ton* wanted me to be. What I foolishly thought you'd want me to be. I was being the real Fanny Epping." She looked at him as if she was afraid that would upset him.

"Well, thank God," he said firmly, meaning it. "I suppose it's time we both stopped pretending so much."

She smiled with relief. "Drury said I should have stopped pretending years ago. He's a very wise man."

Brix cocked his head and frowned. "Since you mention Drury, what exactly has been going on between you two? Humphrey seemed to be under the impression you were about to get married."

"Drury thought jealousy might inspire you to declare your love for me."

Brix was both relieved, and a little annoyed.

"Good God." Then, because all had turned out well in the end, he grinned. "It worked. Well, in a way," he amended. "Humphrey wrote Father that you two were as good as engaged. That's when I realized that I couldn't give you up without admitting how I really felt. I had to confess I loved you, come what may."

She nestled against him. "Then I regret I was so annoyed with Drury when he told me about his plan."

"I'm sure he'll get over it," Brix replied as he wrapped his arms about her. "I don't think you're the first woman to get angry with him, and I doubt you'll be the last. Speaking of anger, Albert won't be happy when he hears about this. Does he have any idea where you've gone?"

She shook her head. "I thought about leaving a note," she admitted, "but I was afraid he'd come after me and try to stop me if he knew."

"I daresay he would," Brix agreed. "Well, we'll get back as quickly as we can and set his mind at ease, about your whereabouts, anyway."

"He'll simply have to accept that we're going to be married," she said, resolute.

Brix's eyes twinkled impishly. "I can't wait to see the look on his face when he finds out you agreed to marry me."

Fanny laughed and looked up into her beloved's face. "Neither can I."

Reclining on the Grecian couch in the drawing room, Elizabeth raised herself on her elbow as her husband, with his injured arm in a sling, marched into the room. "What did they say, my dear?" she asked anxiously.

Albert threw himself into one of the chairs. "They've discovered she took a coach north yesterday morning, toward Lincoln."

"By *herself*?" Elizabeth couldn't have looked more horrified if the Bow Street Runners had found Fanny's body on the banks of the Thames.

"Yes." Albert scowled. "You know what this means, don't you? She's chasing after him again."

Too agitated to sit still, he got to his feet. "What is it about that wastrel? She ought to have more sense. More dignity. More respect for the family name. But no, she goes haring after *Smythe-Medway*, of all men. Gad, I'd just as soon she married my groom."

"Too late!" Brix cried.

His mouth agape, Albert whirled around to discover Brix and Fanny on the threshold of the golden drawing room.

For a moment, Fanny had a moment's sympathy for her brother. He was about to be sorely disappointed.

"Congratulations, Albert," Brix continued as Albert and Elizabeth stared at them, gaping like codfish. "I'm going to be your brother-in-law."

Albert felt for the chair and sat heavily.

"It's true," Fanny confirmed, clinging to Brix. "Brix and I are going to be married, just as soon as the banns can be read."

"But you—but he—" Albert stammered.

Elizabeth suddenly shot to her feet as if somebody'd lit a fire under the couch. She ran to Fanny and, to Fanny's astonishment, threw her arms around her and started to sob.

"I've been so worried about you!" she wailed. "I'm so glad you're safe!"

Feeling rather guilty for running away this time, Fanny patted her on the back. "There, there, I'm fine." She gave Brix a remorseful look. "Perhaps I should have left a note."

"Damn right you should have," Albert said as he, too, rose. "We've been worried sick. And then you waltz in here and announce you're marrying this . . . *this* . . ."

Giving his future brother-in-law a wicked grin, Brix slowly crossed his arms. "Do go on, Albert."

His face reddening, Albert coughed. "This, um, gentleman."

"I'm sorry, Albert," Fanny said contritely while Elizabeth continued to sob on her shoulder. "Elizabeth, let's sit down, shall we?"

Sniffling, her sister-in-law let go and tottered to the couch, where she collapsed. Fanny moved her aching shoulder back and forth.

Albert assumed a pompous stance. "Now see here, Smythe-Medway, regardless of that misunderstanding about the pistols—"

"Albert, I really think you shouldn't offer any objections," Fanny said evenly as she joined Elizabeth on the couch. "Not after Brix and I spent last night in an inn."

Albert gasped. Elizabeth stopped weeping and

regarded Fanny and Brix with wide eyes. "To-gether?" she whispered.

"Not exactly," Fanny said, taking her hand. "But the *ton* won't care about the details, will they?"

"Buck up, Albert, old son!" Brix exclaimed, striding toward her brother and slapping him on the shoulder of his uninjured arm. "No need to look so scandalized. We haven't made love or anything—yet. I can wait for the wedding night." He gave Fanny a look that made her blush to the soles of her feet before addressing Albert again. "As Fanny points out, though, other people won't be inclined to believe that nothing happened. You know how the *ton* loves to gossip. So you'd better get it into your head that Fanny and I are going to be married, and there's nothing you can do about it. Isn't that right, Fanny, my love?"

"Absolutely," she declared. "Now that I've got the Honorable Brixton Smythe-Medway at last, I don't intend to let him go."

"Let them marry, Albert," Elizabeth pleaded, obviously not comprehending that they hadn't come there to ask the duke's permission. "She must love him a great deal."

"I do," Fanny stoutly averred. She rose and put her arm around Brix. "And he loves me, so we're going to get married and live happily ever after. Isn't that right, Mr. Smythe-Medway?"

"Absolutely, Lady Francesca."

"Oh, go ahead!" Albert declared with a wave of his hand. "I have no objections.

"I thought you'd see it our way," Brix said

smugly. He smiled down at Fanny. "Shall we, my love?"

"Yes, let's."

They turned toward the door.

"Where are you going now?" Albert demanded.

Fanny smiled. "To tell Diana and Edmond our good news, of course."

After they gaily marched out of the drawing room, Elizabeth hurried to her husband's side. "It's all right, my dear," she said soothingly. "Nobody will blame *you*."

One look at Fanny's face as she stood in the door of the nursery was all Diana needed.

"Oh, Fanny!" she cried as she held D'Arcy against her shoulder, rubbing his back to get him to burp. "Did he—?"

Brix appeared behind Fanny and put his hands lightly on her shoulders.

"He did! He does!" Diana cried, startling her infant son and making him cry.

"Oh, dear," Fanny exclaimed, both laughing and crying with joy as she hurried into the room. "We've upset the baby."

"Here, let me take the little fellow," Brix said, striding toward Diana and gently removing him from her shoulder. "If I'm going to be married, I'd better learn how to handle a little bundle of mortality, don't you think?"

"Like this," Diana said, showing him how to hold the baby.

"Gad, more wriggly than a puppy," Brix muttered as he strolled toward the window, the baby in his arms. "I had no idea."

Fanny grasped Diana's hands and smiled. "We're going to be married, just as soon as the banns can be read."

"I'm so happy for you!" Diana exclaimed, embracing her. "I know you'll be very happy together." She drew back and smiled warmly. "Maybe even as happy as Edmond and I."

"I say, Diana? Is the little fellow supposed to smell like this?" Brix called out dubiously.

The baby seemed to sense an insult, for he began to wail.

"Here, let me take him," Diana said, going to them. "Why don't you both go downstairs to the morning room. I'll have the nursery maid tend to D'Arcy and I'll join you there."

Edmond appeared at the door. "Ruttles said—" He fell silent when he saw Brix. His gaze quickly swept over the rest of the room. "Is there something I should know about?"

Brix strode up to him and thrust out his hand. "Congratulate me, Edmond. I've persuaded Fanny to marry me."

Edmond gravely shook his hand. Then real comprehension hit. "Good God!" Grinning, he began to shake Brix's hand as vigorously as if it were a pump handle. "Congratulations! About bloody time, too!"

"Edmond, you really ought to watch your language around the baby," Brix said as sternly as a judge.

"He's already an authority on children, you see," Fanny observed with a merry smile. "Even though he hasn't had any."

"*Yet*," Brix noted. He gave Fanny a very wolfish grin. "I intend to have several."

Fanny swallowed hard. It would be at least three weeks before they could be married. It felt like forever.

"Let me get the maid, and we can all go to the morning room. I want to hear exactly how this happy event came about," Diana said.

"All will be revealed—well, perhaps not *all*," Brix replied, giving Fanny a wink. "The pertinent details anyway, as long as you promise not to turn it into a novel."

"I wouldn't dream of it," Diana protested. "I much prefer making up my own plots, thank you."

"Come along, you two," Edmond said, ushering Fanny and Brix to the door. "The sooner we leave, the sooner she'll join us. I speak from long experience."

"You'll be my best man, won't you, Edmond?" Brix asked as they walked toward the carpeted staircase.

"Of course," he jovially replied.

"I'm going to ask Diana to be my matron of honor," Fanny said as they went down the steps.

"I'm sure she'll be delighted," Edmond replied. He spied his butler in the foyer. "Champagne to the morning room, Ruttles, if you please. And in the servants' hall this evening, too. We're having a little celebration. My friends are getting married."

"Yes, my lord," the butler intoned, his expression just as stony as ever. "I realized something of that nature must be afoot when Mr. Smythe-Medway neglected to throw his hat at me because he was too busy kissing Lady Francesca."

Then he smiled.

"Are you sure this is absolutely necessary?" Fanny asked that night as she gathered the skirt of her pink silk dress in her free hand while Brix, firmly grasping the other, led her up the steps to the musicians' gallery in Almack's.

"I embarrassed you in a public manner, and now I'm going to announce that I've lost the wager in a public manner," he declared. "You don't have to come with me if you'd rather not—"

"Oh, no! I'm not about to leave you completely to your own devices when it comes to something like this," Fanny interrupted. "Goodness knows what you'll say otherwise. My mind boggles."

His only answer to that was a boisterous, infectious laugh.

They reached the door that opened into the gallery that overlooked the main ballroom. Brix surveyed her as he put his hand on the latch. "Have I told you how beautiful you are?"

"It must be this dress."

"Dress be damned! It's *you*," he said as he bussed her heartily on the cheek. Then he gave her a roguish wink. "I take that back. I like that dress. Indeed, if it were up to me, I'd have you wear a wedding gown of pale pink silk."

"I'll take that suggestion under advisement," she said, smiling to herself. She'd already decided she would have no color but that for her wedding day.

Brix opened the door and stepped onto the small balcony. "Excuse me, gentlemen," he said to the startled musicians, who stopped playing midbar.

He walked right up to the balustrade and looked out over the assembly as if he were the captain on the deck of a ship about to issue orders.

Hovering in the back, Fanny craned to see the curious, confused faces below. She quickly spotted Albert and Elizabeth, who were deep in conversation with Annabelle Dalyrimple, her mouth open in shock. Humphrey was beside his fiancée, and he looked just as taken aback.

"Ladies and gentleman!" Brix began, his voice easily carrying to the far reaches of the ballroom. "If I could have your attention, please."

He waited for the murmur of voices to die down.

"As many of you are aware, I have made a wager with Lady Francesca Cecilia Epping, regarding the state of my heart. If she was able to break it within six weeks, she would win, and I would be the loser. I must now reveal that I have lost the wager. The lady does indeed have the power to break my heart."

Fanny could see that he was enjoying himself immensely, and couldn't resist joining him.

"As gracious as Mr. Smythe-Medway is in defeat," she announced, "I think we must declare it a tie. Mr. Smythe-Medway has the power to break my heart, too."

Brix smiled at her and reached for her hand, giving it a squeeze. "Fortunately, it seems neither of our hearts must be broken, for Lady Francesca has graciously consented to be my wife."

Then, to her shock, amazement and undeniable pleasure, he tugged her into his arms and kissed her, with a passion that made her weak at the knees. His strong arms held her close, and his mouth moved with slow, delicious, delightful leisure over hers. Her lips parted, and his tongue slipped between them.

He pulled back and smiled at her. "Tit for tat, my darling," he whispered as the noise of excited, scandalized conversation wafted up to them.

She gave him an innocent, wide-eyed look. "I thought you said that was a French kiss."

A liveried footman appeared at the door, his demeanor grave. "Lady Jersey requests that you leave Almack's at once, sir," he declared.

"Oh dear, we'll probably be banned for life," Brix said as they followed him.

"I don't care if we never come here again," Fanny replied, meaning it. "I'd rather spend every night at home with you."

"You, my love, are a brazen temptress. And to

think I was once so mistaken as to call you mousy.
I must have been out of my mind."

News of the forthcoming wedding of the Honorable Brixton Smythe-Medway to Lady Francesca Cecelia Epping quickly made the rounds of
the clubs, assembly rooms and gaming tables.

When the earl of Clydesbrook heard about it,
he laughed, wheezed, shook his head, and said to
the marquis of Maryberry, "That man's going a
long way to win a wager."

"He's welcome to her," Lord Strunk sneered
when he learned of the impending nuptials at a
boxing match.

"Hope she hits him with that bag," Dickie Clutterbuck muttered before passing out.

Buggy immediately rushed over to Brix's town
house to offer his congratulations and decided to
name the first unclassified spider he discovered in
the Amazon after them, provided he got enough
funding to mount his expedition.

Alone in his chambers, Sir Douglas Drury
raised his glass in a solitary toast to the happy
couple, and sat staring at the coals glowing in his
hearth long into the night.

Brix's mother arrived in London a week before
the wedding in a flurry of feathers and perfume.
She kissed her son on both cheeks and said, "I
knew you'd see the advantages of marrying
Fanny eventually. She really is a sweet little thing.
Now let's have tea. I want to hear all about it. Oh,

but first you aren't going to believe what I've just learned about the son of the earl of Byewater."

His father sent a note.

Good for you. Sensible girl. Will be in Town for the wedding. Shot anybody else lately?

Chapter 16

London, the eleventh of July, 1819

Dear Aunt Euphenia,

The wedding was wonderful, and I only cried a little when Brix and Fanny exchanged their vows. Although I'm fortunate to have an understanding of how they feel, given my love for Edmond, I do wish I could properly describe their expressions as they looked at one another and plighted their troth. And their kiss . . . well, I feared more than one young lady in attendance was going to swoon.

Lady Diana Westover Terrington

"**B**rix, put me down."

"I will not. I intend to carry you over the threshold in the very best Roman manner."

Her arms around Brix's neck, Fanny laughed, even as she gripped him tighter. "But you've already carried me over the threshold," she protested as he continued up the curving staircase of his town house.

359

"Of the front door, not our bedroom," Brix explained, barely winded.

Fanny decided it was pointless to protest any further, and truth be told, was excited being in his arms this way.

Nevertheless, she affected a grave demeanor. "What will the servants think?"

"I've given them all the night off and sent them to the theater. They won't be back for hours." He waggled his blond brows. "I thought you'd prefer that we be all alone."

She couldn't deny that, and she told herself there was no need to be nervous. Diana had confided that her wedding night surely would be wonderful, given how much they loved each other.

Still, it was a little . . . disconcerting . . . to think about what was actually going to happen.

At the top of the stairs, Brix put his shoulder against the first door on the left, pushed it open and stepped into the chamber illuminated by several candles.

"Oh, Brix!" Fanny gasped, her anxiety forgotten as she slipped slowly to the ground.

The room was full of roses. Pink roses of every possible hue were in vases on the dressing table, the bedside tables, the windowsills, the dresser, the floor. There were even dark pink rose petals scattered on the white satin coverlet of the wide canopied bed. The scent filled the air, instantly reminding her of the rose garden all those years ago.

Brix took her hand and led her to the center of the room. "Do you like it?"

Delighted, impressed, she turned around in a complete circle. "Oh, Brix, it's like being in a candlelit garden. But I should have expected something like this from you."

He grinned like a mischievous boy. "Except that you didn't, and that's the beauty of it, you see." He loosely embraced her around the waist. "I'm going to enjoy surprising you, Fanny. You look so delectable when I do. Only good surprises, though, from now on. I give you my word."

"And I won't listen at doors," she promised.

He kissed her lightly, his lips barely caressing hers, yet still titillating and making her heartbeat race. "And no more wagers," he vowed.

"No?" she purred as she ran her hands up her husband's chest.

He watched her slender fingers travel over his shirt, the gleam in his eyes exciting her even more. "Were you planning on making one?"

He made her feel as beautiful and seductive as Salome, and she dropped her voice to a sultry whisper. "As a matter of fact, I am."

She moved away toward the dressing table and slowly took off her wedding bonnet and veil.

He didn't stir as he watched her unpin her hair. Aroused by his silent, unwavering scrutiny, she took her time, until her chestnut brown tresses fell loose over her pale pink wedding gown.

"What sort of wager did you have in mind, Fanny?" he asked when she was done.

She gave him a coy glance over her shoulder. "Come here and help me with my gown, and I'll tell you."

"Gladly," he said, and he immediately did as she asked.

She held her hair up to expose the hooks at the top of the back of her bodice. He started to undo them, pressing a kiss to the bare nape of her neck.

His action sent a delicious shiver through her body, and she leaned back a little. "Impatient, Brix?" she asked, her breathing quickening.

"A little."

As he continued and the bodice loosened, she held it to her breasts, resisting the urge to arch back. "I've waited a very long time for this night, you know, and I intend to thoroughly enjoy it," she said.

"Is that what the wager's about?"

"Yes," she affirmed, then she sighed as his mouth continued its delicate, torturous travels while he finished undoing her gown.

She turned toward him. Then, keeping her gaze on his face, she let go of her bodice. As her gown fell in a whisper of silk to puddle at her feet, she watched the play of muscles around his mouth and the growing gleam of desire in his green eyes.

Standing before him clad only in her undergarments, she supposed she ought to feel some sort of maidenly modesty, but she didn't. For one thing, she was still quite well covered. For another, she wantonly wanted to see *him* undressed. *Completely* undressed.

"I'm not an expert in such matters," she said as she stepped out of her gown and picked it up to lay it over the back of the nearest chair, "but I understand that it isn't only men who experience . . ."

She hesitated, wondering just how brazen she ought to be, wedding night or not. "Well, who achieve a certain . . ."

"A certain . . . ?" Brix murmured as he ran his hungry gaze over her.

"Diana called it an orgasm."

Brix's mouth gaped as his eyes widened. He hadn't looked this surprised since that day in Edmond's study when she'd made her impetuous bet. "A . . . *what*?"

"Isn't that what it's called?" Fanny asked, her brow furrowing.

She was fairly certain she'd remembered the word correctly. She was also quite sure, from Diana's description, that it was the same incredible feeling she'd had in the property room of the theater, although she hadn't said so to her friend. If it was, she could hardly wait to experience that sensation again.

Brix's amazement gave way to a slow smile. "I believe orgasm is the technical term, yes."

She strolled toward the bed. "Buggy would know. We could go and ask him."

"I'm not about to run out and ask Buggy to clarify," Brix declared—then he realized Fanny was teasing.

"You little minx," he growled before running after her and pulling her into his arms to kiss her.

Desire replaced her merriment. Need replaced joy, and she had no more wish to tease, or delay. Her pulse pounded, and urgency spurred her on. Her lips still on his, she shoved off his jacket and attacked his cravat.

Panting, he broke the kiss and caught hold of her hands. "What about that wager?"

"It's not important," she replied, gazing up at him, loving every disheveled lock of hair on his head and begrudging the interruption.

"I want to know what you had in mind."

"For some reason, it keeps slipping my mind." She raised herself on her toes and pressed her lips to his. "It's your kisses. They're very distracting."

"I'll have to remember that," he said as he toyed with the end of the ribbon that ran through the neck of her chemise. "Now what were you saying about a wager?"

She took hold of his cravat and drew it off, then tossed it aside. "I'm willing to wager that you'll have one first."

His head bowed so that she couldn't see his face, he started to undo the hook at the top of her corset. "The first what?"

"Orgasm."

He instantly raised his eyes to look at her, and they glittered with desire, and promise. "So if I do, I lose?"

She nodded.

"Although that's a wager I won't mind losing, I'll warn you, Fanny. I'm going to do my very best to win."

She swallowed hard as he left her to sit on the end of his bed. He patted a place beside him. "Come here, Fanny," he said, his voice low and seductive.

As tempting as it was to obey, she clasped her hands behind her back and swayed, shaking her head. "No."

He rose with slow deliberation. "You're right to refuse. It's about time I did the chasing. And the catching."

Her heart nearly stopped. Then it began to pulse with a furious rhythm, part excitement, part fear, part lust.

As he came closer, moving with the cautious glide of a stalking cat, she darted to the other side of the bed.

With a grin of pure male deviltry, he eased off his shoes. "You won't escape me, Fanny."

He'd never sounded so seductive, so determined. So masculine.

Watching her steadily, he slowly stripped off his shirt and tossed it away, his muscles rippling, his stomach taut. She'd never guessed how magnificent his body was.

Excitement surged through her. Then he started to undo his trousers.

"What are you . . . what are you doing?" she asked, realizing how silly that must sound.

"I'm getting ready to catch you."

She shrieked and scrambled over the bed, sending the rose petals scattering, releasing their scent into the air. Once safely on the other side, she tried to remember this was just a game.

A very exciting, arousing one.

So she stuck her tongue out at him.

Still dressed in his partially unbuttoned trousers, he gave a cry and dashed to her side of the bed. Holding out his arms, a little bent over, he blocked her way. "You won't escape me, insolent wench."

She moved to go around him, first one way, then another.

Each time, he deftly moved to block her. "See?"

She feinted, swaying left, then she ran right and passed him.

"Damn!" he cried as he whirled around.

Now by the dressing table, Fanny was giddy with delight that she'd eluded him, although she could scarcely breathe.

Her corset was too tight.

Keeping her eyes on him, she began to undo the rest of the hooks.

"Having trouble?" he asked, his eyes aglow in the candlelight.

"A little," she agreed as she neared the last of the hooks.

"Need some help?"

"No." She removed the corset and let out a sigh of relief as she set it on the dressing table. "That's better."

"I absolutely agree. You must be rather warm in that petticoat, too."

"As a matter of fact, I am," she said. Giving him an enticing little half smile, she untied the tapes that held it around her waist and let it drop to the floor.

Now wearing only her chemise and drawers, she kicked her petticoat aside. "That's better."

His voice was a low rasp. "The rest."

Heady with desire, enjoying the game, and knowing exactly what he wanted, she shook her head. "Not yet."

She saw the subtle change in his expression and was ready when he rushed her. She shoved off from the table and managed to get past him again.

"I chased you a long time, Brix," she said, once more beside the bed. "I'm not going to make it easy for you tonight."

"Promise?" he asked as he walked toward her with slow deliberation.

She got on the bed. With a very purposeful expression, he kept coming toward her. She slithered across the satin coverlet—but not fast enough.

He grabbed her ankle. "Now I've got you!" he exclaimed as he dragged her across the bed toward him.

"Oh no, you don't!" she cried. She wiggled and squirmed, and tried to hold on to the coverlet, but it only bunched in her hand and came with her. She let go and reached for a pillow. She grabbed it and struck him.

Startled, he let go. Freed, and giddily laughing, she dropped the pillow and scrambled away on her hands and knees over the bed. The coverlet slipped and slid as if it were on his side, slowing her progress.

She was still on the bed when he picked up the pillow. "Weapons, eh? Not very sporting, Fanny."

"All's fair in love and war," she gasped, still laughing, and nearly on the other side.

"I'll remember that," he said as he lobbed the pillow at her. She dove to avoid it, falling prone onto the soft bed.

The pillow hit the bedpost and burst. She covered her head with her arms as a flurry of fluffy white down floated and whirled around her. It was like being caught in a blizzard in the bedroom.

Brix landed beside her on the bed, sending more feathers into the air as he threw his arm over her and pulled her close. "Now I've got you!"

"No, you don't!" she cried, passionately excited and laughing even as she struggled to get free.

Ignoring her squirming, he held her tight against him. "Oh, yes, I have. Admit it. I've caught you fair and square."

"You have not," she retorted, although she stilled. Panting, she looked up at his beloved face.

Then she stuck out her tongue.

The next thing she knew, Brix had captured her mouth, and her tongue, with his. The move was unexpected, unforeseen—and tremendously arousing. Passion exploded as he continued to kiss with slow, intoxicating thoroughness.

A whimper escaped her lips when he insinuated his leg over hers and shifted, so that she was beneath him. She welcomed the gentle pressure of his hips against her as she sank deeper into the soft bedclothes, crushing downy feathers and rose petals.

He positioned her so that his knees were between hers, his weight supported by his arms.

Breaking the kiss, he looked into her eyes. "And now that I've got you, Fanny, I'm never going to let you go. I've never given a woman my heart, until you. You have it, and my deepest devotion, forever."

She reached up and brushed back a lock of his wayward hair that had tumbled over his forehead. "I love you, Brixton Smythe-Medway, with all my heart, forever."

Then his mouth was on hers. His lips parted and she slid her tongue between them, slowly exploring the moist warmth. Her fingertips brushed across the skin of his shoulders and the hair of his chest.

His grip tightened, and a low moan escaped his throat when she dragged the pads of her fingers over his nipple.

Heady with this power to arouse him, she raised herself to press her lips there, gently sucking his nipple into her mouth, teasing and toying with the hardened nub, feeling him harden elsewhere, too.

He ground against her, pressing her farther into the bedding. She shifted, pleasuring his other nipple, aroused by the sensation of his erection against her body, her pulse throbbing with passion. And need.

She fell back, and instantly, he grabbed the end of the ribbon of the neck of her chemise and yanked it out. She held her breath, wondering if he would rip the chemise from her, too.

He didn't. Instead, he eased her garment over her head, the soft fabric caressing her skin like his gentle touch. He untied the tapes of her drawers. As he gently pulled them lower, she raised her hips and helped him remove them.

When he saw her naked, he gave a sigh like a hungry man receiving a loaf of bread, and murmured, "Perfect."

He thought her perfect, and her life felt complete.

Then he leaned down again to pleasure her breasts. She grabbed his forearms as his mouth meandered over the rounded top, the sides, underneath, leaving the pebbled nub for last. Her hips and legs moved instinctively, digging into the bed, trying to find purchase to push against him, to feel his body fully.

When he finally took her nipple into his mouth, she gasped and moaned with the sheer pleasure of it. "Oh, Brix," she panted, "now. Please. Now."

"Not yet." He got off the bed and removed his trousers, kicking them away.

She had only a moment to appreciate his naked body before he joined her on the bed. She grabbed his shoulders, tugging him lower to take his mouth again. She was ready, anxious, wanting him to make love with her.

"Not yet," he repeated, pulling away. "I have a

wager to win, remember? You won the last one, so it's only fair that I win this one."

She raised herself to kiss his chest. "Forget the wager. I don't know what I was thinking."

"I do." He smiled at her, proving—as if she needed it—that he could inflame her with his eyes and his voice as much as with his touch. "My wife's pleasure is at stake, as well as my pride."

He laid his hand between her thighs and gently pressed. "I'll do my best to ensure you won't mind losing."

She could well believe it.

He bent down and whispered in her ear, "Lie still a moment, Fanny."

"Why?"

"I want to take my time, and the way you move makes it very difficult for me to be patient."

She thought she ought to protest—there was a wager between them, after all—until he licked and flicked his tongue across her earlobe, and drew it between his teeth.

Then he slid out of sight and she forgot about the wager.

"Brix, what are you . . . ?" Her words trailed off into a sigh of surprise, and ecstasy, as his tongue pleasured her elsewhere.

Diana hadn't told her about *this*.

Excitement and suspense combined, shattered and combined again as he used his tongue to arouse her. She closed her eyes and bunched the bedclothes in her fists as one of his hands moved with excruciating leisure up her leg toward her hip. The other cupped her breast, gently kneading. His thumb swayed back and forth over her pebbled nipple.

"I love you, Fanny," he murmured.

"I . . . love . . . you . . ." she panted.

"I want to make you happy."

"You do. You will."

"In every way."

She opened her eyes to see only the top of his blond head and his disheveled hair, and then his tongue thrust—

"Oh, Brix!" she gasped, clutching the sheets.

He stopped and moved upward, so that she could see his face. "Is that . . . have you . . . have I lost?" she asked, not caring if she had.

"Not yet. That was only a prelude," he replied with a look that heated her blood.

A prelude? If that wasn't an orgasm, she'd probably die having one.

It seemed a good way to go.

"I think you're ready for me now, my dearest, sweetest Fanny."

She smiled with pure wanton, joyful wickedness as she put her hands on his chest. "Me? What about you? I don't want to give you an easy victory, even if you are my husband and I love you. I think you need more . . . provoking."

"Provoking? Good God, Fanny, you've been provoking me for weeks."

"Have I indeed? Well, well," she murmured as she dragged her fingertips down his body. She found his erection and ran her hand over the smooth shaft.

"Fanny, what—?"

"I'm exploring."

"Gad!"

"Should I stop?"

He closed his eyes. "Yes. No. Damn, Fanny, how . . . ?"

"Diana. I didn't want to come to my wedding bed completely ignorant," she explained as she continued to stroke him. "She's told me several very interesting things since you and I became engaged."

"So I see," he said through clenched teeth while she continued to stroke him.

"I asked a lot of questions."

His eyes suddenly flew open and he grabbed her hand. "It's time for you to stop that."

"Don't you like it?" she asked, confused. "I thought you were enjoying it."

"I do, but there's a time for everything, and—"

The truth burst in on her. "You're afraid you're going to lose!"

"Like I said, I'm determined to win this time."

She forgot what she was going to say to that when he put one hand on either side of her head and eased his hips forward, so that his erection was against her. "It might hurt a bit the first time, Fanny," he cautioned her, his expression concerned.

"I know. Diana told me that, too. Don't worry, Brix. I love you."

He kept his adoring gaze on her face as he pushed inside her.

She grimaced, for there was pain. He immediately embraced her, and gently kissed her lips. "I'm sorry. It should be just this once," he whispered, his voice tender, just like when he was a boy and she was crying.

Remembering the boy, loving the man, she held him close as the pain diminished.

"I'm fine," she assured him when it was nearly gone.

He studied her face, then he smiled in a way that made her heart throb with yearning as he rocked forward, the sensation startling, but not painful. Stimulating. Thrilling.

That wondrous tension began to build again, and his kisses grew more heated, his passion more intense. She returned them with an answering, fervent desire.

He thrust his hips with more force, and she gasped with the primal pleasure of the feeling, the masculine power of his body.

"Again," she commanded in a husky whisper as she grasped his forearms and pressed against him.

He obeyed, pushing harder. Bending her legs, she shoved herself against him, meeting him. Encouraging, wordless little noises burst from her throat as his thrusts grew in intensity, hard and strong, as virile as he. Every muscle in her body seemed to tighten, expectant with need. Give and take. Push and pull. The rhythm strong, powerful, primitive in its force and urgency. Making them one. Man and woman, husband and wife.

And then it was as if a taut line snapped. She cried out with pulsating, throbbing release.

He groaned deep in his throat as he bucked.

Then he stilled.

His body sweat-slicked, his breathing labored, Brix laid his head against her breasts. Too sated to speak, blissful in release, they both lay quiet as the candles burned low, and the scent of roses filled the air, and bits of white down swirled around them.

Then Fanny felt Brix's lips twitch into a smile. "You lost."

She ran her fingers through the tousled mop of his hair and laughed softly. "No, I haven't. I've won everything I ever wanted."

He raised his bright green eyes to look at her with love and contentment. "So have I, my darling Fanny Epping. So have I."

The best in romance can be found from Avon Books
with these sizzling March releases.

ENGLAND'S PERFECT HERO by Suzanne Enoch
An Avon Romantic Treasure

Lucinda Barrett has seen her friends happily marry the men they chose for their "lessons in love." So the practical beauty decides to find someone who is steady and uneventful—and that someone is definitely *not* Robert Carroway! She wants a husband, not a passionate, irresistible lover who could shake her world with one deep, lingering kiss . . .

FACING FEAR by Gennita Low
An Avon Contemporary Romance

Agent Nikki Taylor is a woman with questions about her past assigned to investigate Rick Harden, the CIA's Operations Chief who is suspected of treason. Yet instead of unlocking his secrets, she unleashes a dark consuming passion . . . and more questions. Now in a race against time, piecing together her history can get them both killed.

THREE NIGHTS . . . by Debra Mullins
An Avon Romance

Faced with her father's enormous gambling debt, Aveline Stoddard agrees to three nights in the arms of London's most notorious rake, a man they call "Lucifer." Once those nights of blistering sensuality and unparalleled ecstasy are over, will Aveline be able to forget the man who has stolen her heart?

LEGENDARY WARRIOR by Donna Fletcher
An Avon Romance

Reena grew up listening to the tales of the Legend—a merciless warrior who is both feared and respected. So when her village is devastated by a cruel landlord, she knows the Legend is the only one who can rescue her people. But the flesh-and-blood man is even more powerful and sensuous than the hero she imagined . . .

REL 0204